Too Many S| Case

Book 1 of The Files of Doug McCool

*To Roth,
Have fun with this
Thanks,
Miles Archer*

Miles Archer

Clocktower Books

San Diego, CA USA
www.clocktowerbooks.com

Too Many Spies Spoil the Case: Book 1 of The Files of Doug McCool
by Miles Archer

Clocktower Books

San Diego, CA USA
www.clocktowerbooks.com

Copyright © 2000 by Miles Archer

This book is a work of fiction. Names, characters, places, and incidents either are products of the author's imagination or are used fictitiously. Any resemblance to actual events or locales or persons, living or dead, is entirely coincidental.

CLOCKTOWER and design are trademarks of C&C Publishers.

Cover art by Ariana Overton

ISBN 0-7433-0112-9

Prologue

San Francisco, 1973. The Roe v. Wade decision was handed down by the Supreme Court on January 23rd. The country was furiously split.

It was beginning to look like we would never extricate ourselves from Vietnam. The news was a constant barrage of demonstrations, arrests, conspiracies, and violence.

As if things couldn't get any worse, *Alias Smith and Jones* was canceled and there were clouds gathering over the White House surrounding the Watergate burglary case.

The previous fall, Palestinian terrorists from the Black Septembrists slaughtered Israel's Olympic team with German security forces watching helplessly. Israel grimly swore revenge.

I was working for AAA Legal Process Service and idly wondering when I was going to get serious about my life.

Chapter One

Wherein Our Hero Eats Breakfast

The fact that I knew I was dreaming didn't change the reality of the dream. There was something comforting about the familiarity of it. I'm face down in the mud, mortars exploding all around. There iss this horrible feeling of my back and ass being exposed. My ears are roaring with the noise—screams, explosions, counterfire from all around me. I'm trying to become one with the mud. There is a tremendous roar near me and simultaneously I'm splashed with warm sticky stuff. The rest of the dream is chaos—men shouting in my face, hands pulling at me, the sound of distant screaming, my legs not there, I can't feel my legs. A shout—I'm awake.

My face is sweaty and my heart is pounding. It takes me just a second to remember that I'm alive. My legs are asleep; they get that way if I sit or stand too long. It takes a few more seconds to remember where I am.

I suppose it is best to begin at the beginning. The beginning of this story is breakfast.

I was eating in Pacific Heights that morning, my coffee cup wedged between the windshield and the dash. I want to tell Volkswagen designers they should have made the dashboard on the Microbus flat instead of sloping. It's not easy to keep from spilling Tommy Lee's scalding brew on a dash that's slanted. I was attempting to eat only pastry and avoid the paper wrapper of the jelly doughnut in my left hand, and keeping my right ready if the coffee container should start to slip.

I was parked. More precisely, I was staked out. Interesting term, "stake out". One thinks of the goats hunters use to lure tigers. The term "sacrificial lamb" comes to mind next. In any event, I was the hunter, not the hunted. It was 6:30 a.m. and Mr. George Barron, Jr. was going to back out of his two-car garage and drive his Lincoln Mark III to the high-rise office in the Standard Oil Building. My particular interest in this event was that when it occurred, I would present him with a communication from his loving wife. That is to say, I was going to serve him with a Summons and Order to Show Cause in the Superior Court of the State of California, in and for the County of San Francisco in the matter of Barron v. Barron.

I washed down the doughnut with a cautious sip of Tommy's coffee. Tommy brews a good cup and it stays hot cradled in the indestructible white plastic. I told Tommy some day he would be sued for injuries sustained from the strength and temperature of this stuff. Little did I know I was prophetic, although it turned out to be McDonald's. Deeper pockets.

Tommy with an air of frantic innocence said, "No sue me. I just little guy try to make a living. No money, no money!" Tommy didn't have much of a sense of humor when it came to money.

He owned about four square blocks of the Avenues, where he rented flats and apartments. I was sure that Tommy was right when he indicated "no money". It was all set up in dummy corporations with interlocking directorates. Anyway, I gingerly pried off the plastic lid and impatiently waited for the coffee to reach drinking temperature. I wanted a cigarette badly by now, but my little rule is no cigs until after that first sip of coffee. I am not one of those smokers that fires up a cig immediately upon waking. I like to play little games of self-denial once in a while. Makes up for the indulgences. In any event, as I slurped down a large glob of jelly I could see the garage door start to tremble, preparatory to rising. "Shit", I said out loud. I grabbed a sip of coffee, burning my tongue, and tossed the doughnut on the dash. I grabbed the neat packet of legal mumbo jumbo from the passenger seat, adding a slight patina of strawberry jam, popped open the door, and trotted over to the house.

The door was up and I could see into the darkness of the garage through the swirling fog. It was July in San Francisco so I wore a sweatshirt. I love to watch the tourists freezing in their shorts and tank tops when they come to "Sunny California" in July. This is not Redondo Beach.

There was a plume of vapor emerging from the Lincoln's tail pipe. A man who let's his car warm up is a great gift to people in my line of work. I waited beside the open door, heard the light clunk of Barron Jr. shifting into reverse. As the white car slid into the driveway like a ship being launched, I tapped on his window. He jumped, of course.

"George Barron, Jr.?" I shouted at him through the glass. He nodded yes, instinctively. Then his eyes narrowed as the realization dawned on him that he was nailed. When you ask a person their name, most people instinctively answer correctly. Barron was nodding yes even as he was realizing why I was there.

"This is a Summons and Order to Show Cause for you." I tapped the window with the packet. In response he floored the accelerator and cranked the steering wheel. The big car leaped back and turned to the right, the side of the car pulling away from me.

It was a good maneuver and would have left me standing there with a bunch of paper in my hand and looking ridiculous, except for one thing. He had forgotten or misjudged the location of the short retaining wall that ran along the right side of the driveway. It was only about ten or twelve inches high, but that was enough.

His right rear wheel rode over it and then sank into the flowerbed on the other side. There was the grinding crunch and scrape of the chassis on the concrete and the tire spun in the flowers. Dirt and pansies flew everywhere before he realized what he'd done.

I stood admiring the situation. Barron burst out of the car in a tidal wave of wool suit and wingtips. He looked back to assess the situation. What he saw was not a cause for happiness. He started swearing, nothing creative, but it was steady and growing in both pitch and volume. I took a couple of steps closer and held out the summons.

He turned on me. "Look at this mess, you fucking son of a bitch!" Words to that effect.

"Here you go." I held the papers out to him.

"I'm not taking those! I refuse to accept those!" He was almost screaming.

"You don't really have a choice, sport. I've identified you and you're served." I tossed the fat little packet at his feet. It fell on the concrete like a miniature morning paper. "Have a nice day," I said, pointing to the smiley-face button on my sweatshirt. I stepped around the beached Lincoln and headed across the street, Barron's foul language following in my wake like debris floating in the Bay.

"I never touched those! You didn't serve me legal, I never touched those. I'm not accepting this." Barron was demonstrating his vast legal knowledge. Many people are under the misapprehension that for service to be legal they must touch the paper in some way. This is not true. No doubt Barron's attorney would so inform him. At one hundred and fifty bucks an hour.

I noticed another garage door open and a car half out of its space when I reached my bus. The driver was standing with his hands on his hips, glaring at me as I walked up. My bus was parked across his driveway and he was waiting impatiently. As I opened the door and started to climb in he yelled, "You can't just block a driveway like that! I've called for a tow truck, you're getting towed."

"Thanks anyway." I smiled. "I don't need a tow. But your neighbor over there seems to have a problem. That's right neighborly of you." The fellow gave me the one-fingered salute. I laughed and fired up my bus, pulled the cup down from its perch on the dash, and drove away. I spilled coffee on my hand when I made the shift from first to second and cursed, oddly echoing Barron.

Chapter Two

Reflections and Musings

I drove down California Street just easing along with the morning traffic. I held the coffee in my left hand and a cigarette in my right, and glanced at the pile of papers on the passenger seat. I had four or five stops to make. I realize that seeing me is probably the beginning of a bad day for most people. If they want to blame somebody, they can blame the attorneys. Process serving is not my calling, not my avocation if you will, but it certainly is my vocation of the moment, and a good one, too. I pull in about three fifty to four hundred a week and even after gas and car insurance, it's not a bad living.

We process servers live in our cars, naturally, and mine was made for living. My VeeDub Microbus is the perfect vehicle for this work - roomy, comfortable, reasonably economical and provides me with a "home-away-from-home". I could sleep, eat, urinate, spy, fuck—all the necessities of life, and on a long stakeout it is heaven to fire up the stove and make a cup of coffee or reach into the AC-DC fridge and pull out a snack. It isn't fast but in this line of work, speed is not my first consideration, comfort is. I could get the thing up to seventy-five or so and that's fast enough for me. You can go to Hell in your own way. The bus's faded green and white paint and ubiquitous nature rarely caused people to take note of me. It was plain enough to fit into the poor neighborhoods and common enough to fit into the rich ones. I take very good care of it and devotionally see Jerry at Bug World every three thousand miles.

The last few serves were uneventful—a couple of summonses on little stores, received with weary resignation by the owners whose attempts at capitalism were about to meet head on with the banks' and their suppliers' lack of faith in their ability to ride out the recession.

One place had been closed some time, the dust on the display of nic-nacs in the window a pathetic comment on the tardiness of this particular supplier's attempt to recover his misplaced faith.

"Another tax write off," I thought.

By now I was downtown and it was only 8:30. I crossed Market Street and drove around to my favorite parking area, the block behind the Palace Hotel. So far the earnest efforts of the City of San Francisco to eliminate all on-street parking by slow strangulation was working; there were few places left where you could park for more than an hour, outside of the rip off parking garages. This little alley was not yet posted and you could actually park for four hours. An oversight by some official that would no doubt be rectified. I locked up, hoisted my cheap black briefcase, and ambled to Market Street, the highest risk activity of my day so far.

Market Street, the main north-south thoroughfare through the heart of downtown San Francisco, looked like a war zone. It is the destruction that is billed as progress: the eternally late, eternally over-budget Bay Area Rapid Transit. This paean to progress was going to revolutionize mass transit by providing computer-controlled electric trains running from the suburbs of the City, through the downtown, and all the way to the border. The border of San Francisco, that is. When you're a native San Franciscan, any other place doesn't really count.

I crossed Market Street, threading my way through barriers, across traffic islands, street car tracks that were functional or not, depending on the whim of the contractor on any given day, avoiding buses driven by psychotic Muni drivers, cars trying to ram their way through crosswalks—Market Street circa 1973 was a no-man's-land of transportation, yet a half million or so hapless drones were required to navigate the area daily.

I reached the lobby of 450 Market, a nondescript brick office building, prewar (I'm not sure which war), supported by reinforced masonry neighbors of many more stories than poor 450's five floors. This gave her occupants some reassurance that during the next big quake, 450 would probably only lose the front and rear facades, the middle would be held up like a drunk between two cops. It was worth your life to have a desk near either front or rear wall, and the wisest occupants chose the internal rooms. Unreinforced brick buildings fall faster than a ten-dollar whore goes down. When I reached the fourth floor I stepped off the wheezing elevator and followed the staccato sounds of the ubiquitous IBM Selectric typewriters to AAA's door. This is before the days of word processors and the voice of the Selectric was heard throughout the land.

The office door was one of those rippled glass jobs right out of a Thirties movie, with black lettering painted on by a no doubt long dead sign painter. "AAA LEGAL PROCESS. Enter." I entered. The office was an odd, trapezoidal shape. This was necessitated by the fact that 450 Market was not a square, but a semi-wedge shape caused by the intersection of Sutter Street with Market at an acute angle. This kind of odd intersection is common in the City, due to the steep and irregular topography. This irregular polygonal shape caused the offices to be rather haphazardly arranged.

To the right, immediately upon opening the door, was a blue vinyl couch and a couple of mismatched chairs, steel and plastic, not selected for comfort, but rather the obvious relics of a used furniture store. I believe the couch to have been the one that Harry and Dorothy used in their first apartment. It was as tired looking as the rest of the place, and so drew no attention to itself. The Silvers were not people who put up much of a front. Clients almost never came to the office in person and were only familiar with AAA by phone or messenger. Six figure per annum lawyers do not leave their offices for idle visits. Lawyers, like cabbies, only make money when the meter is running. "Billable time" is the attorney's mantra.

The black and white check linoleum "foyer" had gradually deteriorated to charcoal and tan paths that showed the casual visitor where the internal offices were located. This 'deer trail' was an unintended map through the warren of tiny rooms.

Taking the right hand fork led to Darrell Prince and his mousey assistant crouched at tiny desks. They handled the document processing. Directly in front of the entrance was the office of the proprietors, Harry and Dorothy Silver. It was the only room with a door and a large window in the front wall that commanded a view, not of the city to the rear, but of the entrance to the office. It was flanked on the adjoining wall by another window, allowing the occupants a broad visual field of fire. When you got to know the Silvers you realized that this was deliberate. Their office also had a pair of smaller double hung windows in the brick wall facing the street. These would have had a nice view of the financial district except for two things: they were obscured by piles of books and papers that blocked half their height and they had not been washed since Eisenhower was delivering his military-industrial complex speech.

Immediately in front of this office, in fact, her chair would block the door if she were to stretch, was Barbara Brown's desk: office manager, receptionist, typist par-excellence, personal secretary, marketing manager, den mother, corrupter of youth, charmer of hostile intruders, massager of lawyers' egos and typists' sore shoulders.

Mary, Bernice and Layla sit directly past Barbara, sharing a space that allows three desks and walk around room. They're all going at it with their Selectrics like BAR men in a fire fight. The noise becomes a kind of background rhythm. They can type, talk, smoke and flirt at the same time. It's a little disconcerting to talk to them while their fingers are flying over the keyboard, as though their hands functioned independently from their brains. Through the doorway on the left is Lowell's office. You enter through a curtain of blue cigarette smoke. A large map of the City dominates the wall facing his desk. He could have faced the windows, but this would have been too much competition for Lowell's wobbly attention span.

Lowell Van Duzee is a pasty little guy, perennially ill looking, with watery blue eyes, thin hair, stooped shoulders, and wet, trembling lips. He is a very nice guy, just not much to look at. He's my direct boss. "Van", everyone calls him, was a lawyer. He was disbarred years ago in Michigan, I think it was. Van doesn't exactly brag about his past. Anyway, having seen Van's ability to put away booze, I have no doubt he was involved in some sort of major fuckup. I doubt if he came out of it with anyone else's money or anything like that. He probably just fell down drunk in court. He's long since divorced and lives in a one of those residence hotels in the Tenderloin. You know the kind. Cheap linoleum paved lobby, a guy that's badly in need of a shave sits behind a wire cage and one old elevator. Broken down old men sitting around the TV. Smells you don't want to catalog. I'll depress you with a more complete description some other time.

"Hi Doug. How's your morning going?" Van is solicitous to those servers who move a lot of paper.

"Van. How are ya? Watch the game? Can you believe those fuckin' Giants? I've never seen a sorrier bunch of losers in my life." I hate baseball, myself. Don't watch much television either, but I know that Van's evenings are spent getting blitzed in front of his set.

"They were pretty disappointing, all right." He probably never saw the end. He held out his hand to receive the stack of cards I held. The girls record each subject's name, address and such particulars on a card and paper clip the card to the papers. We leave the papers and retain the card. There's a space for a description and notes if we feel the need to write such down for future testimony, if we suspect that the subject might deny service. Most of the time we don't bother.

"Doug, I don't like to bug you, but the client is asking about this one." Van hands me a note with a name I recognize right away.

"Van, this guy is a royal pain. He has a chain of pizza joints, look at all the addresses they gave us. Every time I go to one of them, he's never there. 'Just left' or 'Never comes in on Tuesdays' some shit like that. I've been to every place a couple of times and you know I can't sub him until I've been to each one three times. That takes a while."

"I realize. I just want to be able to tell this guy we're working on it. Is he ducking?"

"Can't say for sure. I get the feeling that he's given his employees instructions to shine on anyone looking for him, but it could just be that he's really not around. I don't know." The last statement is a sigh of frustration. I'm not making a lot of money hunting this guy all over town for three dollars and fifty cents. "I work it when I'm in the area, but you know I'm not going to chase him."

"Well, if he's ducking service I can tell the attorney we need to make him a special."

"If they want him done fast, then they're gonna have to cough up the money." Van nodded and put the note in a pile. If there's a system to his desk, it's not one that would be apparent to anyone other than Van's slightly addled brain, but he generally gets things done.

Van handed me my Monday pile of papers. There were about fifteen or twenty. I stuffed the bunch into my briefcase for later sorting by area. Van held one piece of paper in his hand.

"This is a hot one." He handed it to me.

I looked at the very thin folded paper and the name and address on the card. Didn't set off any bells or whistles, a cloud didn't suddenly cover the sun. "What's the big deal?"

"That's a Federal Order to Show Cause."

"So, I've served these before."

"Look at who the plaintiff is."

I pulled off the paper clip and opened the stiff papers. It was a very thin document, just a rather generic order asking for the subject to appear and show cause why the order previously entered into should not be carried out. I'd seen this kind of legal document fifty times, but not one where the plaintiff was the Government of Iran. I looked up at Van. He looked back at me through his glasses, eyes watering, and smoke curling up from his cigarette. I lit one too. "This is a big deal, huh?" Van nodded.

"Look at the attorney."

"Ooo. I'm all a-twitter." I was sarcastic but my pulse picked up when I saw the name: Belli and Associates. Mel Belli was the most notorious litigator in San Francisco. You know him. The guy that defended Jack Ruby. Yeah, *that* Jack Ruby. Mel could smell million-dollar publicity a mile away. Since it didn't really matter who defended Ruby (he was in the unenviable position of having committed his crime on live national television) Mel saw a good thing. However, Belli also represented widows and orphans of people in plane crashes and the biggest of the big corporations those widows and orphans were suing as well. His personal office faced Montgomery Street and was filled with antiques. Large windows allowed passersby to see the great one at work.

"Himself?"

"I'm given to understand that."

"Time and mileage?"

"It's a City job, smart guy."

"Yeah, okay, then just the usual rate?"

"Of course. They want this ASAP."

"So what else is new?"

"You'll get right on it?"

11

"Your wish is my command, sahib. Mel Belli and Associates now commands my very soul. For ten dollars an hour. I've got an address in the TransAmerica Pyramid and an address on Powell, how hard can this one be?"

Van shrugged. "He might be avoiding service."

I just looked at Van and smiled an evil little smile. "You know how I love a challenge."

Just then Bill Walters came in and plunked down on the couch in front of the windows. I was sitting in the chair next to Van's desk.

"Hey Dougie, hey Van." Bill's a big, handsome, friendly guy. He radiated natural charm and flashed a ready smile. Would have made a good car salesman or bartender and might have done both in the past, for all I know. At present he was the best (or perhaps second best) process server in the house. He and I were the dynamic duo, the Batman and Robin, the crème de la crème. When the paper needed to get laid, Van called Bill or me. When the shit hit the fan, he called us both. I nonchalantly put the Big Deal paper in my bag. Van had been giving me a lot of specials lately, and I didn't want Bill to realize it. Van noticed my move and a ghost of smile flickered across his face.

"Bill, how the Hell's it hanging?" I was genuinely glad to see him as he was the kind of guy who always cheered me up.

"Long and low, my boy, long and low." Bill was a good fifteen years older than I, forties to my twenties, about six foot-two, solid but not a exercise nut. A full head of surfer-style straight blond hair, green eyes and Robert Redford looks caused women to adore him and men to want his friendship.

I moved out of the chair and wandered around the office while Bill turned in his papers and chatted with Van. Dixie was on the phone and I couldn't bug her while she was working. Dixie did our skip traces and she was a genius. She worked with a reverse phone book, endless contacts in low places like the DMV and the phone company. She could lie like no one I'd ever heard and looked like your grandmother.

Out in the main office the girls were hammering away. Mary is a thin blond sitting in the far corner. Pretty, quiet. Married to a medical student. Bernice was the newest addition, a matronly African-American moved out to the Left Coast from Detroit. Divorced. I perched on the edge of her desk and made idle chatter. I turned on the bullshit and soon she was laughing and blushing. She was really kind of attractive. I found myself speculating idly about her possibilities as a recreational partner. My taste in women is catholic.

Layla, an exotic-looking Eurasian mongrel, part Russian and part Chinese, she said. High cheekbones, slightly epicanthic folds, with Russian coloring- auburn hair and pale skin. Fabulous body, with a great wardrobe of tight pants and revealing blouses. Thank you Dorothy, for not having a dress code. This day she wore skintight stretch pants that revealed the creases of her hips, and a silk blouse without a bra. I tried not to stare while I worked on Bernice's ego. Layla would look up from her typing every once in a while and give me a little half smile, like we shared something. We didn't, but oh how I wish we did. I caught Mary and Bernice glancing at each other, then at me. They both laughed that kind of laugh that women have when they share a thought about a man and the man has no clue what they're thinking. I beat a quick retreat to Barbara's desk, their giggles following me.

I am a healthy male, 27 years aged, and not particularly well behaved. I like women. On occasion, women like me. I try not to dissuade them from that. I poured a cup of coffee from the pot on the table next to the ramshackle couch and lit a cig. Dorothy and Harry were in the inner office, the door closed. I idly speculated on what they might be talking about. I'm curious by nature, nosey actually, and also slightly paranoid about my employers.

Dorothy Silver is your nice Jewish neighbor lady, the kind that you would be happy to have next door- responsible, neat, watched your house while you were on vacation, looked at your grandkids' pictures as long as you liked. She did not take crap from anybody, and she was in a business that provided a lot of crap. Office rumor had it that she was an aggressive process server in her own day and laid more paper in this town than most men. I could believe that.

She was medium sized, kept her figure well. Her black hair was assisted by Miss Clairol. Wore nice clothes, but not expensive. Did have a white stone ring that I'm guessing was in the $5-10k range. Not being a jewelry type myself, I couldn't say, but it was a nice rock.

Harry was a nondescript fellow. Brown suit, good but not expensive. Thin hair combed straight back over his bald spot. He did not try to cover it with fancy combing, just combed his hair back, that's all. You could say he had "the map of Jerusalem" on his face. They both wore their Jewishness as a fact of life. They make no effort to assimilate. I respected that. They left the office promptly at three thirty on Fridays, so that Harry could go to synagogue.

"What's doin', big boy?" Barbara hung up the phone and looked up at me.

"Hangin' around bein' big."

"I'll just bet you are." She delivered this line in a flat and noncommittal way, leaving me to guess what she meant. We liked to tease each other.

"Are we payin' the bills this week, or should I look for honest work?"

"Honey, honest work don't suit you at all. You just stay here and I'll keep you in beer and pretzels."

"What more could a man want?" I looked straight into her eyes. She did not blink.

"If you think of something, I hope I'm the first to know."

"You're definitely on the list, Barb."

She winked broadly. "What would it take to move to the top?"

Before I could respond Bill clapped me on the shoulder. "Doug, come on. Enough schmoozing with the girls. Let them get on with their typewriting and phone answering. You and I must labor in the fields."

"*Adios* ladies. Keep a warm place in your hearts for us." They all allowed as how they would and Bill and I left like knights off to the Crusades.

When we were safely in the hallway, the door closed behind us and the typewriters drowning out any possibility of being overheard, Bill spoke. "Is that not about the finest collection of pussy to be seen in any office, anywhere?"

I smiled. "I couldn't argue with that, not at all, Billy. I'd say that Harry had good taste."

"Dorothy lets him have his scenery, I guess."

"Well, Bill, let's face it, it keeps us interested as well."

"Maybe you, but I'd leave in a heartbeat if there were more money to be made. Fact is, Harry pays the best and he isn't a creep like that Murphy."

Bill had worked for two or three other process services in town and was willing to share his opinion that compared to these others, Harry was a jewel

"You going somewhere now?" This was a prelude to an invitation to slip into *The Office* for a morning eye opener. I didn't make it a practice to drink in the morning, but lately I had picked up some bad habits. Additional bad habits.

"A quick one, Bill." I almost mentioned the hot one over on Montgomery before I remembered I didn't want him to know. I swallowed the first vowel.

He could see that I'd started to say something and had changed my mind, but he was discreet enough not to comment.

Chapter Three

Plots and Plans

We repaired to the dark hole that was *The Office* and took sides in one of the back booths. *The Office* was on the street level, of course, and had doors that allowed entry from either the Sutter or Market Street side. This was convenient for more than one reason, but I felt that it's primary feature was that should an undesirable encounter be approaching from one direction a tactical retreat was afforded in the other. Bill particularly insisted on spending his time here, although Jan and I were equally partial to the *Hoffman Grill* and other hangouts nearby.

After we ordered up and were quietly sucking down our tranquilizers Bill looked around quickly, then a serious expression crossed his placid face. "You know, McCool, you're a pretty smart fellow, I think."

I said nothing. When someone says they think you're smart, it's best not to open your mouth and disabuse them of the notion immediately.

"How much do you suppose Harry and Dorothy pull out of that dumpy little office a year?" He glanced upward, indicating either heaven or reminding me of where the office he was referring to lay. His voice was quiet. "I would guess they are probably pulling in at least a mil, net." He waited for some look of astonishment to cross my face. He was disappointed.

"Well, Bill, yeah, I would guess it's a pretty good piece of change. If you figure the number of serves we make a week, and the number of guys on the street, not to mention what the couriers bring in and Darrell's operation. I suppose it's a pretty nice income. So?"

"Well, look, what's involved here? What do you need to run a deal like that?" He meant this to be rhetorical, but I had an answer ready.

"Money."

Bill's expression changed. He started to look even more serious. "What kind of money, do you think?"

"Okay, you've got the front money for the lease. You've got telephones, furniture, typewriters, an office manager, pagers, stationery - shit I don't know, a lot of stuff."

"Yeah, well, it's not a fortune, is it? You've got two months office rent up front- that's about seven hundred; the phones you lease and the up front on that is a hundred bucks; the office furniture you can buy used; the pagers and all that shit is nothin'."

"You're right so far, but I'll tell you the one thing that's most important." I paused for effect. His eyebrows went up. I couldn't tell if he was thinking the same thing I was. "The office manager. Without somebody who knows their shit we're just a couple of jerk offs who know how to lay a lot of paper."

"I got that part figured out." He paused. This dramatic pausing was wasting a lot of time but we were both Irish, what can you expect? "Barbara."

I drained my glass and waved at Sharon to fix another. "You think she'd bail on Dorothy and Harry?"

"Well, why not? She's not getting any younger, I'm not getting any younger. You're young and you've got smarts. With the three of us working eighteen hours a day we could get it done." He smiled in a self-deprecating way. "Besides, she thinks you're all right, you know what I mean?" He winked.

"What *do* you mean?" I knew but I wanted to make sure I understood what he knew.

"She likes you. C'mon, don't play innocent. She has the hots for you."

"She's married."

"Yeah right, like that ever stopped a woman from anything."

"Well, Bill, I don't know your experience with women, but I'm fairly sure my mother never cheated on my father. So there must be some women who are faithful."

He conceded the last point with a wave of his hand, so as not to be drawn into a ridiculous debate. I was feeling like a dumb kid for having brought up my mother anyway, and Bill gracefully let it go. "Well, anyway, I think she would do it. Three way split- even Steven."

"One minor problem. My assets are what you might call limited. Like, zip, zero, nada. I've got a few hundred in the bank in case the Bus blows up or something, that's it."

"I've got that part covered. I've got five grand." He tossed out the number like it was nothing.

I choked. Literally. After I recovered from inhaling some gimlet and then coughing it back up I looked at Bill from under my eyebrows. "Do I want to know where this came from?"

"It's no big deal. I got lucky when the Nicks took the Lakers four games to one."

Bill was where he was in life because of a gambling jones. He knew too much about odds and spreads, followed sports like it was the breath of life itself. I've seen this before. Guys who needed the rush. Loved to be on the edge of disaster at all times. I didn't care one way or the other *about* Bill's lifestyle choices but now we were talking about being partners.

"Who's going to talk to Barbara?" There was nothing else but to a least string along with the idea for now. What could it hurt?

"We will. Tonight after work."

"Okay."

"I'll meet you guys here. Say about six fifteen. You lay out the idea to her and then I'll show up and fill in the details. If she isn't interested you just give me a little high sign and I'll back off."

I understood now. Bill wanted me to be the stalking horse. If it got back to Dorothy and Harry, it would sound like it was my idea, not his. Oh well, I thought, what the Hell. I didn't think that Barbara was the type to tattle to Mommy.

We left separately. I went out the Sutter Street side and headed up Montgomery. It's pretty fair walk to the TransAmerica Pyramid but I enjoy the hustle of the City and the day was turning warm. A nice breeze off the Bay meandered through the skyscrapers and every once in while a pretty secretary would walk by and improve the scenery. I stopped at a corner newsstand and decided on the spur of the moment to celebrate the possibility of becoming a raging capitalist millionaire like Harry Silver and bought a box of Sherman's.

Drawing on the elegantly thin brown cigarette and feeling very sharp I waited outside the outlandish pyramidal tower owned by the giant insurance conglomerate and gazed at the huge buttressed walls. The thing looked like a space age medieval cathedral, buttressed at the foot and narrowing to a sharp top, with a couple of wings sticking out like ears to accommodate the elevator shafts. I finished the cig and walked into the lobby and checked the directory. I found the office I wanted on the forty-second floor. I took one set of elevators to the twenty fifth and then changed to the set of elevators that ran on the outside of the building to continue on up. This was required due to the ridiculous design and I marveled at how the corporate need to satisfy its ego with a distinctive building could overcome the design requirements of function. I had to admit that the pyramid gave the skyline distinction, but as a practical matter it was silly to have to change elevators every time.

The second elevator deposited me directly into an office reception area. This was that unique design again. No hallways in the narrow levels near the top. Only one office on each level, one on one side of the tower, the other on the opposite, each served by the elevator on that side. It was cool in one way, when you left for the day your office was very secure - the only access by the public was from the elevator, which you locked off when you left. There was an emergency staircase, but it was locked and monitored.

Directly in front of the elevator doors, about fifteen feet into the room sat the receptionist at a large polished black desk. In fact, the entire room was furnished in black and white. As I stepped in, my shoes sank into deep carpet pile. I waded through this to the desk. The woman who sat there observed me with an expression of neutrality that bordered on insolence. I suppose I was not dressed according to her standards. She was wearing an outfit that color coordinated with the room - white blouse, open enough to reveal skin that was only a shade or two off the white of the blouse, black suit, fitted closely to her very thin body, unnaturally platinum blonde hair, pale blue eyes, minimal makeup except for rather startling dark red lipstick. It drew all attention to her mouth, which was set in a firm line.

This is not going to be a gal I could snow into letting me back to see her boss. The serious official approach would be required. Unfortunately, my jeans and t-shirt were not conducive to intimidating this kind of lady but I didn't like to dress up, most of the time comfort and ruggedness were more of a requirement than elegance. I mentally shrugged and slogged to a halt in that mire of carpet. I noticed that there was no company name on the wall, or any other feature that would tell you whose offices these were.

"I have a delivery for Mr. Gunter. Is he in?" Always try to take control by asking a question that has to be answered, it fosters an attitude of unconscious cooperation.

"Just give it to me." She extended a perfect china hand, palm up. So much for unconscious cooperation.

I smiled apologetically. Sometimes you have to try to get sympathy, one working stiff to another. "Gee, I wish I could. But, well, my company requires that he sign for it. I'm sure he's busy but this will only take a second." Slight whine in the voice, not enough to be annoying, but trying to seem bound by powers beyond my control.

"Not here." Her helpful manner was charming the shit out of me.

I stood for a moment, trying to look baffled by what I should do next. Hoping she would come up with something that bordered on helpfulness instead of doing a passable imitation of a stone wall. She stared back. She was good. Also it was occurring to me that she was perhaps not totally unfamiliar with people coming to see her boss that he did not wish to see. Ever. I made a little looking around gesture of helplessness like maybe he would materialize unexpectedly. Just then a guy in shirtsleeves and tie walked out of the back. "Christine..." He stopped when he saw me.

Unlike many people who, when encountering someone in their reception area would have some sort of reaction, this guy just stopped. He didn't change his expression, didn't look at me directly, didn't say another thing, like "could he help me" or "good morning". He hung a quick u-turn and walked right back down the short corridor that ran behind the receptionist's right side. I heard a door close firmly.

"That Mr. Gunter?" I didn't expect the truth. I just wanted to gauge the lie.

"No." She looked convincing, so I was sure that was him.

"Know when he'll be in?" She had me talking in short hand now.

"No."

"Could you narrow that down a little." I dropped any pretense of charm or helplessness. I could see already that this was going to be a pissing contest.

"Try tomorrow."

"Tomorrow's a long day, honey. What time does he get in?"

"Can't say."

"What time does your office open?"

"Ten."

I backed up, nearly tripping in the expensive fiber mush. I wanted to get naked and roll around in it. Not with this girl of steel, but I could think of a couple of candidates.

"Thanks for your help. Have a lovely day." I tried to sound like I meant it. I was not interested in really pissing this lady off. She looked like the type that could think of many ways to make life difficult. I had to turn my back on her to punch the elevator button and then wait, exposed to her baleful examination. I could feel her drawing a bead on my spine with those blank blue eyes.

I tried to leave with as dignified a carriage as possible, but I'd lost round one. During the ride to the mezzanine to change elevators and escape this joint I mentally noted the appearance of the guy who'd said "Christine" and then beat it.

He was on the long side of 45, could have been a fit fifty. Medium brown hair flecked with gray. Square face, nothing particularly distinguished about it. Very steady eyes. Don't know what color. Good shoulders and only a little thick in the middle, rather the thickness of a man who has pumped a lot of iron, not a body builder but a power lifter who went for the maximum clean-and-jerk type lift. I would not have wanted to take a punch from him. I had a vague feeling that I'd encountered an ex-military type. Controlled. Disciplined.

I wandered back toward the office, reflecting on how I'd done. Tried to think of another scenario and how I could have played it. Not that this would help now. I had already been made. They knew who I was and why I was there just as surely as if I'd announced my purpose out loud. But I always liked to think about these things and figure how I might do it better next time. Of course, I hadn't *known* he was ducking service. If I had known that, I might have come up with something more elaborate. Like carrying a box. That really worked. You tell the front person you've got this delivery, and there it is, this small box. But the guy's got to sign.

When he comes out, you keep the box and hand him the papers. It never failed. They would be confused. "Hey, what about my package?" they'd say, as I turn away. "You've got it. You've just been served," I call out over my shoulder. But that wouldn't work now. Hell, the ice queen and Gunter probably wouldn't have fallen for it anyway.

I spent the rest of the morning listlessly passing out paper. By a quarter to twelve I was starting to get the "He's out to lunch" answer and called time out. Wandered to the *Hoffman*. I was feeling bored and wasted and wanted the noisy solicitude of the *Hoffman Grill*. The heavy wood and glass door with the shiny brass handle felt like the hand of a good friend.

I stood at the bar and waited until the server could spare a moment. The *Hoffman* started lunch early and the pace just kept building until late afternoon. At about one thirty, after the market in New York closed, the stockbrokers flooded in. They couldn't wait to celebrate or mourn. Either way was good for the liquor business.

The *Hoffman* has been in the same spot since before the Earthquake and Fire. This block of buildings had miraculously escaped destruction. Now it was an institution. There were no bar stools, only a worn brass rail to rest a foot. San Franciscans, a dying race, believed that bar stools were for women and sissy boys. Men stood while they drank or, if they needed privacy they retreated to a booth or table. Liars' dice was the preferred method of determining who paid for the drinks and a true San Franciscan was an accomplished liar. The menu offered the usual hearty kinds of food that an unfashionable place would have, like hamburgers, steaks and pork chops with mashed potatoes. But *The Hoffman* also offered chili and fettuccini, a truly unique combination of flavors and perfect in every respect as a lunchtime meal. With a couple of gin and tonics and chili you could face the world or take an afternoon nap, which ever seemed appropriate.

I guzzled my first gin and was working on another when Bill and Jan walked in. Jan is a Yale dropout, a thin, rather dissipated figure, with hard blue eyes and quick sarcastic style. An expert photographer with thousands of dollars in arcane equipment, he came to work for AAA about a year after me and I had shown him the ropes. He caught on quickly and for some reason, perhaps because he dressed well and was not as aggressive, he was doing a lot of document subpoenas, where all he had to do was go to some doctors' office or whatever and photocopy files. I waved and they pointed to a table.

When we were all set up with gins and the formalities of ordering food were over we gossiped and chatted until the food arrived. We then set to the serious business of diminishing our appetites and expanding our waistlines. There was nothing of consequence that occurred and I mention lunch only to indicate that I had good reason for returning to the van and stretching out on the bed in back for a mid-afternoon siesta. I realize that this may seem incredibly indolent to those of you who work at a real job, but I would be out serving paper until at least ten or eleven tonight and up at six the next morning.

My system of catching people required me to be up early and out late. Most people are home in the evening so that is a good time. They are off guard and watching TV. I appear at their door with "a delivery". Oh goodie, a present! I'm down the front steps before most of them realize what they just received.

Other targets of my attentions are hip. They are waiting for me to show up and have no interest in a "delivery". "He's not home." "She's at her sister's for a week." So I reappear in the morning before they leave for work. Now they're bottled up in the house. They have to get to a job, take kids to school to, etc. When they back out of the garage or walk down the front steps, I've got them. It's easy for me and keeps the long, expensive process of skip tracing and staking them out down to a minimum. Stakeouts are profitable for me and the company, but our clients are obviously not interested in paying for them unless absolutely necessary. If AAA can't nail people the regular way, they figure, then a stake out or skip trace is really required. We have our pride. And competition to think of. Don't want that asshole Murphy over at Reliable Process Service to get too much business.

I woke up about four thirty and sorted through my evening's work. Using a Thomas Brothers' map I arranged my work by area. I would work commercial addresses until five thirty, lay low until the commute traffic cleared up, around six thirty or seven, then pick one area of the City to work and go up and down the streets, trying to minimize my travel and all the time working towards home. By nine thirty or ten I'd be close to my apartment and could knock off.

Gunter lived on Nob Hill, on Powell between California and Sacramento Streets, right behind the Fairmont Hotel. Flats that rent for more per month than many people earn in six months. I thought I'd try to catch him at home around seven thirty. In the mean time I was supposed to meet Barbara and Bill at *The Office*.

I re-parked the van and headed for the bar. From four thirty to six thirty was happy hour and the food there was so good that most of the time us regulars made it dinner. As a group, we were pretty good elbow-benders and Sharon, the owner, couldn't complain that we were freeloaders. She served those little chicken wings in barbecue sauce, and garlic bread cut in little pieces and cocktail hot dogs on toothpicks, miniature spring rolls and various raw veggies with ranch dressing. A complete meal. I loaded up a plate, snagged a booth and ordered two gin and tonics. Might as well save the poor waitress a trip.

Miles Archer

When Barbara came down she was with Bernice and Layla, so I skipped making Bill's pitch. The four of us chatted and laughed about this and that. The girls tried to convince me to buy a leisure suit. I wasn't sure about that, but I told them I'd think about it. Bill never showed and I left at seven.

Chapter Four

The Man with Platform Shoes

There is never any place to park in the City. Never. But I had commercial plates and these pretty much kept me immune from parking tickets. I could put on the four way flashers and double park. Of course, any loading zone was legal for at least a half hour. I never hesitated to use my target's driveway. On Nob Hill I found Gunter's building easily, right on the corner. Six stories, very nice, each floor with balconies facing the Bay. Older building with double doors of heavy glass, brass handles gleaming. Black awning extending to the curb with a white zone in front to allow passenger loading only. I parked there and left the flashers going.

When I got to the door I was a little surprised to be greeted by a doorman, an old-fashioned feature. He smiled nicely enough and opened up.

"Yessir?" An African-American guy, he looked about a hundred years old if he was a day.

"Hi, delivery here for Mr. Gunter."

"Oh he's not home yet. I'll sign for it."

"Sorry, I wish I could do that, but he's got to sign personal. Is he home?" I smiled and shrugged.

"Nassir, not home" he repeated. I had tried to catch him fibbing and it didn't work. Or else Gunter really wasn't home.

"You see everyone when they come in or go out?"

"Well, yes, I do. See, they parks their cars in the garage around the side here and then they comes through the door there and takes the elevator. So I sees 'em all, comin' an' goin'".

"Gotcha. You know what time he comes home?"

The doorman gave me a curious look. "You can't just leave it for him then?"

I shook my head.

"Well, he comes and goes, sometimes he's out of town for a while. I don't know if I can say." He looked like he didn't want to say too much.

"Well, hey, no problem. I'll just try later on tonight. You think he'll be back by, say, nine?"

"Don' know. Maybe. Sorry you have to make another trip. Maybe you should call him and make an appointment. Or take it to his office. You got that address?"

"The one in TransAmerica?" Maybe there was another office.

He nodded. "That's the one. Try there."

"Yeah, I just missed him there earlier. Oh well," I turned to go. "Thanks anyway." I paused. "What's your name, partner?"

"Jerome."

"You be here at nine, Jerome?"

"Oh yes." He said it in such a way that I got the feeling he was there forever.

Gunter's set up was pretty good. He was secure without being obvious. No guards or locks and bars, but hard to get to. Slippery without coming across as sneaky. Just a busy executive who doesn't want his time wasted. By little things like showing up in Federal court to talk to the Government of Iran.

The documents didn't say anything interesting. The papers themselves, which I had looked at out of curiosity, were just a generic order, no supporting documents, nothing. All I could surmise was that the Iranians had sued this guy, gotten some sort of order or judgment and so far hadn't gotten any action. A Show Cause order required Gunter to appear and explain to the court (or rather, his attorney to explain) why he was or wasn't doing what the Iranians wanted. In other words, to show cause why he shouldn't get his nuts twisted, in a legal sort of way.

Back in the van I headed toward the Western Addition to lay a little ordinary paper. The Western Addition is a rough part of town, so consequently fertile ground for people being sued. Mostly collections stuff, poor bastards who got in over their heads with Macys or BankAmericard. I love the credit industry. They'll sign up anybody that breathes, then when they can't pay, they sue them. Like they'll ever get the money. Most of these saps never show up for the hearing and the company gets a judgment, then tries to collect. Occasionally they attach some working stiff's wages and actually get some money, but most of the time these people never had a pot to piss in anyway. The company can then write off the bad debt and show they tried their best to make it good. Anyway, "ours is not to reason why..."

I went from dilapidated tenement to dilapidated tenement. Most of the time some tired looking man or woman would answer the door, opening it a crack, worried it might be a drug-crazed neighbor there to rip them off. I would hand them the summons which they would take either with exhausted resignation or with a confused look that indicated that they knew it was bad news of an undetermined nature. I would try to be polite with them, but I didn't stick around for longer than it took to make sure they were the person I wanted and hand over the paper. Once in a while they would stop me and ask what it was I'd given them. I would explain that it was a summons for them to appear in court and that the information would be on the paper. Frequently I was sure, by the way they looked at me, that they wouldn't be able to read it. Sometimes they would ask me what they should do. I used to say they should see a lawyer, but given their circumstances, I felt idiotic even making the suggestion.

An old black lady stopped me this night. "Who's this from?" She was gray and bent, with deep, sad eyes and a look of perpetual resignation.

"Ma'am, I'm sorry, I don't read these things. It's just my job to see you get it properly. The law says you have to be notified personally and that's what I'm doin'." I tried to make my voice innocent and gentle.

"What's this mean?" She fumbled the paper open and glanced over it. From the way her eyes moved over the paper, I could tell she wasn't taking in its meaning. "I don't understand. Am I in trouble?"

I reached out for the summons and read it over. I turned toward her and moved my finger along the words. Like all legal documents it contained more words than necessary. "See, this is from a lawyer. He works for the Sears company. They say you owe them money. See, here, $385. It says you borrowed it on your charge card and never paid it. So you got to go to court and tell the judge why you didn't pay the money."

"But that was when my nephew, Ralph, he borrowed my card, see, to get a TV. He told me he would pay, but then he lost his job and now he in Georgia with my sister and her people. He sold that TV to get the money to go. An' I can't pay no $385. I tol' them Sears people that when they called and called. Oh Lord, now they gonna take me to court. They'll put me in jail." She was crying. I was torn between feeling like a shit and wondering how this lady thought the system worked. I was angry too. Angry with the collectors who don't listen and angry with people getting themselves into these fixes.

"Look, ma'am, I can't help you out here. I can't give you legal advice. You can call the Legal Aid people. They're in the phone book. You can just show up at this hearing at the time and place it says and try to explain to the judge. Why don't you get a friend to help you out. Get somebody you know to look it over for you, okay?" I just wanted to get on with my work and here I am being a social worker.

"Yessir, yes, I'll call my daughter. Maybe she'll know what to do." She turned into her apartment and absently closed the door. I continued spreading joy.

And so the evening went. I really didn't like working these tough neighborhoods, not because they were tough, but it's a hassle to find a place to park. I would have to lock the bus, climb the stairs, find the apartment. Wait for someone to come to the door. About a third of the time I would be told they didn't live there any longer. About a third of the time the answerer would get that nervous look liars get and tell you that the person you wanted wasn't home. If they claimed they weren't living there anymore, I would take the paper back to the office and Dixie would do her thing, using the various means at her disposal to determine if they were lying or not. If they were, I would be back in a few days and keep going back. At the third trip, I would simply leave the summons with whoever was there. It was legal service and they would have to prove in court that they really didn't live at the address where we served them. Most of the time they weren't that sophisticated. Once caught in the lie they would accept the summons and "justice" proceeded. But it was a big hassle. Not the easiest way to make a buck. But what is?

It was past eight thirty by now. I was on my second pack of Marlboros. Fifteen pieces of paper. Fifty-two bucks richer than when I'd started. I was already thinking about my apartment, a glass of tequila and perhaps a toke before bed. I had a couple more summons left for this area and then I would stop by Gunter's again on the way home.

The apartment buildings are all about the same here. A hundred years ago this had been the first development outside of the core of San Francisco. Fine Victorian houses, three and four stories, frantic detail trim picked out of builders' catalogs by middle class San Franciscans. Sometime between the wars they had been chopped into two or three room apartments and shotgun flats and rented to the poor flocking to the coast during and after the war. They smelled of stale grease, cigarettes and roach shit. Some of the really bad ones smelled of urine too. I walked up two flights and found the apartment I was seeking. The scarred brown door looked like any other. A stereo played disco. I tapped and stood back.

The door opened the usual crack and a brown, bloodshot eye peered out. "Whatch' wan'?"

"Delivery for," I peered at the name on the card in the dim hall light, "Elias Jackson."

"Wha' kin' delivery you got?" The crack stayed at a paranoid width.

"Just papers. Don't know what it is, man. I just deliver the shit." I was trying to sound bored and nonchalant. These are the kind of crack-door interviews that seldom go well. Tried to take the initiative. "You Mr. Jackson?"

"Maybe." Brilliant answer. You don't know who you are?

"Well, if I could just give this to him. Is he in?"

"I'll take it." The decision was sudden and unexpected. The door swung wide. I had no idea what prompted Mr. Jackson's sudden trust, but I didn't care. I extended the summons into his hand.

He was a medium size guy with a ratty Afro, dressed in yellow polyester bell-bottoms, no shirt and three-inch platform shoes. He reached out with a trembling hand. He wasn't old, but he looked old for whatever his age was. Rheumy eyes, veins standing out on his arms and hands, so thin you could see his ribs. He took the paper and immediately started to open it.

I turned to leave. I never like to let people start reading these things while I'm there. They tend to get angry and take it out on whoever might be around.

I sensed rather than saw something come at my groin. I was already in mid turn, however, and heard as well as felt a blade make a kind of crunch as it sliced its way into the meat of my ass. Adrenaline instantly spewed into my bloodstream. I whirled back toward him, saw him standing with the knife, looking kind of surprised at himself. I'm pretty sure I said, "Fuck!" Then, on autopilot, I seized the guy by both arms and lifted him bodily off the floor. He was a featherweight in my arms. I tossed him in the direction of the hallway. He landed on his feet for a moment, but lost his balance with those stupid shoes, stumbled at the head of the stairs and fell over the top step. He landed like a load of wet laundry on the landing below. Twitched once or twice and then did not move.

I stood trembling. My overcharged heart was thumping wildly. I walked down to the landing like a puppet in the hands of a poor puppeteer. I didn't have to get very close to see that he was dead. The knife was sticking out of his chest, between the third and fourth intercostal space. They taught us about that in the Army.

I tottered back up the stairs and into his apartment, intending to find his phone and call the cops. I swear, I was going to call the cops. But what I saw on the table in his living room brought me to a stop. There was a quart plastic bag on the table filled with a "suspicious white powder." I didn't need to taste it to know it was about a fifty grand worth of cocaine. And on the table next to it was a neat stack of bills bundled with rubber bands. A whole bunch of them. Bills, that is, not rubber bands.

I tell you, your mind can work at lightning speed when it has to. I sized up the money, the dope, the corpse on the landing. You know what I did. I closed up that plastic bag and stuffed it under my sweatshirt. The money went into a pocket on the other side. There was so much it wouldn't all fit and I had to stuff some in my jeans' pockets. Then I blew out of there and down the stairs as fast as my shaking legs would take me. As I stepped across the threshold I noticed the summons I had given Jackson. I picked up the accusing paper and stuffed it in a pocket.

Incredibly, not a door opened. The whole thing was like a silent movie. I fumbled the door of the van open, jumped in and roared away, hardly paying attention to the direction I headed. I fled quickly, but without speeding.

I got about a dozen blocks away, turning twice, instinctively heading for the brighter lit parts of town before my shaking got so bad I pulled into a loading zone and stopped. I lit a cigarette with twitching fingers and rolled down the window.

I couldn't get enough air. The fog-tinged evening breeze struck my sweating face like a slap from John Wayne. I smoked the cig so fast it made me dizzy and sick. I lit another and tried to calm down.

That was then I noticed my right hip was stinging. I felt my jeans. They were a little wet and sticky. I turned on the dome light and surveyed the damage. Couldn't see anything except a dark wet spot on the fabric and a small hole. I concluded I would live a long time with this wound. My heart decided it was not going to pound itself into a coronary attack tonight and I caught up with myself.

Why did I do what I had done? I don't mean throwing Jackson down the stairs- that was pure reflex and it wasn't my fault he tripped over those shoes. He struck first, anyway, I reasoned, so he paid a tall price for his short temper. Why had he stabbed me, anyway? Cocaine induced paranoia or rage, I suppose.

What I marveled at was that I'd decided in that flash of situational ethics to grab the dope and dough and leave. Why? Haven't a clue, really, although retrospective analysis suggested that I was afraid the cops would have given me a major bad time, even arrested me, and that I would have been charged with something. I could even make a case for them accusing me of going to Jackson's for a dope deal that had gone bad. It wouldn't have fit the facts, but in my experience, cops solve the case first then look for the facts to support the solution they have developed.

I don't know. Does it matter? There was no going back to change my decision. My conscience gave a mental shrug. I may have actually physically shrugged. But the next thing I knew, I lit another cigarette and was mentally going over the scene, trying to remember if there was anything that would tie me to the crime. Fingerprints? I didn't think so. The cops were not going to turn this into a major homicide investigation. The scene was self-explanatory to them. Drug deal gone bad. There was enough spilled cocaine around to show what Jackson's business was. The knife was Jackson's and didn't have my prints on it. I had even remembered to grab the summons on my way out the door.

I drove home slowly. Stopped for every yellow light. Watched my speed. A ticket in the vicinity could prove to be an awkward piece of evidence and I needed to drive slowly so that I wouldn't overtax my brain's processing ability. It was running at ninety miles an hour, going nowhere.

I felt like it took two hours to cross San Francisco. I parked the bus, careful to curb the wheels on the hill, grabbed my briefcase and went through the gate into the yard of Rick's house.

Rick, my landlord, rented me the basement studio. There was a little garden in the front of the door. My front door was just next to the steps that led up to the main house. I opened up, flipped on the light and dropped my case on a chair. I emptied my pockets of drugs, money, cigarettes and miscellany onto the kitchen table. The drapes were drawn, as always. I went into the bathroom, pulled off my shoes and jeans, then turned toward the mirror to assess the damage. There was a neat little slice in my right buttock, just behind the hipbone. It was no longer bleeding much. I ran the water and washed the whole area with soap, using a corner of the towel. I pulled the wound open and scrubbed, then opened the medicine cabinet and took out some wound stuff, the kind they advertise on TV. Stingless. Until you pour it into a two-inch deep knife wound. Then it will give you a whole new meaning of pain. I practiced my foul language vocabulary and then dressed it with a couple of band-aids. I didn't have anything bigger, but vowed I would get some more sophisticated first aid supplies tomorrow.

Back in the main room of the apartment I first poured a good slug of tequila. I usually fool with the lime and salt and all, but not now. I took a big gulp. It burned its way down to my gut. That's what they always do in the movies, right? I sat down at the little dinette table and turned on the lamp overhead. For a minute I just sat there looking at the heap of money and drugs. I lit a cigarette and started sorting through it.

The bag of powder was one of those zip up jobs, nearly full. I tried to guess how much it weighed, and concluded maybe a half a kilo. I opened it and gingerly took a taste. Yep, coke. I opened my pocketknife and took a goodly pile onto the tip and conveyed it to my nose. Deep sniff. Wait.

Nose burning. I felt the kick of the stimulant entering my brain. Whew, it was righteous shit. I am not a choirboy. I have done bad things with my mind and body. Oh, and you haven't? Goody for you. I am what I am. (Who said that? Oh yeah, God.)

My body was now cruising on the twin and countervailing influences of alcohol and coke. My glistening eyes turned to the stacks of money. I lit another cigarette, cocaine always causing me to become a terrible chain smoker. See, I thought, they're right, using one drug does lead to another.

I methodically counted each bundle. There was exactly the same amount in each. Each a bundle of twenties. Fifty twenties in each bundle. Sixteen bundles.

I sat there for a while, my mind doing its running in place routine, like a mad jogger going nowhere. I rummaged through my cabinets, found some plastic sandwich bags and parceled the money out into them. It took six bags to hold it all. I sealed up the cocaine bag and then opened my tiny freezer compartment and took out little packages of leftovers and frozen dinners until there was room in the back. It wasn't the most original hiding place, but would have to do for a while. I walled the loot up with frozen foods. Put the food that wouldn't fit back in the freezer into the refrigerator section. Thought foolishly for a second about how it would thaw and spoil before I could eat it all.

Two more slugs of tequila and I went to bed. In spite of the coke, I fell asleep right away.

Chapter Five
The Tradeoff

I woke up thrashing and moaning. They come as a series, the jungle one, the helicopter one, the weird one with the girl that shoots... what the Hell, I told you, I'm used to them. I staggered into the bathroom, my bladder hurt so bad my back ached. Of course, my back always aches to some degree. It let up a little after I pissed, "like a racehorse" the saying goes. Do you know why racehorses piss so grandly? Well, of course horses piss pretty magnificently anyway, but they give racehorses lasix, a diuretic, before they run, to get the weight off of them, so they piss even more extravagantly than usual. Just one of those little pieces of trivia that pools in my poor sodden brain.

My butt was really sore. I couldn't see it too well, the mirror in the bathroom was just the door to the medicine cabinet. I didn't have a big mirror in the place. Not that vain. Or so vain I thought I didn't need to check my appearance. Which was it?

I touched the wound lightly. It warm and hot. And I felt warm all over and a little wobbly. I peered at the alarm clock- seven thirteen. I was not going to make it to work today. I could feel any desire to face the world draining rapidly away. I'd call after eight. I laid back down on the bed but couldn't get comfortable. My butt hurt pretty bad now and my back was chiming in. Must have tweaked it when I tossed my victim down the stairs. Christ, I hope I hadn't done anything to the fancy hardware that resided in there. I could tell things were probably okay, since I wasn't weak or numb in my legs. I knew from experience when it was serious and this was just the slightly increased misery of having overdone my activity level. I groaned to myself and went back to the medicine cabinet and took three Vicodin. I have a system for them. One for just getting to sleep. Two for a regular sore back. Three for a miserable back. Four and two shots of tequila to hold me until I could get to the ER. See, I could be a doctor.

I dozed off after a while and woke again to a knock on the door. I eased out of bed and looked through the peephole. It was Rick. I opened the door, turned back into the room and eased into my recliner, wincing when my sore butt hit the chair.

"I saw your car here so I thought I'd see what's up," Rick explained. He didn't like to impose on me. "You look like shit."

"Thank you. I feel like shit."

"Well, I hope it was worth it, whatever you did to earn that face." Rick was smiling and imagining some decadent adventure.

"Well, actually, I got stabbed in the ass and killed a guy."

Rick obliged me with a pretty good double take, right on cue. "You shittin' me?"

"'Fraid not. My butt hurts like Hell, I screwed up my back a little bit and there's something in the freezer you should see."

Rick and I go back to 'nam. He dragged me to the helicopter after the mortar attack. He thought I was mangled and he was saving my life. It wasn't his fault that what he was seeing was some other guy's guts all over me. They loaded a bunch of us in the Medivac chopper and it took off. About 50 feet up it got hit and crashed. That's when I wrecked my back. I woke up in a Navy hospital ship. Between the mortar attack and the ship was just one long nightmare. It wasn't Rick's fault. He was saving my life, or so he thought. But he felt guilty about it anyway and after he got back to the States he tracked me down. He owned this house on Potrero Hill with a nice little basement studio. He was a good guy, even if he was a fag.

Rick went to the kitchen area, which was just one corner of the living area and made coffee. While he filled the coffee maker he called over his shoulder, "Drop your shorts and let me take a look at your ass."

"You know I'm not of your faith."

"Don't be a wise guy, I wouldn't fuck you if you were the last man on earth."

"Well gee, you really know how to hurt a guy's feelings." I dropped my shorts and turned my butt to the light coming in the front window. Rick inspected. He was our company medic, a conscientious objector who never carried a weapon in the whole damn war, the bravest son of a bitch I had ever known. He worked as a nurse in the ER at the county hospital, SF General.

"Christ, Doug, it's pretty nasty. Did you clean it up?"

"Of course, best I could. What do you think? Need stitches?"

"It's too late for stitches now, you should have gone to the ER."

"Uh, Rick, I need to point out that they report suspicious wounds in the ER and I had just tossed a fellow down the stairs. I really didn't want to get into a long explanation with the police. Besides, you haven't looked in the freezer yet."

"What's in the freezer?"

"About a kilo of cocaine and something in the neighborhood of sixteen grand."

"Holy shit!" Rick went to the freezer and looked behind the frozen peas. "Jesus fucking Christ! Doug, this is some serious amount of drugs."

"I'm hip".

I filled Rick in on the incident with the late Elias Jackson, coke dealer and fashion plate.

"Why'd you take it?" Rick was kind of weighing the plastic bag with one hand and the money with the other. "What the Hell were you thinking?"

"I didn't really stand there and reason it out, you know. I checked the guy and he was extremely dead. I went into the apartment to call the cops and there the shit was. Before I thought it through it was in my pocket and I beat feet outa there."

Rick looked at me in a speculative way. I could tell what he was thinking because when you spend a lot of time with people under stress you get kind of telepathic. "Help yourself. Then come here and fix up my butt, will you?"

"Uh yeah, sure. Look, I'm off today anyway and I was just going shopping." He laid the baggy of drugs on the table and put the money back behind the frozen peas. It took him all of ten seconds to fix himself a nice little heap of coke on the end of a pocket knife and administer it. To himself. "I'm going upstairs to get some supplies for that wound."

He was back in ten minutes. I lay face down on the bed while he cleaned the wound with Betadine and then dabbed it with antibiotic cream. He dressed it and then straightened up. It hurt like Hell and I had squawked plenty.

"Here, this will perk you up." He offered me a big toot of coke.

"No, thanks, I don't think that's such a good idea."

"Well, suit yourself." He took it. "You know, this is fantastic. What're you gonna do with all that dough."

"Save it for my lawyer."

"You think they'll find you?"

"Actually, no I don't see why they will. I'm sure they'll figure it was a drug rip-off and I'm pretty sure nobody saw me. So all I have to deal with is my own poor conscience."

"Yeah, well, you know how I feel about killing and war and all that, but this was self defense. You should have called the cops."

"Uh huh. And when they found the money and the drugs they would have spent all night hassling me about it. Maybe charged me anyway. Then I would have to deal with lawyers, and court dates and bail and all that crap. No, Rick, I'll tell you. Only a sucker goes to the cops if he doesn't have to." The self-justification was growing in my own mind. "As for taking the stuff, well, I told you, it just kind of happened. I don't know what I'm going to do with the shit."

Rick took another toot. "I'll tell you what I'd do, honey. I'd call every pair of hot pants in the City over for the biggest party you can imagine."

"Yeah, I'll bet you would. Look, go ahead, take some. Take as much as you want." I sat next to Rick at the table and helped myself to the pile, in spite of my previous abstinence.

Rick looked at me, then looked at the bag. He didn't wait to be asked twice but got one out of the drawer and took about a quarter of the stash. "I'm going to very popular this weekend on Folsom." That was the gay area that Rick preferred. Lots of leather bars and such. I'd been there with him once, but it was much too weird for my head. Those guys liked their sex rough and ready. I always felt like it was dangerous to do anything besides sit down. I'd been felt up once or twice in the crowd and it was pretty intimidating to have some muscular guy with a leather jacket and various parts of his body pierced leering at you. I tried not to think about Rick in that environment. My relationship with him was so different from his gay friends that I sometimes forgot that side of him. Not that I really cared. What a guy does with his dick is his business and Rick never came on to me. Well, one time, but that's another story.

Rick pulled a joint out of his pocket and we smoked. Then dipped into the coke. Then started on the tequila. "Shit!" I remembered the office. Called in and told Van I was sick and wouldn't be available for any special runs. He stuttered out a fair imitation of concern.

We continued our impromptu drug orgy; drinking, smoking and snorting the morning away. My wound was only a dull throb and my back was a forgotten misery. We laughed like a couple of goofs and talked about the war and the guys we served with and what a bunch of idiots we all were. We bragged and lied like guys do. About noon we staggered out to the corner store and bought sandwiches and beer and wolfed them down. We sat in the little courtyard in the sunshine and just enjoyed being alive and stoned. We wasted time and ourselves in fine fashion. My guilt ebbed away along with my pain. After lunch I took two more Vicodin just for good measure and went to bed. Rick went back upstairs with his little portion of the stash, waving merrily and telling me he'd come down later to "check my butt" with a lewd wink and laugh. I laughed too and passed out.

The knocking at the door broke a perfect, painless coma. I rolled out of bed and took a couple steps before the wound in my butt reminded me it was there. "God damn it," I told myself, and then called out, "Coming, coming. Hold on," to the doorknocker. A quick peek through the peephole told me it was just Sammy Feinstein, another one of AAA's fine corps of servers. He reached up to knock again and I timed it so he was knocking on air. He almost fell forward when the door disappeared under his knuckles.

"Oh!" was all he could muster.

"Hi Sammy, what's up?" Sammy was not exactly a social acquaintance; we just saw each other in passing. He was about sixty, not more than five foot three and round about the middle. He walked like a penguin; a round head littered with a few thin gray hairs. His '68 Caddy was parked at the curb, dented and rusty.

How he could afford gas for the thing with all the driving we did was beyond my understanding but it was none of my business how he spent his money.

Sammy was trying to organize his explanation. "Uh, Doug, Van told me come by and see how long you was gonna be laid up, 'cause if you're gonna be laid up very long he wants me to pick up one of your jobs Geez you look like shit." He needed to take a breath here and wheezed for a moment.

"Come on in, Sammy." I turned back inside and planted my wounded butt gingerly in a chair at the table, waving him in for a landing.

"So how you doin'?" He grunted as he sat.

"A little rocky. Guess I got the flu or somethin'".

He fished a crumpled little piece of paper out of his pants pocket. I recognized one of Van's notes. Sammy peered through the magnifying section of his bifocals. "Van says if you can't get to this one you're supposed to give it to me. It's..."he stopped to decipher Van's writing, "...Gunter. An OSC."

"Yeah, I know the one. Just a sec." I retrieved it from my case and handed it over. "Hey, this guy is playin' games, Sammy. I've been to the office and got blown off by his secretary. He lives in a building with a doorman and I couldn't get to him last night there."

"Yeah, well, Van says the client called this morning, so since you didn't work it, he wants me to take a stab at him at the office and at his residence tonight. It's a stake out." He added the last sentence with great relish. I understood. Sammy liked stakeouts cause he could make ten bucks an hour for sittin' on his ass. I liked them too, and for the same reason.

"Well, great Sammy, don't forget to take a bottle."

"I use a milk carton." He sounded proud, like there was something superior about pissing in a milk carton instead of a bottle.

"Well, to each his own. Look, I'm gonna crash, I feel beat." Sammy took the cue and waddled his way out. I called to his back, "How're the legs?"

"As bad as always. Doc says he wants to cut them off."

"Oh." I felt bad for asking. "Well, tell the doc to fuck himself."

"I did." He made it to his car and I watched him pull away in that monster, muffler roaring and valves clacking. "Christ," I shook my head as I closed the door, thinking about Sam trying to drive all over San Francisco in that piece of shit and having to climb stairs to deliver crap to people who cursed him. I don't think anyone was actually mean enough to take a poke at Sammy, he was such a pitiful broken down old guy. In a way that was his protection. A depressing vision of myself in thirty or forty years flickered in my mind.

Chapter Six

Death is Nature's Way of Telling You to Slow Down

Rick checked in later that evening, poked at the wound and clucked, changed the dressing. We discussed the possibility of a party. Rick threw a party almost once a month, or more, and with the windfall I provided him he was hot to throw a big wingding. I'll tell you this, there are no more dedicated partiers than fags. I've never seen anything to beat them, including R and R in Bangkok. Halloween was three months away and Rick and his pals were probably interested in warming up for the "queer New Years Eve", as Halloween in Frisco is known. Anyway, Rick was all excited and twittery about what a big party he was going to have Saturday night and all the food and decorations he was planning. I said I'd stop by sometime that evening. But Saturday was two days away.

I passed a quiet night and slept the sleep of the unjust (which is just as good as the sleep of the just, in my opinion). My pager beeped while I was shaving. It was Van.

"Hi Van. Good morning."

"Hey Doug. How're you feeling?"

"I'll live."

"Go relieve Sam on that stakeout, would you?"

"Was he there all night?"

"No, but he's been there since five and was there last night. He's probably beat."

"Sure."

"You know where he is?"

"Yeah, I remember." I told Van I'd be there within half an hour.

I circled the block before I saw Sam's Cad parked across from the garage entrance of the flats. He hadn't worried about which way the guy would turn, since Sacramento Street is one way downtown and he could only have turned right out of the garage.

I double parked just behind him and got out. Sam didn't look back when I pulled up. As I got closer I saw his head back and his mouth open. Asleep. Asshole, how could he know if our subject had taken off or not? I rapped sharply on the window, intending to scare the crap out of him.

He didn't react. I yanked the door open. He started to fall out, his head landing in my arms as I reached out to keep from being knocked over by his dead weight.

Too Many Spies Spoil the Case

Dead was the operative word. I propped Sam back behind the wheel. I could tell he was dead without any fancy pulse checking or eyelid raising. He was cold, slightly stiff, and didn't make a sound. As quiet as the dead. That's the thing about corpses- they don't make the slightest sound.

I glanced around but didn't see anyone or anything that would prove to be of immediate help. Leave Sam here and go find a phone? The faces of all the buildings were as blank as an executioner's. I decided to go to Gunter's lobby, since there would be a doorman and he would have a phone.

I left the van there, double parked, and ran around the short corner to the door. Sure enough, there was the old doorman, Jerome, sitting at his desk, looking tired.

He took forever to get to the door, and a second eternity before he understood what I wanted, but he got the "police" part and "dead". I told him I would wait at the scene.

When I came back around the corner there was a meter maid scooter pulled up in front of my car, right next to poor Sam. A fat meter maid scribbled in her ticket book.

When I walked up she gave me a dirty look and handed me the ticket.

"You can't double-park here, even if you got commercial plates." She was pronouncing sentence.

"Yeah, well, that's cool." I gave her a big smile. "Of course, you didn't happen to notice that fellow you're parked next to?"

She glanced around and noticed Sam.

"So what. Some drunk asleep in his car. He's parked legally."

"He's not drunk, he's dead."

She shrank back like I'd threatened her and looked at Sam's corpse more closely.

"Shit, he sure do look dead. Shit. I got to call a patrol car."

She was back in her little cart and I could hear her squawking into the radio hysterically. I leaned against the van and waited. I didn't want to get in, I was afraid Miss J. Edgar there would report me for trying to flee.

A couple of minutes later a radio car pulled up, casually blocking the next lane. Now there was only one lane for cars headed downtown to use and traffic backed up fast. The officers got out, listened to the junior G-man for about a minute and then sent her out to direct the rubber-neckers. The other one went up to the car, walking as though he expected Sam to jump out with a machine gun, and knocked on the window. Sam remained as responsive as before. The cop opened the door and this time Sam stayed put. Either this cop hadn't seen many corpses before or else he was putting on a show of thoroughness, he checked Sam's neck for a pulse before turning to me.

37

"Did you find him?"
"Yes."
"Know him?"
"Yes."
"How?"
"How do I know him?"
"Yeah, how do you know him?"
"He works for the same outfit I do."
"And that would be...?"
He pulled out his notebook. "AAA Legal Process, on Market Street."
"Number?"
I started regurgitating statistical information about Sam and myself. While he took shorthand his partner called for the morgue and a homicide detective. When I got to the part about coming to relieve Sam the cop got interested.
"Relieve him of what?"
"He was staking someone out."
"What for?"
"For ten bucks an hour."
"All right, smart ass. Why was he staking someone out for ten bucks an hour." He was getting unpleasant and I was already sick of the bored, routine way he was taking everything down, like Sam was just an inconvenience in his morning.
"We've got some legal papers to serve on a guy that lives in that building," I nodded to my right. "He was ducking service and our client wanted him served ASAP."

An unmarked detective's car arrived, further screwing up traffic. Now not only was the street reduced to one lane, but the rubber-neckers were in full observation mode, ignoring the frantic "move along" gestures of the fat meter maid and getting a good eyeful to share around the coffee machine as soon as they got to work. I could see that most of them were carefully looking at my face, as though to recognize me again when I appeared on the evening news as the perpetrator of some heinous crime.

The detectives consulted with the uniforms for a few minutes, not seeming to be in any hurry. I figure the reason cops don't hurry is they are paid by the hour, and get overtime. My "the officer is your friend" days were clubbed out of me in the San Francisco State riot of '68. I've been looking to get even ever since.

The older detective rounded on me. "So you know this guy, huh?" He said it like it was an accusation.

"Yes, I knew him. He worked for the same company I do. As I explained to your fine colleague there just a moment ago."

"Are you a smart ass or don't you like cops?"

"Both." His face said he was looking forward to making my life miserable.

He turned back to Sam's car and gave the interior a cursory look. He and his partner whispered like they were discussing state secrets and then he told the uniforms to arrange for the car to be towed as soon as the morgue took Sam away. They took a few photographs with a Polaroid, made a couple of notes and then the first detective turned back to me.

"You, come to the Hall. We need a statement."

"Sure. Of course." He handed me his card and after giving my van a cursory search, like they would find a bloody weapon on the seat, we arranged to meet in an hour.

"Do you think you know what killed my partner there?" I asked.

"Looks like his heart, to me. But we have to investigate this kind of thing." Yeah, no kidding.

I handed him the ticket. "Think you could get this taken care of?" He grimaced and thought about it. "Come on, don't make me go to court." He relented and jammed it in his pocket.

I drove the van around to the front of Gunter's building and prevailed upon Jerome for the use of his phone one more time.

Barbara answered. It was just as well it was her and not Van Duzee, who would need the story three times before it would penetrate. I boiled it down to: "I found Sam dead in his car when I got there this morning. I've been hung up with the cops for an hour. I have to go give a statement downtown. Put Harry or Dorothy on will you, I need to ask 'em something right away." Bless her, Barbara took it all in with only an instinctive "what" once and Harry came on the line in thirty seconds.

"Doug, Sam's dead?" Harry needed to hear it from me, I guess.

"That's right, dead. Found him behind the wheel, and he's been gone for a while. Look, Harry, I didn't tell the cops anything specific about why we were there, just that we were trying to serve somebody. Can I tell them everything or is there some confidentiality thing here?"

Harry paused for a second. "No, you can tell them anything they ask. There's no confidentiality in a civil case when there's a possible felony involved. You're not violating any kind of client privilege."

"Okay, just wanted to check with you first."

"Thanks for asking. You go ahead and go to the police station and, Doug, try not to be a smart ass." He said this last kindly.

The morning ground on its inevitable way with heavy glass doors and marble hallways and old wooden furniture and lots of waiting around. The detectives treated me okay and we settled into a fairly businesslike relationship of they asked and I answered. They got a little interested when the Government of Iran bit came up but when they saw that I wasn't a player in that case except in the most minor way they dropped their interest. They were professionally contemptuous, which is all I expect of cops anyway. They certainly don't respect process servers, in principle. They think of us as a bunch of idiots or losers. Gee, not all of us are. I hope.

It was noon before I made my way back to the office and of course when I walked in there was general pandemonium. I gave the story to Harry and Dorothy in private, then I had to go through it all again for everyone in the office. By the time I finished, I was talked out.

Finally Bill appeared to rescue me, declaring that he was buying me a drink. I was ready for lunch as well, so we repaired to the *Hoffman*, considering the gravity of the moment. We were barely seated five minutes when Jan came scurrying in and spotted us.

Bill and Jan settled for the Reader's Digest version of events. We quickly drank a round and then started another. We ordered perfunctorily and went on drinking through our meal. By the time the food was gone we were all feeling pretty mellow.

Bill said, apropo of nothing, "It was probably his heart."

"Why would it be anything else?" Jan asked.

"Yeah, Bill, he was in his car, window up. The cops found his half full piss jug and some food and a carton of milk. If he were down on the street, I would have thought maybe somebody popped him, but like that, well, you know Sam was pretty far gone, anyway." I felt guilty that Sam was working the paper I should have been working. I had been too screwed up to work, after fighting with platform shoes and getting crazy with Rick the next day. The guilt was mounting fast.

It was two thirty when all our pagers went off, one after the other. We got up en masse and walked back to the office.

Life, and more likely work, goes on. Van sent Jan to San Jose on a filing, Bill on a special to Marin and he told me to stop by Mel Belli's office for another copy of the OSC, since the cop's took all of Sam's paper. I was to pick up the new OSC and get over to the Pyramid and try to nail the guy coming out of his office.

Mel Belli was the quintessential San Francisco trial lawyer. Mane of white hair, wide girth, expensive suits and an avuncular manner. His office on Montgomery Street was in the North Beach area, just down from all the titty bars and jazz joints. If you walked uphill half a block you could be at Enrico's coffee house in five minutes, where Belli had his own table and would hold forth on occasion.

His personal office was on the ground floor of a three-story building, with big windows so anyone walking by could see the great man at his desk. The room was packed with expensive antiques and mementos of a long and colorful career.

I picked up the papers from the receptionist and headed to the Pyramid. Parking was the usual impossibility, but I managed a place in a loading zone and parked myself on the mezzanine level where Gunter would have to pass when leaving his office elevator.

I hung around for an hour and a half before a security guard finally asked, politely, if he could help me. I told him I was there on court business, waved the OSC under his nose without showing him anything, and he nodded and went away looking like he'd learned something.

Twenty minutes later his supervisor showed up and we went through the story again. He wanted to look at the papers, which I politely declined to permit. We reached agreement that I was not going to cause any trouble and had a legal right to be there, at least until closing.

I hung out the whole afternoon, but Gunter did not pass me and I knew there was no point in dealing with the ice queen in the office. About four forty five my pager went off. I went down to the lobby and phoned the office.

"Hi Van, what's up?"

"Doug?" Van's wavering voice told me he was running out of steam for the day.

"Yeah Van, it's me, you called?"

"Can you come into the office now?" There was something nervous in his tone.

"Sure, I suppose. This jerkoff at the pyramid hasn't shown, though, don't you want me to hang here for a while?"

"Well, Harry wants to see you." Van said Harry's name like he was the Pope.

"What Harry wants, Harry gets. Can you tell me what's going on?"

Van's voice dropped to a slurred whisper. "He's got a couple of suits in his office. I don't know for sure, but Barbara thinks it's about Sam."

"Cops?"

"Don't look like cops, too well dressed. I think they're Feds."

"What would fucking Feds care about Sammy?"

"Just come in." Van had said all he was going to say.

"On my way."

On the way back to the office I tried to arrange the facts I knew into some scenario that explained things, then gave up. "Find out soon enough" I mumbled to myself. When you want an intelligent conversation, talk to yourself, I always say.

I breezed through the door. The girls were putting the covers on their typewriters and picking up their purses. They glanced at me like I was walking to my execution. Barbara's machine was still uncovered. She was sorting out tomorrow's work and trying to divine what the suits in Harry's office were saying. They were sitting in front of his desk, Dorothy was sitting next to Harry, and everyone was looking really grim.

I whispered to Barbara as Harry caught my eye, "What gives?" but she just gave a little shake of her hair and motioned me into the office. "Make it a nice funeral, will you?" I muttered over my shoulder.

Dorothy was already up and opening the door for me. She smiled tightly, "Come in Doug. We need to talk."

I plopped into the only available chair. With the five of us the office was packed. I crossed my legs and tried to look nonchalant. "Okay, what's up?"

Harry spoke first. "These gentlemen are Federal Marshals. They want to talk to you about what happened to Sam."

I looked at the two marshals. They looked like TV actors playing the part of Federal agents. They were both tall, athletic, unsmiling, with quick intelligent eyes and a no-bullshit attitude. I tried to put my smart-ass persona into storage.

The right hand marshal spoke. "Why was Mr. Feinstein working the case you were assigned?"

"Working the case" I thought. We were hardly "working a case" but it certainly made it sound important. "I wasn't feeling well that day, so Van had Sammy pick the paper up from me". I tried to keep my voice totally without expression, since I didn't want to go into why I wasn't feeling well. The wound in my butt was throbbing in guilty sympathy.

"Sick?" The other one questioned. He couldn't seem to take his eyes off the 'Have A Nice Day' smiley button on my sweatshirt.

"It happens."

"When you were working this particular case, did you ever come in contact with Mr. Gunter?"

"Well, maybe. I saw a guy in his office that was probably him but he scooted into the back office and the receptionist gave me the bum's rush. Haven't seen the guy since. Tried his flat, no luck."

"Describe the man you saw."

"Sure. About 45, five feet nine or ten, sandy hair shot with gray, looked pretty athletic, something military about him. Light eyes, I think. Blue and white striped shirt with gold and onyx cufflinks and matching tie tack with a white stone in the center. Gray slacks, no suit coat. Black shoes. Wears his hair in a brush cut, I guess that's what made me think military."

"You're pretty observant." The left one spoke.

"For a dumb process server, you mean." My suspicion and guilty conscience were making me irritable. The Fed guys gave me a look and Harry said: "Now Doug, don't take that attitude."

"Well, how about we get some story from their side of the room now?" I tried to keep my voice even, probably not successfully.

The Feds looked at each other, then Harry and Dorothy, then me. "You are aware that this is a case that involves a foreign government?" Mr. Left spoke.

"Yeah, I can read." I was getting pissed off with this step-by-step approach.

"Did you ever develop the sense that you were being followed while you were attempting to effect service on Mr. Gunter?" Mr. Left again.

"No. So what's going on?" They ignored me.

"You didn't observe anyone else who might have had Gunter staked out?" Mr. Right. They were the regular dynamic duo.

"No again. Not the kind of thing I run into in my line of work, you understand. Was he being staked out by you guys?"

They ignored me.

Harry spoke up. "Under the circumstances, gentlemen, we are going to inform our client that we are no longer going to attempt service on this man. We'll let you take it from here."

"Was Sammy killed?" My voice grated out of me. I hadn't meant it to sound that rough, but it came out that way.

Mr. Left was apparently the spokesman. "We have no indication of foul play here. The autopsy is scheduled for sometime tonight." He intended to leave it at that. He turned his head toward Harry and Dorothy. "Look, we don't think that the death of your employee had anything to do with Mr. Gunter. The police believe he died of a heart attack. However, since this is a Federal court case we felt that we ought to inquire. I don't think you need to withdraw, Mr. Silver. The Marshal's office doesn't have the time or manpower to serve civil process. We just wanted to look into it. That's all." He stood up and his partner was on his feet at the same time. They smiled in unison, turned and squeezed out of the office without another word or look back. Leaving their huge load of bullshit behind. Why would Federal marshals know when Sammy's autopsy was scheduled if they weren't interested in this?

Harry, Dorothy and I sat looking at each other. She spoke first. "I don't like this, Harry. Let's give it back."

"Wait," I butted in. "I want to work it."

"No," Harry looked at Dorothy, then at me.

"Why not? You gonna let these spooky Fed guys bother you? They said go ahead. Who cares what they're up to. I want to nail this guy. Besides, we should stay in tight with Mel, shouldn't we?" I was grasping at straws.

Harry and Dorothy exchanged glances. "We'll think about it."

I gave up trying to make my case with them, stood up and walked out, closing the door behind me.

Barbara was still in the office, just fooling around waiting for me. As soon as I came out of Harry's door, she said, "Let's go get a drink."

"You got it."

"I think the rest of the gang's down there."

Chapter Seven

A Kiss is Still a Kiss

When Barbara and I walked into *The Office* it was thick with drinkers. Bill, Mary, Layla and Bernice had a booth and Barbara and I crammed in with them. We were plastered up against each other, but no one cared. I could tell that they'd been drinking steadily since closing the office and Barbara and I hurried to catch up. As soon as we all had drinks in front of us they started grilling me about the Fed guys. There wasn't that much to tell and we discussed the whole thing from every angle, the speculation becoming more creative the more we drank. We gorged on the free hot hors d'œuvres and got pretty well blitzed. By seven thirty Bill excused himself, mumbling something about working, but after he left Barbara laughed about the excuse he gave.

"Bullshit," she snorted, "He's going to his bookie's. He'll lose his shirt tonight." She glanced around at the other three women and then she laughed. "I'd like to see this guy lose his shirt tonight too!" They all started laughing and their eyes were dancing from one to the other. Mary and Bernice both gave Barbara an appraising look, and Layla stared intently into my eyes. I looked around the table.

"Now ladies, I'm not sure I'm up to handling that kind of thing." I joked along with them. I was intrigued with the idea of how I could make it with four women at once, and the image suddenly shot from my brain to my crotch, which responded enthusiastically.

Just as quickly the conversation suddenly changed to how this one and that one needed to get going. Layla left first, then Mary. I offered Barbara and Bernice a ride, but they both wanted to be dropped at their bus stops. We walked to my van. Barbara sat in the back, Bernice next to me. We chatted for a minute or so, then Bernice looked at Barbara strangely, looked at me with the same strange look, reached out one soft brown hand, took my head with it, and pulled me to her lips. I was so startled I didn't know what to do except cooperate. She kissed me until I was gasping for breath. The soft intensity of her lips was deep and urgent. I barely had time to inhale when Barbara, who was now kneeling between our seats took my head the same way and kissed me too. Her tongue flickered about mine, then she sucked it firmly. I felt Bernice's hand on my thigh, and it slid right up to find my cock and, reaching it, started squeezing it determinedly. It leapt to her touch.

We kissed, the three of us at once, tongues dueling from one to the other, laughing and teasing. Both women were rubbing me, and kissing me, and each other. The windows fogged.

Suddenly we stopped. The women looked at each other and smiled. Barbara said,"Oh God. I really want to finish this, but I have to get home."

Bernice looked down at the floor. "I've never done anything like that before." Her voice didn't sound regretful, more like surprised.

My poor cock was throbbing with anticipation and now was disappointed. However, the brain part of me was slightly relieved. I needed to think about a threesome with two women I work with. There were elements that could prove to be serious complications down the road. A little drunken groping between friends was okay in my book, and didn't necessarily have to lead anywhere. Although, the prospect of getting Barbara in bed had thrilled me. Not to mention adding Bernice to it. Well, I could reflect later.

I dropped them off in good order, stopped by my favorite burrito place and picked up giant pork *carnitas* with everything and wolfed half of it down in a few minutes. These things were huge, filled with rice, beans, meat, guacamole, sour cream and jalapenos. Then I went out and laid paper until nine thirty. I stopped by Gunter's building on my way home, fenced with the old doorman, knocked on Gunter's door with no response and left. I started to drive home, but on a whim I circled Gunter's block, went up three streets, then came back down slowly. As luck would have it, I found an empty loading zone that gave me a pretty good view of the corner where his building sat and settled down to watch. I didn't know what I was expecting to see, but I just sat there and let my eyes roam around.

Cars came and went, stopped for the stop sign at the top of Sacramento Street and then accelerated away. They came down Powell Street past me, slowed for the intersection and then continued on. I was looking for something that didn't fit, that was out of the pattern of ebb and flow of traffic, either vehicular or pedestrian. There was little foot traffic on those streets, the area being mostly high-income flats with garages. A car would occasionally come up to a garage door, the door would open in response to the automated opener, the car would enter, the door would close again. A couple of cars pulled away from street side parking places. I was not smoking. It hurts your night vision and the telltale odor on the night wind would reveal my presence. I thought it a good idea not to do that, in the light of Sammy's misadventure. I always lock my car doors.

The Powell Street cable cars ran past every ten or fifteen minutes, ferrying their load to Fisherman's Wharf. A few dedicated San Franciscans would ride them to and from work, although they were mostly for the amusement of tourists. Kind of like a ride at Disneyland. San Francisco is an amusement park with booze and hookers.

The ancient cars rattled and clanked, the grip man would clang the bell wildly and then the thing would clatter away up or down Powell. I wondered how much it cost the City each year in lawsuits when people fell off, which happened pretty regularly.

I was about to give it up around eleven when my patience (or was it inertia?) was rewarded. I noticed a pale little stream of smoke coming from a car on the cross street, down from the corner. I then focused on the windshield and sure enough, the telltale brief glow of a cigarette being drawn upon told me a fellow addict just lost the wrestling match between nicotine and discipline.

Now I was no longer the idle observer, but the hunter. I could only make out that the vehicle was a generic American sedan, four door, brownish. Rental? Cop car? Certainly the kind of nondescript vehicle favored by those who like to remain unnoticed. How could I come upon it without them noticing me?

I waited until a cable car came past, using the racket it made to cover the sound of my car door. The cable car blocked the view of the watcher so I could hustle up the street out of sight. I then walked away from my target and around the block. It was quite a hike, uphill and down, and took a few minutes to realize, but soon I was coming up the hill on Sacramento Street, behind the watcher. It was dark and he was not likely to see me in a side view mirror, I reasoned. I sauntered my way closer.

As I drew nearly even with my quarry, my heart gave a jump and for a moment I stopped in surprise. There was another car, four door, nondescript, with two men in it, parked on the other side of the street, in position to watch the car I was approaching. I recovered my attempt to look like an evening stroller working his way uphill. As I drew close to the first watcher I recorded the letters/numbers in my head, then casually glanced at the occupant as I passed.

I couldn't make out much. Male, dark clothes, dark hair. He had stopped smoking after the one failure of will power. I didn't dare glance backward at the windshield after I passed, but decided to stop at the corner, two cars past, and turn to cross the street. That let me stop just off the curb and look up and down the street, as though looking for traffic. I got really lucky, several cars were coming down the hill, and I, cautious pedestrian, waited for them to stop at the sign before I crossed. I looked straight at the figure in the car for a good thirty seconds, but in the dark, I really couldn't see much more than my first impression.

I crossed the street, then walked around to my car. That was six long blocks so as to come from another direction. I even approached from the opposite side of the street, as though I was coming out of one of the buildings. As I opened the driver's side door, with dramatic inspiration, I turned and waved enthusiastically to no one in farewell. It's better to be noticed and dismissed than noticed and wondered about. I took a few minutes to start up, then drove away briskly, not looking toward the two sets of watchers.

Chapter Eight

The Dark Side of the Moon

On the way home I reviewed what I knew versus what I suspected:
 1. Obviously, Gunter was involved in more than just some big buck civil lawsuit.
 2. Obviously, at least to me, Sam had been in the wrong place at the wrong time and being suspected by someone of being a player in whatever this other drama was, they killed him. That may have been a burst of over-enthusiasm on someone's part.
 3. Okay, we know the Feds are interested. Were those guys in Harry's office really marshals, or were they some other agency that could supply any identification they chose?

After asking and not answering these and many more questions I flipped on the tube, surfed channels for a minute, lucked into one of my favorite movies, *The Maltese Falcon,* and watched Sam Spade handle everything with assurance and panache.

After Sam sent his love off to jail I went to bed.

Friday morning I decided to give Gunter's office another shot. After the tedious routine of parking, walking, elevatoring, changing elevators, I rode the final leg of the marathon.

The doors opened and I took three steps forward before I processed what I was seeing. Gunter's receptionist, Christine the Ice Queen, was sprawled in her chair, her head back at a ridiculous angle. For someone alive. However, in her case, the angle of her neck was the least of her problems. The small hole in her forehead and the shower of blood and brains on the wall said more.

I stood there frozen in shock. Two corpses in two days is a hard way to start your mornings. The elevator doors had closed behind me, so it was just me and her. She was not good company. I tiptoed past and went into the first office I found, picked up the phone and called the cops. Then I sat down and waited. I figured that whoever the shooter was, he/they must be gone by now, or else I would have the same problem as the Ice Queen.

This time with the police was an all day affair, and Harry wound up coming down to headquarters and talking with the detective lieutenant to get them to ease up on me. Since I was innocent, at least of this crime, there really wasn't any place for their interrogation to go, the repetition of questions and denials was becoming tedious.

They really wanted to talk to Gunter, of course, but I could shed no light on that problem for them. In fact, I didn't have a clue why two people in two days had been knocked off.

Harry and I finally walked out of there about four thirty. I thanked him for his help and headed for home. I was very glad to curl up in front of the TV and watch Frank Cannon solve crime for me. I put my brain on hold for the night.

Saturday I woke up early and got ready for Sammy's funeral service. I wore my favorite dress up clothes: gray flannel slacks, white-on-white pattern shirt with French cuffs and a pair of ornate knotted white and yellow gold cufflinks that were my Dad's, black knitted silk tie with a tack that matched the cufflinks, black cashmere sport coat with one gold button, deeply cut with narrow lapels. Black spit shined boots. With this on, I felt invulnerable and wealthy. Didn't look half bad either. I pulled my hair into a tight ponytail with a black holder.

The service was held at Sammy's synagogue, an old building in the Mission, surrounded by Mexican restaurants and plumbing supply places, oodles of kids playing in the streets. No place to park. Walking to the old building I looked as out of place as a man from Mars. Dozens of brown eyes followed my progress. A couple of gays smiled and eyed me as I passed them in the street- I guess I'm not used to being checked out by men, it still makes me feel a little weird to be appraised in the same way that a woman might be by a construction worker.

Those of us from AAA were clustered in the worn lobby area. Harry and Dorothy were the self-appointed managers of this affair, and they directed, instructed and arranged us according to their sense of decorum and protocol. I watched Bill hustle in, just making it before the doors to the sanctuary closed and fumble with the *yamica* that Harry handed him frantically as Bill sailed past.

I suppose my coworkers were surprised when I walked up to the small dais with Harry and two short gray men with *tallis* over their shoulders. The four of us, together with six old men, made up a *minyan*, the ten men required to have a service. We did the necessities dictated by the God of Abraham, Issac and Jacob. I sang the *Kaddish*, rather well, I thought, and Harry delivered a short eulogy that seemed to have to reach for something significant to say about Sam's small life. His widow's face remained buried in her hands the entire time. I could not tell you what she looked like, a little gray haired woman in a lumpy black dress constantly surrounded by three similar women who never lost contact with her. Guides for the blind, as she seemed to be sightless in her grief. Well, thank God someone loved Sam. He deserved it. Don't we all?

After the service we stumbled out of the house of sadness and into the bright warm day of the Mission, busy and populated as thickly as ever. We broke up into groups, by who was to ride with whom, and I was not required to chauffeur anyone. Barbara and Bernice were appropriately subdued. We exchanged widely innocent looks and neutrally pleasant greetings, as custom would require. Barbara whispered, "You clean up pretty nice," and winked at me.

Her appearance startled me, when I spotted her in the audience at the service. Her plain brown hair had been magically transformed into billows of blond curls styled like Farrah Fawcett. "I can't believe how gorgeous you look." I stuttered. "Wow!"

She smiled coyly, "Oh, well, I'm glad you like it," patting her hair.

"Well, I like the whole package. It's just...I wasn't expecting the hair."

"I thought I could use a change. Glad you like it." She sailed off with Dorothy and Harry in their car.

When we reassembled at the Silver's house everyone expressed their feelings in muted tones, gave their formal expressions of grief to Mrs. Sam (I don't think I ever did get her name) and then hit the booze and food. The bar and buffet were generous to a degree, as though the Silverman's had reached some agreement as to Sam's value in death- plenty of food and booze, but not caviar or canapés, more the roast beef and lox style. Sam would have eaten himself to death, were he not already the subject of this wake.

I was complimented with varying degrees of surprise on my performance in Sam's death ceremonies, seems many of my fellow employees felt that the name McCool was not a fair advertisement of my ethnic background. I was obliged to tell the family story of how Meir Kuhlschtein admired the last name of the Irish immigration officer that he encountered on Ellis Island and had "Americanized" himself and his descendants on the spot. To make matters worse, his son, my father, married a saucy Black Irish girl, so I was more deserving of the McCool moniker than one might think. I had, at my mother's insistence, been raised and educated in the faith of my fathers, although, by strict Jewish law, I was not Jewish due to my mother's Catholic roots. The random interaction and conflict of these genetic gifts made for many misadventures and some lovely times.

Jan sidled over. "Hey, what's this about another body you found?"

"Yeah. Pretty weird."

"Who was it?"

"Some chick."

"Really! Geez, and Sammy the day before." He smiled crazily, "I hope you don't ever come to find me. You're the angel of death."

Thanks.

Harry made his way over to me. He held a small plate of goodies and a glass of red wine. "Doug, come with me, we need to talk."

I followed him down the hall to a small office. There was a plain wood desk, a wood swivel chair with a red cushion faded to a dusty rose, several filing cabinets, tan, four drawer, very scarred. One wall was books, mostly legal stuff, references, their spines making a nice collage of maroon, black and brown leather, the gold lettering on them glinting in the light of a cheap fluorescent fixture. Harry was not pretentious, you could say that for him.

He slid between one wall and the desk and planted himself in charge. He set the plate and glass down and motioned to a plain gray steel straight back chair, with black vinyl padding. I sat.

"About those men..." Harry waited for me to appear to be up to speed. I was immediately a little more attentive in appearance. "Well, look, I'm not interested in adventure, here, Doug. You understand? We aren't private investigators, you see? Yes, I have a license. Got it many years ago when it wasn't so hard. But that's not the point."

He paused to let me absorb the argument so far. I nodded to him to go on.

"I talked with Mr. Belli's office and, he, uh, they, made it clear that their client urgently wanted the order served, and that they did not want to rely on the, uh, mercies of the Federal marshal's office to get it done. Those guys have their own priorities, and serving this stuff is not one of them."

"So, what did Mel say?" I knew that Harry had talked to *the* man. They were friends. It would bug Harry for me to call Belli by his given name.

"*Mr. Belli's office...*" he emphasized, "would appreciate it if we could continue to attempt service. However, given the nature of the situation..."

"Meaning Sammy's unfortunate demise...and yesterday's, uh, incident."

"Yes, of course, that. But given that certain of my staff could operate under my license..."

"In other words, as private investigators rather than just process servers..."

"Exactly. This would also mean your pay rate would be, ah, significantly higher. On a per hourly basis, you understand. The budget is reasonably liberal in this regard, so you could consider yourself relieved of most of your routine work for the time being. Van might need you for a special of one kind or another, but you could work that in."

"Okay. I work the Gunter paper full time until he's nailed. That the idea?"

"Exactly. However," he raised his voice a decibel here, and spoke real slowly, so even one as stupid as I could understand, "We are *not investigating* the events surrounding Sammy's death. We follow and poke around on finding Mr. Gunter until we find and can identify him, if need be, in court. Just keep it up until you can serve him."

"Of course." I sounded innocent. This was like leaving ground beef on the floor with a dog. I had been after Harry to expand into PI work, he owned the license and I owned the ambition. Process serving was pretty crude in terms of a career, as Harry and Dorothy had both lectured me.

Harry continued, picking up on a discussion that we'd had before. "Ever since California instituted the 'no fault' divorce laws, the gravy work for PI's is gone. There are two or three big PI outfits in town, and they eat up most of work available. The big dollar cases are investigating accidents and occasional fraud. Undercover work catching crooked employees. There are even companies that want PI's for undercover drug investigations. It's mostly crap work and not like in the movies."

"I understand, Harry. I know I don't have the background for the business, but I can't be a process server forever." I hoped.

"Well, I just want you to understand that this is a one-time deal."

"Yeah, I understand. I'll get started right away."

"I told Mel we'd start on Monday. There's no point wasting time staking him out over the weekend. If he's holed up you're not likely to catch him, unless you get lucky."

"Mel" I thought. I was working, indirectly, for Mel Belli. Okay, not a bad start.

"Starting first thing Monday I'm on this guy like stink on shit." Harry winced.

When I eased back into the living room, Barbara slid up to me, eyes shining with liquor and empathy, and asked for a ride. She was dressed in a black knit dress, probably the only dress of suitable color she owned, and it was a little too flattering for a funeral. The neckline scooped down to reveal a good deal of bosom. The hem was short enough to show her legs to good advantage. She wore spike-heeled patent leather pumps and stockings with seams. The seam drew your eye from ankle to mid thigh in one smooth, delicious swoop. I had not appreciated before how important a delicately formed ankle could be. I wanted to kiss and stroke those ankles like breasts.

We made off together as soon as we could, trying to look innocent, failing, and receiving looks that ranged from curious to envious. After getting in the van, we looked at each other and started to laugh.

"My place?"

"Oh yes."

Chapter Nine

Wherein Our Hero Finds a Friend

When I drove up to my apartment I was startled to see all the cars parked around. I had forgotten about Rick's party. The garden was twinkling with lights, the front door was open. Music and smoke wafted out. Disco, cigarettes, and pot floated on the evening breeze.

"Oh, I forgot. My landlord's party. I told him I'd look in. Do you mind?"

"As long as I can get a drink and dance."

"'You can get anything you want at Alice's Restaurant.'" I quoted.

"Oh goody!"

"Uh, by the way. It's going to be mostly guys."

"Gay." It was statement. She knew the answer.

"I'm afraid you won't be in much danger. But then, the way you look, who knows. You could cause a couple of conversions." She laughed.

We walked up the steps to Rick's place and wound our way through the crowd in the hall, the crowd in the living room and the crowd in the kitchen before Rick waved across the room and squirmed through the mob.

He was always a little more obviously gay when he was around his friends and relaxed. I realized he felt the need to tone it down around me when we were alone. He hugged me, hugged Barbara, waved us to the booze and then whispered to me, "The good stuff's in the bedroom, I'll take you two back there anytime you want."

Barbara grinned and said, "Hell yes, take us back there first."

"I like this girl already, Dougie."

So we followed him back to the master bedroom, twisting through rooms packed with men, Rick stopping to hug and kiss half the guys on the way. In the bedroom there were two fellows making out on the bed, but Rick ignored them and took us into the bathroom. There we all fed our noses and laughed in conspiratorial delight.

When we came out I was a little embarrassed to see the two guys were now doing more than just kissing. Barbara looked at me and ran her tongue over her lips wickedly. "Looks like they're having fun."

"I can't look." I pretended to be shocked.

We danced in the living room, jammed among the sweaty bodies. I think we were the only heterosexuals there, the few women danced with each other. They admired Barbara and she smiled at them and wiggled provocatively. I enjoyed watching her. Soon some of the guys were dancing with her, rubbing against her with their crotches while she laughed.

She lurched over to me and pulled my ear to her mouth. "Let's get the Hell out of here."

I took her arm to help her negotiate the brick path with those deadly heels. We went inside my dark little place.

"It's nice."

"It's home." We seemed to be like people who have just been thrown together by accident as opposed to co-conspirators. I took her sweater, put my coat over the back of a chair and pulled off my tie. She slipped off the heels and instantly shrank two inches. I always forgot how small she actually was, since Barbara's impact in a room was always twice what another woman's might be. She drew eyes to her, both men and women, not always with feelings so different from each other. People lusted after Barbara instinctively, there was something about her look and carriage that said, 'touch me, explore my secret places, see if you can turn me on'. She was not young, being north of forty, but her manner was saucy and energetic and her mind and mouth uninhibited and witty. Looking into her eyes you saw that indeed the lights were on and someone was home. But there remained around her an aura of guarded sadness.

I fixed drinks and rolled a smoke. "So tell me more about you."

"Oh Hell, you don't want to hear all that shit, do you?" She waved a hand with a cigarette in the air, sweeping away the words that hung there.

"Actually, yes, I do. I want to know who you are."

"Ah, I'm just a good ol' gal from Missoura," she accentuated the Midwest twang.

"Would it freak you out if I said I thought you were kind of special?" I hadn't felt this way since high school.

"No. Would you be freaked out if I said you were special too?" Her eyes held a hint of fear and they were shiny again.

"No, that would be nice." We circled our attraction like wary dogs.

We sat on the couch; I put the stereo on KJAZ and turned off the lights. Lit a candle here and there. We knew enough about each other at this point that we discussed what we'd do, as though checking that each had accurately become attuned to the other. We immediately agreed on another joint, a little coke and ice cold vodka.

"I have to warn you though," she looked at me from the couch while I was assembling our drugs of choice, "coke makes me crazy."

"Crazy?"

"Yeah, you know, in bed."

"No need to apologize for that. I can hardly wait." Mr. Happy stirred in my groin, he was anticipating a good time too.

"Do you have something I can wear, beside this?"

"Like what?"

"One of your shirts?"

The image was in my mind instantly. "Oh yes."

I found my favorite well-worn corduroy shirt and she stepped out of her dress in a flash and stood revealed. She had picked out her best lingerie, I was sure. Her black lace bra was generously filled, and she wore a tiny garter belt that held up her stockings and framed her pussy.

She had shaved herself so that her fur was a small strip that accentuated the lips of her vulva. It stood out against her pale skin like an exclamation point. She was not wearing panties. When I realized that all day, in the synagogue, at the wake, while we were eating and talking, that soft hot pussy had been there, available for the taking, I was even more aroused.

She slipped on my shirt after having given me a good look at what lay in store, and smiled with a knowing smirk and wink. "Like that?" She knew the answer without asking; she just wanted to hear me say it.

"Oh yes," my voice was thick, husky. I had to clear my throat. "Oh yes, very much."

"You're such a nasty boy." It came out a compliment.

I decided to change as well, since I felt dumb dressed up. I pulled a robe over my shorts, no t-shirt, and took off my socks. We proceeded to self-medicate with my selection of stimulants and alcohol. Our minds soared away and soon our bodies joined. We came to each other almost violently, our mouths exploring, tongues probing, hands testing for those special places we could learn about and exploit. The back of her neck, stroking her spine, the inside of her thigh. I had promised myself to make love to those beautiful ankles, and I did, while she moaned and cooed. She came while I was stroking the promontory of her ankle with my tongue and she fell back with a groan.

"That's a first," she breathed.

"How's that?"

"I never came without even having my pussy touched before. That was incredible."

She drew me up to her and I removed her bra, caressing her nipples and weighing the size and shape of her with my hand. Her breasts were large, a feature which by itself is not all that important. It was their shape that drew me. They sloped down like ripe eggplants, the curve of their shape pleasing, like those parabolic shapes one sees that have perfection in their harmony. Women cannot understand

Too Many Spies Spoil the Case

the feeling that these curves inspire in men- that need to stroke and examine, to softly taste and bring the nipple erect as a perfect termination to that shape. How satisfying a feeling it is to hold a full breast in the palm of one's hand, like a baby's butt, soft, innocent, vulnerable and arousing.

While we started like this, slowly testing and experimenting, it wasn't long before our bodies leapt together and we fell into bed. She pushed me to my back and spun on her knees, diving head first to my cock, which was standing proud, through the open fly of my shorts. She tugged at the material and used both hands to withdraw my rampant member from the tangle of fabric. With a satisfied moan she flung the shorts across the room, seized me with one hand and without ceremony plunged her hot mouth onto me, then slowly slid further and further. I was impressed me with the depth and enthusiasm with which she was able to take the thing, which seemed to have a mind of its own, pulsating with a need independent of any brain or control.

I pulled Barbara on top and wrapped an arm around her waist. When my lips and tongue contacted her, her hips reacted instantly, bucking frantically while she moaned around my cock in her mouth. She swallowed it all the way to the root, her tongue massaging it on the way down. I took her clit carefully between my lips and sucked gently, flicking it side to side rhythmically. She came over and over, and as she came she would suck my cock deeper into her throat. I had read how sword swallowers mastered the trick of relaxing their throat and suppressing the gag reflex. Barbara had apparently learned it as well. A woman of many parts.

After driving each other crazy in this manner, we switched, Barbara moving around and poised above me, then slowly easing herself down, flexing hot and slick, taking me into her. Once we were completely joined, she rocked slowly forward and back. We melted together, become one flesh. Her eyes were half open, gazing down at me. I found it incredibly exciting that she looked at me while we coupled. Her expression was ecstatic, and from time to time her whole body would convulse with pleasure. Her capacity for orgasm was something I had never experienced with any woman. We were able to merge into each other in a way that only two people who care about each other can achieve. When I came, the explosion felt like my entire body was drained by spasm after spasm.

We fell asleep, wrapped together. Later, recovering groggily, Barbara staggered to the couch, took a slug of her watery drink, shuddered, and lit a cigarette. She picked up the lighter, the pack and poured two ice-cold vodkas. She sauntered through the half-lit room, letting me follow her every movement, the way her breasts jiggled, the way her little strip of pussy hair glistened wetly, winking at me as she approached with the supplies and a smile that stretched from ear to ear. She knelt on the bed, with almost geisha-like grace, and handed me a vodka. I shuddered slightly just breathing the fumes. She said firmly, "Drink it. We might as well, right?" with a slight shrug and a little half smile.

I drank. The icy liquor hit me like a slap. I had to admit after a minute that she'd been right- it woke me up. She lit another cigarette and handed it to me. There was something about that gesture that touched me. I could not recall any woman lighting my cigarette for me, or offering me a lit cigarette. They might shake one out of the pack, but this small habit of hers was something strange. Barbara liked to serve me. I felt instantly guilty, an ability I attribute to Grandpa Meir. But at the same time, it gave me a thrill of pleasure.

So we talked and smoked and drank and told the truth to some degree, and lied to each other one when we thought that would please. We talked about our sexual histories, mostly, we were candid. As candid as a man might be when talking with another man he trusts. Or as perhaps two women would be.

"I've never talked this way with a woman before," I said, surprising myself a little.

"I don't want to pretend with you. I want to be as I am. If you like me, great. If you don't, well, that's your privilege." She shook her blond curly hair with emphasis. "Look, I'm too old to fuck around with that crap. And you don't strike me as a man who needs to be fed a load of bullshit in order to believe in himself. I think you're a man I can trust, and believe me, honey, I know as much about men as any woman can."

I drew her close to me. Suddenly, she was crying softly. My first reaction was that male thing: ask a question; you know, "What's the matter, darling?" but somehow I knew that was not what she wanted. Instead I just held her. After a few minutes she drew back and wiped her eyes. "I'm sorry, that's stupid. Men hate a crying bitch."

"Cry all you want. I'd probably feel better if I had a good cry myself."

She pushed at my shoulder. "I thought you were a tough guy."

"Ah, I'm just a cream puff."

About three AM we ate breakfast. Barbara cooked eggs and ham and made biscuits. I couldn't believe the biscuits, but they just appeared. She buzzed around the kitchen, in the corduroy shirt, the tails flapping and giving me delicious little peeks at tits, ass and pussy.

I made us coffee and we ate, then she looked at me and winked. "Want to try one more time?"

I put down my mug, took her hand and led her to the bed. Gray was misting the window facing east and we were together in a black and white movie.

She told me sexy stories of her past and brought up things I had told her about other women. She would ask me what a certain one was like in bed, and want explicit details. She would then try to duplicate the event. We talked while we fucked, letting each other gradually merge our fantasies together, spinning a story that drew in people we both knew, doing things that we may have only thought about, all the while gently fucking away, watching which part of the fantasies we spun seemed to excite and which seemed to go in directions that made the listener uncomfortable. A slight stiffening or break in rhythm was enough to let the ideas ricochet from one forbidden fruit to the other. Soon we were laughing and trying to make up outrageous ideas that were impossible or silly. Then we got down to some serious fucking and came together, with grunts and moans. We slept.

Sunday we were both wrecks. We realized that we would have to stop our orgy of talk, drugs and sex, but ignored the impending doom of the approaching workday. We read the Sunday *Chronicle* and drank coffee. Later, showered and dressed, we went for Chinese. I took Barbara home. She refused to let me take her to the door, gave me a quick kiss, said, "That was the most fun I've had in years," and was gone. I went home and missed her, even in my sleep.

My mind was swirling with overload. The past few days presented too much in the way of experiences to be absorbed. I slept like I had died, but woke up with my back locked in spasm like a board. I had hoped that I would be okay, but all the jumping around of the past weekend did its work. I had avoided the worst abuses, and Barbara wordlessly tracing the scar that ran like a white ridge down the lower third of my spine. It had been a pretty good workout and I was paying in spades. I swallowed three Valium and four Ibuprofen and went back to bed. I added two Vicodin in an hour and finally slept until morning. I dragged out of bed Monday morning at five. I felt like warmed-over shit, but showered, dressed and staggered to the van.

I stopped for coffee at *Nice Buns*, a bakery run by Ed and Ed, a nice couple. That was the thing about a gay couple; they could both have the same first name. Thus fortified I traced my way over Potrero Hill, down and then up to Nob Hill, to lie in wait.

I waited. I sat. I smoked. There was no sign of the other watchers. I had circled the block both ways first without seeing them. There was a plumbing van that seemed suspicious, but a few minutes after I got there a guy in coveralls came out of one of the apartment buildings and drove off. I guess I underestimated the pay of plumbers. I didn't think they could afford this neighborhood. It was certainly too early for a service call.

I waited until nine thirty, then got impatient and left for the TransAmerica Pyramid. I parked in the lot and hung out at the mezzanine where Gunter would have to change elevators to get to his office, but by ten thirty he hadn't shown. I didn't even know if the cops ever talked to him or not. They weren't going to share that information with me. I didn't hang around long, thinking that Gunter would be crazy to come back to this place after what happened. I decided to sic Dixie, our ace skip tracer, on the guy.

I gave Van my other work to distribute. It would be a bit of a load for the other guys, and Van didn't want to tell them what I was up too, (if he actually knew that much) so he arranged the idea that I was on a "special" that would last on and off for a few days. I casually tossed the Elias Jackson summons into the pile with the rest.

Harry came in and told me he wanted to talk to me. We went into his office and he signaled for me to sit or stand with a little equivocal wave. I stood, wanting to keep it short.

"Report." To the point.

"Staked out the apartment Sunday evening anyway, no love there. Started at six this morning. Don't see how he could have got by me, I was across from the garage door. Either he took a cab, parked outside on the street or was never there to begin with. I couldn't watch the garage and front entrance from an available position. Hung around the Pyramid until ten thirty. Didn't pass me there. Who knows?" I shrugged to indicate the vagaries of tailing someone.

"See anything else?"

I didn't really wanted to tell Harry about this, but since he had directly asked about anything else, I felt compelled to. So I mentioned how I thought *maybe* there were these other stakeouts. And that I had bothered to get the license number of one of them. Oh, and could Dixie run a skip trace on the guy - car license and make, other addresses he might have, regular office hours and exactly what was his business, all that good stuff that an old lady with an honest sounding voice can get over the phone. Dixie was so sincere sounding that people told her information they only told their mothers.

"Yes, I'll put her on it right away." I was surprised Harry hadn't suggested it first.

I returned to the Pyramid about four and hung around the mezzanine. I didn't actually expect Gunter to return, but I had to try something. The guard was the same one as before and he just nodded to me. After a while, on his next pass, he stopped and nodded again. "Still on that stakeout." He was observant.

I resisted a smart-ass answer. Why else would I be hanging around here? But his comment was meant in the same spirit as "Nice weather we're having?"

"Yeah."

"Got something to do with that girl that got killed?"

Too Many Spies Spoil the Case

"No. This is just a civil thing. Trying to beat his old lady out of support." I looked seriously at him, like I had shared some forbidden knowledge.

"Oh yeah, sure. You never said nothin' to me about it." He winked and smiled his trustworthiness. We were pals, comrades in arms.

"Hey, you want to make a few bucks on the side?" I offered. He raised his eyebrows. "Just call this number if he shows. I promise we'll make it worth your while."

He slipped the card into his pocket and winked. Perfect. Now I had a friend at the Pyramid. Just like the company's ads said. Only this friend might actually be useful.

I left at seven. It was a long, boring time. Trying to watch each load of passengers come and go, but trying to be inconspicuous too. I didn't want Gunter to see me first. I looked for furtive movements among the crowds or someone changing direction to avoid me, but nothing happened. The combination of tension and boredom was excruciating.

Chapter Ten

Win Friends and Influence People

Two days passed with no change in this routine. The only interesting event was when Harry shared with me the results of Sam's autopsy. His neck had been broken. Apparently by someone with the training to effect this quickly and skillfully. How nice. No one else in the office was to know.

Harry reminded me where our interests lay. Yes, the police were investigating. No, he hadn't heard back from the "marshals". He called the number on the business cards they left behind. It did not correspond to the number for the Federal Marshal's office in the phone book but a woman answered "Marshal's office" and could put them on the phone or give them a message. When he called the phone book number, they said they did not have those names in their listings.

On Thursday, Dixie presented me with some useful information.

She handed me two pages of notes. James Gunter, Major, USAF, retired. President, Midland Surplus International, a Delaware corporation with offices in Texas, California and, interestingly enough, Geneva and Tehran.

There was a little more information about the company, but being closely held, not a public corporation, there really wasn't much information available. Good rating with Dun and Bradstreet.

Residence. Well, we had that. Oh, well, looks like he has a place in Tahoe. Cool. Maybe a trip to Tahoe would be in order. Car registration- two cars: a 1972 Jaguar sedan (the XK12L-the long wheelbase, 12 cylinder job) and, this guy possessed great taste in cars, a 1965 Cobra. Boat registration. And a boat! The surplus business must be great.

Dixie apologized. "There isn't a Hell of lot there, honey. This guy is very low profile." His credit was good, he had no criminal record in California, his license had two speeding violations in three years (naturally, with that high performance hardware), he had not married or divorced in the state. Remember, this was in the dark ages, before computerized Internet databases were available at the touch of a few keys.

He possessed a passport (surprise) but Dixie couldn't find out where he had traveled. She didn't get far with the calls she made, and the phone at Midland would ring until the answering service picked up. All they would do is take messages. She'd located the boat, so now I had three places to try to cover.

"Did you show this to Harry?"

"Sure."

"Did you point out that we have four possible stake out locations and only one guy working?"

"Harry was aware of that."

"Okay. What about that license number?"

"Oh yeah. A rental."

"Wonderful." That was a dead end.

I asked Barbara if Harry was around but he and Dorothy were out and she didn't think they would be back today. We took a moment to make a date for Friday. And Saturday. Sunday would be a given, I guess.

I could hardly wait to see her. At the same time, I had to figure out how I was going to attend to Major James Gunter, etc. I decided I would work it out somehow.

That afternoon, late, I went to the boat location. It was a "marina" of sorts located in the Third Street Slough. Known to yachtsmen in the area as "Shit Slough." This turgid ditch of semi-stagnant San Francisco Bay was surrounded by landfill- offices, railroad tracks, streets and a high bridge separated it from open water. There were a few houseboats tied up to floating docks, and about a dozen boat slips. I didn't know which slip was his, I only had the registration number of the boat and couldn't see those from the parking lot. I sat for while trying to figure out an angle. I noticed there was a wooden board with faded notes, most of them illegible with weather and sun.

I hung around the board for a while, and finally a hippie couple came out the gate. "Hi, excuse me." I called politely.

They stopped and turned their glazed eyes to me. They were a zoned-out looking pair. Their faces indicated they were listening as attentively as they could.

"Uh, there's a notice up here about a boat for sale, but I can't read which one it is. The owner's name looks like Hunter, or Gunter or something?"

They looked at each other for a long beat. The girl's eyes began to focus on the problem. "Oh yeah, I think that's that guy. You know," she urged her companion. She did not address me. "That guy!" she shook a little with impatience, as though she had explained everything to him twice already.

"Oh yeah, I know which guy he is." Thank God. "He's got that nice teak lady." He waved his hand in the general direction of the boats.

"Gee, I'm sorry to be so dumb, but which one is that?" I couldn't have told you a "teak lady" from a rowboat.

He turned, with the girl rotating along with him, and pointed.

"Cool, thanks. Can I go down and get a look at it?"

"Sure, man. But don't go on it or nothin'?" It was a plea and a warning.

"Oh no, no way. Just want to see if I want to give him a call about it. You know, see if it's worth my time."

"Oh hey man, it's a cool boat. He's got a new Jap diesel, radar, generator, the works. It's a sweet boat. All mahogany inside. I work on it for him sometimes."

"Wow, sounds nice. Probably more than I can afford." I pulled a sad expression.

"What's he want for it?" Uh oh. This was getting too complicated for a quick little lie to get onto the dock.

"I can't read that part." I turned and pulled a card at random off the board. "But I can make out the number, so I'll give a call later on."

They started to walk away. "Hey, can you let me in?"

"Oh yeah, sure man. Sorry, I forgot." Well, short-term memory loss comes with the grass, friend.

I walked down the steep walkway. The tide was out, revealing a shore of filthy muck punctuated by garbage. The dock bobbed enthusiastically up and down, back and forth, with each shift of my weight from left to right. I could get sea sick in ten feet. I settled into a rhythmic sway that rolled with the dock and sauntered my way toward the boat.

The day was almost evening now and no lights shone onboard. I slowed as I approached, resisted the urge to look behind me and walked up to the slip.

She was a lovely vessel. Anyone could tell that. All gleaming white paint on the hull and shining varnished wood. Brass fittings glowed. The white ropes that controlled the sails were neatly coiled.

She had two masts. I dredged up from my memory the term "ketch" and it seemed to fit the picture I was seeing now. The cabin stepped up twice, the aftmost (I did know that it was *bow* and *aft*, not front and back) cabin tall enough so one could stand at a gleaming brass wheel visible through the glass. There was another wheel, made of varnished wood that shined like polished glass, in the open part in back of the cabin. The stays that supported the mast were running here and there, from a bow spirit to a graceful narrow stern. I couldn't see the name without leaning way over the end of the dock and I didn't want to attract any attention.

I looked around the area, pretending to be critically inspecting and admiring the sailboat while I looked at sight lines and unobtrusive places I could park and still see the entrance to the dock. I made a mental note of a couple of likely spots, walked to the end of the dock, stood there as though admiring the filthy view of smelly water and then walked back. I slowed as I past Gunter's lovely little yacht as though lingering wistfully. I always think it's important to do some method acting. Your actions and mannerisms should match your cover. No point in making people nervous or attracting enough attention to gain a mention to Gunter by some observant dock neighbor.

I got back in the van and sat, thinking. How was I going to cover four possible locations, one of them in another state, for Christ's sake? It was a rhetorical question. The only answer was to get Harry to put more guys on the case or else just do a hit and miss until I ran across the guy.

I noticed an abandoned van in the lot. It had been lurking around my consciousness. It sat on blocks, no wheels. The windshield was cracked. But I noticed that every once in a while, it vibrated a little. Like someone was inside it. Homeless hippie?

I looked around. There were no other cars or interesting looking places for a watcher to hide. There were actually three abandoned vehicles scattered at the fringes of the lot. I decided that there was no point in hanging out any longer. If the abandoned van was actually a duck blind for someone watching Gunter, they made me when I went down to the boat. No one would think that was a coincidence. They might even have seen me hanging out somewhere else.

I drove off, circled the block and came up across from the marina, on the other side of the slough. I parked far down the block and walked up the street until I drew even with the marina on the other side. I was about a hundred yards away. There was a bus stop and little train station that served the commuter trains that ran up and down the San Francisco Peninsula. I could hang out there for a long time without attracting attention or being noticed.

I took my pocket binoculars with me. They were real handy for reading house numbers and street signs. I focused on the abandoned van quickly, then put them in my jacket pocket and settled down to watch.

Eight cigarettes later my patience was rewarded. A four door brown sedan, the rental car of the previous day, pulled up on the parking lot side of the van. I raised the binoculars to get a better look. The side door of the van popped open, a man got out and another got out of the sedan. They exchanged places. The car pulled away. The whole thing had taken less than ten seconds.

Okay. I didn't figure that I was a step ahead of anyone, given AAA's limited resources. But who was this? Feds or someone else? How could I find out?

It wasn't likely that anyone had noticed this set up at the marina. It was dark by now, and the exchange was quick and quiet. How could I screw up their little hideout?

I thought about calling in a complaint about an abandoned vehicle. But it was on private property so the police wouldn't care. I would have to represent myself as the owner of the property and get a tow company to take the thing away. That would take days.

Then I saw a little knot of secretaries walking to their cars in the lot of the office building across the street from the marina lot. I went to a pay phone in the station and called the local precinct house number.

"Third Street station, Sergeant Adams."

"Yes, Sergeant. I want to report a man exposing himself."

"Where was this?"

I filled the good sergeant in on the location, told him how the poor secretaries had seen this derelict wagging his weeny and how I thought he was hanging out in an abandoned van. When it came time to give my name, I obliged him. "Gunter, Jim Gunter. I work in the big blue office building across the street." What the Hell, one name was a good as another.

The sergeant said they'd get a car out there as soon as possible. 'Possible' turned out to be about fifteen minutes. A black and white pulled into the marina lot; the two cops walked around, looked at the office building and the van, and walked over to the van. In a few moments they yanked a guy out of it, and were vigorously talking to him.

I used the glasses quickly to get a better look my victim. He was dressed in dirty clothes, unshaven and uncombed, looking the part of a derelict. I could see him denying, shaking his head, waving his hands. The cops cuffed him and put him in the back of their car, then drove over to the office building. When they got there, however, they could not locate the Jim Gunter complainant, could they? They radioed, sat around for a while, then drove off with the guy in the back. I suppose they could get him on a vagrancy charge.

I hustled back to my bus and drove back over to the now abandoned blind. I parked a few feet away and quickly looked inside.

It was a pretty slick set up. There was a stool, a large piss jar, empty, and the debris of a stakeout: discarded cigarette packs, and butts, junk food packages, coffee cups. A thermos. And a notebook! I put it in my pocket for future examination.

The cops hadn't even looked in the van, just a glance inside like there might be a dead body or something, then hauled the poor schmuck away. I wondered if he would keep his cover or not. I thought so. After all, he would be out of jail the next day, or even that night. They might just take him to a shelter. I decided to return to the train station and see what happened next.

I waited two more hours. By now it was almost ten and no activity. I reasoned that the car would not return with a relief until morning, so they wouldn't find out about the roust for hours. I decided to come back early Friday morning and see what I could see then.

Too Many Spies Spoil the Case

I was restless all night. My back ached, I was thinking about my date with Barbara and getting frustrated with my lack of progress with the Gunter thing. I just couldn't figure out how to break something loose. Something that would expose Gunter to me so I could serve him. And maybe find out something about what was going on that was so important that Sam's insignificant life had been swatted down like a fly.

I assumed money was at the root of it. After all, you didn't get a whole country suing you for peanuts. I didn't know anything about the suit, although Harry might. I didn't know exactly how close he and Mel Belli were, or if Belli would confide something about a client like that to Harry.

Who were the two sets of watchers? The Iranians could be one set. They might want to make sure their target didn't blow the country, although how they thought they would stop him was not clear. They obviously wouldn't want him harmed, or else they could never collect their money.

The other set could be Feds. What brand of Federal involvement was open to debate? Was this a national security case? Likely. And that could mean anything. The US government dabbled in revolutions, misinformation, arms smuggling, assassination by proxy, election rigging, and on and on. So what was their angle?

I sat in my recliner, tilted back, getting my back adjusted so the spasms were not so bad, smoked a joint and sipped tequila, with lime and salt. Did I want to continue with this whole thing? It seemed to be way over my head and what would I accomplish? Serve a crummy piece of paper on a guy that probably would be in Switzerland the next day? Or might already be there. Avenge Sam? Not bloody likely. I fell asleep pondering such great questions, woke up in the middle of night and stumbled into my bed for a couple more hours of restless sleep, marked with intense dreams.

I was up early and was back at the train station by four thirty. I figured since they relieved their man at nine last night, eight hours later would be about five. God, I love it when I'm right! About five minutes before five the sedan pulled up and the relief jumped out. There was visible consternation when he found the van empty. He went back to the car, talked for a few minutes and then looked around the area, as though trying to find some clue to his missing partner's location. One of the guys in the car got out and looked around as well, they got back in the car and it sped out of the lot. You almost feel their confusion and frustration. Well, in a few hours they would no doubt hear from their wayward man and I expected their confusion and frustration level would jack up another notch or two when they heard that story. They would know they had been made by somebody, but they wouldn't know who.

I drove over to the other side, to stake out the marina. I couldn't park in a good position. I could see the lot, but not the gate or Gunter's boat, unless I kind of craned my neck from time to time.

All this sitting and watching was getting on my nerves. I was used to being busy all day, not playing games hour after hour. Usually a stake out resolved itself quickly in our business or didn't resolve at all. Most of our clients were far too cheap to spend much on staking out an evading subject. A few hours was all the commitment we usually made, and that was all it usually took. The subject would come out of his house to go to work or whatever and bang, we'd hand him the paper and blow.

So I shifted in my seat restlessly, glanced in the side view mirror once in a while, and mainly tried to stay alert. I'd not slept well and was bored to tears. I played the radio, one of those talk stations, but the host was a jerk and the callers were even dumber than he was, so I tried some music. I sat through the thousandth play of Roberta Flack singing the Lori Leiberman poem about Don Mclean, *Killing Me Softly*. I had heard it so many times that I was beginning to wish he *had* killed her with his song. I snapped the radio off in frustration.

I guess I'd spent just a little too much of my attention on the radio. There was a blur at my left and my door popped open. Before I could react, or even realize that I'd forgotten to lock the damn thing (it's always that one time) a big guy yanked me out of the seat. A car pulled up, another guy grabbed me from inside the car while the first guy shoved me like a sack of laundry.

I made a preemptory move to fight the two off, but my right arm was pinned very firmly and excruciatingly far behind my back by the shover, and the guy inside the car whacked me once across the ribs with a short billy club.

"Okay, okay, relax. I'm not going to fight." I went limp to show that I meant it.

"Sit back, shut up and you won't get hurt." Mr. Left instructed. Sounded like a good plan to me.

Chapter Eleven

He Who Fights and Runs Away, Lives to Fight Another Day

We drove out Third Street until we reached an area of vast vacant lots punctuated with nondescript industrial buildings of enormous size. There were truck trailers parked on the streets, little traffic and no one visible for blocks. The driver took us up a side street and pulled over. The whole ride the two guys next to me remained silent and watchful. Mr. Right released my arm from the painful lock, then frisked me thoroughly. Mr. Left looked disheveled and tired. Being rousted and jailed will do that. He seemed in a bad mood.

"I don't carry." I assured them.

In the front seat next to the driver was a dark haired fellow that hadn't even turned around when they hustled me into the car. He remained silent and facing forward for the ten-minute ride. Even after we stopped alongside the curb in the middle of an empty block of broken concrete and weeds he did not turn or move for a full minute. I remained quiet as well, assuming that I would learn more that way. Besides, what could I say, "Unhand me you louts"?

Mr. Dark finally turned around to sit sideways on his seat, turning his head to look at me. He removed a pair of dark glasses and let his eyes do their thing. His face was rather narrow, kind of ferret-like, although I hate to offend ferrets - they're kind of cute, and Mr. Dark could not fall into the column headed "cute things I have seen".

He was pretty much a Semitic type, black, wavy hair, olive skin, but not real dark, prominent nose accented with a David Niven mustache, large black eyebrows. He was altogether a type from central casting, except for a feature that did not suit his line of work - he had very light, hazel eyes. They were impossible to miss and captivating in the contrast they offered to his dark, narrow face. You wouldn't forget this guy, no matter how you met him.

"You have evidenced some interest in a James Gunter." It was not a question.

I nodded. Raised an eyebrow. I was determined to be cool. The ten-minute ride to the boondocks was been a small mistake on their part. They gave me time to let the adrenaline ease down. My face throbbed on the left cheek where Mr. Right had shoved me into the doorframe while doing the stuffing bit, and my ribs were bruised from the tap with the billy, but I was not in bad shape. I was concerned but not particularly scared. There was plenty of time to get scared later.

"You're not much of a talker, are you?" His tone sounded irritated.

"On the contrary," I piped up. "I like to talk. Indeed, sir, I like talking to a man who likes to talk..." He didn't recognize the source of that line. I had to entertain myself somehow. His lack of reaction told me a lot about who or what he might be.

"Yes well, you will get an opportunity to talk, now. Tell us who you work for and why you are shadowing Gunter." There was no hint of compromise in his demand.

I was a little surprised by the question. I assumed that these guys knew more about me than I knew about them. Maybe that was not the case. They were foreign, although they spoke unaccented English perfectly. Actually, that's why I realized they were foreign - their English was far too grammatical for an American.

I didn't really have time to make up a lie. Besides, I have learned through hard experience, that it's better to conceal small lies in the context of general truth than to try to create something out of whole cloth. It's too hard to structure all the details of a complex story without lots of time to work out any inconsistencies.

"Okay, sure. No big mystery. I work for AAA Legal Process Service. Here in San Francisco. I'm supposed to," I chose my words carefully, "deliver some legal papers to Mr. Gunter. But I haven't been able to find him."

Mr. Dark flicked a glance at Mr. Left who, without any warning, brought the billy club whistling across my chest and right arm. It smarted quite a bit. I hollered, quite satisfactorily, I'm sure.

After giving me a minute to recover, so he could be sure he had my complete attention, he spoke: "That is to remind you that your tone of voice is as important as the information you give. We do not like disrespect from crap like you." I nodded to indicate that I was thoroughly chastened.

"Now, this legal document you are to, *deliver*, you know what it is concerning?"

"Very little. All I know is that it's an order to show cause in a judgment in a civil case brought against Gunter in Federal Court." That was mostly true. I did not want to appear important in any way. Besides, I wasn't important. In any way.

"What do you know about the case?"

"Not a thing." The billy club wavered. "I only know the other party is the Government of Iran."

"You have not seen the other documents involved?"

"No." The club wiggled. "Look, you guys need to understand, my company just delivers this stuff. We don't know or care what it's about. We just get hired to take the papers to the parties involved."

"You seem very dedicated for a mere delivery boy. I have never seen a delivery boy stake out his recipient's home, work and other haunts. Nor have I seen a delivery boy who managed to interfere in someone's surveillance." So they guessed it was me who had gotten their man in hot water. Probably saw a green and white Volkswagen van one too many times. "I believe you are not what you seem to be at all. I believe you are an agent for another government that intends to interfere in this matter."

I didn't like the sound of that conclusion. "Hey, you're dead wrong, pal. Look, I can prove it." I regretted the choice of the word 'dead'.

He ignored me and turned to the front, telling the driver to pull up to the next building. It was a huge industrial building with no activity around it. The car nosed into a small side street between this building and another across from it and stopped. I had a bad feeling about what was coming next.

Mr. Right took hold of my right arm firmly and opened the door. Mr. Left held my left arm and the billy club in his other hand. They started to pull and push me out of the car.

You know, when you see the hero take some terrific beating and then go on to solve the case, that's just acting. But this was reality, and in the real world, a beating like they seemed to have in mind could either kill me or put me in the hospital for weeks. AAA did not offer a health plan. Besides, I have experienced pain before. Don't like it or plan to get used to it.

In a crisis situation, the best time to do something is right away. Most people don't fight for a living. They have to get themselves worked up for it. You know, name calling and threats and pushing and what not. That is not the right way to deal with impending violence to your person. At the first sign of a threat, strike as hard as you can at the first opening. Exploit any hesitation as weakness and deliver the most destructive blow possible.

Of course, that's a lot easier when you don't have two big goons holding your arms and waving clubs and God knows what else. But that was just the way this cookie crumbled. As soon as I got to my feet outside the car, I struck.

It's hard to describe it in sequence. I became all feet and elbows, lashing at the softest parts that I could see or feel. I do know that Mr. Right, the first guy out, had stepped back to give me room to get out, and at that moment he appeared to be a little off balance, as stepping backward in the street is liable to make you, and I shot out of the car in one leap, dragging Mr. Left along with me. He was off balance as well, kind of on his side, laying half out of the car. My right arm broke free and I grabbed the door, slamming it as hard as I could. I guess that to be pretty hard, as I was scared shitless and my adrenals were pumping overtime. Mr. Left's hand dropped from my arm like a dead branch.

Mr. Right fell with the shove I had given him, and as I slammed the door on Mr. Left I leaped close to the fallen giant and kicked him full into the diaphragm.

Miles Archer

If you have never been struck in the diaphragm you do not know one of the seven circles of Hell. By striking just below the sternum, the nerve plexus that serves the diaphragm is temporarily paralyzed. The diaphragm, by the way, is that tough large muscle that lets you breathe. Yes, it's just as bad as it sounds. You try to inhale, and can't. You feel like your entire chest has been crushed and the pain is enough to make you pass out, but you can't breathe so you are choking and thinking you will die. Indeed, you may. That blow, delivered forcefully enough, is fatal.

So, in a second and half, I was free. I spun and ran like a son of a bitch. I ran like it was the Watts riots and I was carrying a new TV. I ran like all the hounds of Hell were behind me. I knew that I would not hear the sound of the bullet that hit me and I turned as soon as I could and rounded the building doing sixty. I wish I'd time to say, "Feet, don't fail me now!" but I was busy.

I was not exactly a star athlete in school. I didn't like the abuse that substituted for coaching ability in organized sports. I prefer to avoid being verbally or physically abused by men not related to me by blood. However, in my junior year I discovered fencing. Foil fencing demanded the intellectual and physical talents I possessed. Cunning, strength, quick reflexes and, if I may modestly claim, a not unimpressive amount of wit.

So to make a long story even longer, I ran on the cross-country team in order to build up my stamina for fencing in the spring. So I knew that somewhere in my life I had run three miles up hill and down at a full gallop. Not just jogging, but full-tilt-boogie running.

I ran like that now. I wore my felony flyers and I flew. I cut across the concrete wasteland. By the time they got the car going in reverse, I was already half a block across the lot covered with big blocks of broken concrete. No way could they follow me over it in a car. It would have hung up on a piece of concrete right off. So they were forced to pursue on the street, which I was angling away from.

I was not seventeen anymore, and had been abusing my body in loathsome ways for ten years. I knew that any minute now I was going to be running on empty. What high speed long distance running taught me was that no matter how bad it hurt, very few young men dropped dead of a heart attack while running. So I kept going, slacking off from a full sprint to a serious lope.

The only problem was, where would I run to? The only possible goal was Third Street, which might be busy enough to have traffic, although at late morning was not heavily traveled, but still, steady enough. So I angled toward that four-lane boulevard. They anticipated me and drove to the corner, waiting to see which way I turned when I reached the street. They knew I couldn't evade them long on foot. My chest burned fiercely, telling me I had run up a debt my body could not pay. I glanced wildly up and down the street. There weren't any public-looking kind of buildings. You know, the kind you can run into when the bad guys are after you. (Damn it, they're never there when you need them.)

Then I saw a cop car coming down Third. It was going to pass me. I tried to speed up, but my legs said no. As I reached the curb the black and white was already past. I came to a dead stop, found a fist-sized chunk of concrete and ran into the street. I flung the concrete at the retreating cruiser. It struck the trunk with loud thunk and the car came to a screaming halt.

I almost fell to my knees in gratitude when two uniforms jumped out, batons in hand. They were mightily pissed, and I just stood in the middle of the street with my hands on my hips, trying to catch up to the oxygen debt my body wanted paid now.

I tamely put my hands behind my back and gasped while they cuffed me and put me in the back seat. Then we pulled over to the curb. I coughed out, "Some guys, trying to rob me. I thought they were, gonna, kill me." I telegraphed a rough approximation of the truth. I did not want to complicate it with secret agents and civil lawsuits and dead process servers. That story would have me answering questions all day. As it was, they eventually got the idea that this was an act of desperation to save my life from a gang of kids set to rob me. Eventually they believed my story. The "robbers" took off at the first sign of the cops. I got a ride back to my bus and a firm warning to try waving my arms up and down instead of throwing chunks of concrete. I smiled and nodded and thanked them and God profusely the whole way.

I headed for my cave forthwith. I just wanted to get somewhere with four walls and phone. I didn't want to go to the office with my face bruised and my clothes torn. I know Harry would freak if he saw me and call the whole thing off. Just when it was getting good.

After a lot of water, an apple and cheese sandwich and half an hour to recover I tried to think things out. I possessed a lot of information and hadn't much time to think.

I took four ibuprofen and a Vicodin. I was just starting to feel my aches and pains. I decided there was no point in martyrdom. It would get worse before it got better. I'd sworn to quit smoking at least ten times during and after my run, but I lit a cigarette anyway. The spirit was willing, but the flesh was weak. I smoked some dope too, just for good measure and to get the cerebral wheels up to speed.

Okay. Now we had confirmed bad guys. It hadn't been a cozy chat, so what did I know from their manner and what they'd said?

1. My guess was they were Iranians. That seemed to be the only logical answer.

2. Apparently they didn't really understand the legal system here and just what was what. At least, in the details. I would assume that Belli talked attorney to attorney, with some Iranian attorney general or whatever. Then I remembered Jack Ruby. The consensus was that Mel had been grandstanding when he volunteered to represent Ruby after he shot Oswald on live national television. Maybe he was wired into more than met the eye?

3. In any event, these guys didn't know that the delay was being caused by our inability to track down Gunter. And they were interested in finding him as well. Or at least in knowing where he was at all times.

So where did the US fit into this? There was no doubt now that there was some serious shit connected with this little piece of paper. And I but a pawn in the great game of life.

None of this told me where to find Gunter or whether I had any chance of finding him.

I nodded off and slept the afternoon away. By the time I woke up I was stiff, sore all over and late to pick up Barbara. Fuck! I hobbled over to the phone and called. I told her I'd gotten hung up on a job but would be there in an hour. She was sweet and forgiving.

"No problem," was all she said.

I took more ibuprofen and put a couple of Vicodin in my pocket. Showered and changed clothes. I was underway in forty minutes and outside her place in fifty-five minutes flat.

We ate at a great little restaurant in Polk Gulch called the *Casablanca*. Decorated around the theme of the movie, with posters of the actors in case you didn't get it. They served a mix of French and California cuisine with a vaguely Mediterranean flare. I have a theory about restaurants. When you find one you like, go there regularly and get known to the staff. Paul, the maitre d'hotel, remembered me, although he certainly did not mention that the last time I'd been in with a particularly breathtaking blonde. Thus being identified as a regular meant that we were given some treats not on the menu, a pâté de foie gras en croûte that melted in your mouth. Barbara asked about the red mark on my face.

"I bumped into a door." Well, that was true.

On the way back to my place, I swung by the marina. I looked at Gunter's boat as we drove by. It was dark. I didn't stop.

We got into bed and Barbara melted into my mouth and I into hers.

Chapter Twelve

Wherein Our Hero Goes for a Drive in the Country

Sunday I was up early and decided that since the boat location hadn't been that helpful, so I would try the flat again. I dropped Barbara at home, reluctantly, and went on up Nob Hill to the apartment. There was a car with two men watching the garage, but they couldn't park where they could see the front door too, so I parked up the block and walked back to the building.

Jerome was on duty.

"Yessir, I remember you right away. You got that important delivery for Mr. Gunter." He drew the words out with a lovely Southern drawl. Mississippi Delta I would guess.

"That's right, sir. Good of you to remember." I stuck out my hand. "Name's Doug, glad to meet you."

"A pleasure to meet you, Doug," he shook my hand warmly.

"Is he home today, that you know?"

"Ain't seen 'im in a week, and that's a fact."

Great. I've been chasing a shadow all week.

"Could he be up at the Tahoe place?"

"He got a place in Tahoe?" Jerome's yellow eyes revealed nothing he didn't want to reveal.

"Uh, yeah, but I hate to drive all the way there if he's somewhere else."

"You could always call him, couldn't you?"

Good point Jerome. "Well, Jerome, fact is, Mr. Gunter isn't exactly enthusiastic about what I have to give him." I decided I would try the honest approach. "I have a court order to serve on him, Jerome. It's a Federal Court Order." I capitalized the words with my voice. "It's a pretty big deal and I'm not supposed to discuss it with anyone, but I know you won't blab."

Jerome shook his head sincerely. "Nassir, I won't breathe a word. He in trouble?"

I didn't know how Jerome felt about Gunter. Did he like him and want to help him out, or did he dislike him and wouldn't feel guilty about helping to get him in hot water. Jerome certainly understood that Federal court orders were something that didn't mean good news.

"Yeah, I'm afraid so." I tried to be neutral in tone and expression.

Jerome smiled slowly. "Good. That son'bitch. Fuck him." He went on. "He out cruisin' around the wine country in that hot blue sports car he got."

"The Cobra?"

"Yeah, that noisy little thing he drive on weekends and shit."

"Any idea where he would stay?"

"He goes to that Silverado Country Club place and stays there a lot."

"Think he'll be back Monday?"

"Who knows? That son'bitch comes and goes like a wild pig. Could be gone a month. I hope."

I pulled a twenty out of my pocket and put it in Jerome's leathery wrinkled palm.

"Oh no sir, not necessary," he protested.

"Just consider it my way of saying thanks," I insisted.

"Yessir. Thank you sir."

"Take it easy, Jerome."

"Yessir. Take it any way it comes, I will. You take care yourself, Mr. Doug."

"That I will, Jerome, that I will," I thought, and turned to go out. Then another question struck me. "Say, Jerome," I said, turning back, "Have there been any other people inquiring after Mr. Gunter?"

He smiled a little smile. "Well, since you ask, yes. There was two men looking for him t'other day. They said they was marshals, showed badges and all. They was pretty rude about it, tol' me I be in trouble if I helped Mr. Gunter hide from them. Shit, I told them I didn't know nothin' 'bout him bein' anywhere." I thought I heard him mumble something about crackers, but I wasn't sure.

"So you didn't happen to mention Silverado?"

"They didn't ask."

It pays to be polite, Mom always said. I waved a hand and went out.

Well, a guy in a classic sports car, especially one as distinctive as a Cobra, shouldn't be so hard to find. I knew roughly where to look. A nice drive through the wine country would be pleasant. It was only ten in the morning. I could be at Silverado by two.

The drive was lovely. It was August, and the weather in the Napa Valley hot. I drove with the windows down, the radio up. I enjoyed zipping along the two lane winding roads. Motorcyclists would zoom around me from time to time, and the occasional aggressive sports car driver would impatiently pass, not being able to stand the thought of being behind a VW bus. I was rolling along at a very good clip, but after all, it was a box on wheels, with a 70 horsepower four banger. I don't blame them.

I stopped at a convenience store and bought some lunch, eating while I drove. I was in the town of Sonoma by one thirty and driving through the gates of Silverado by one fifty.

I cruised around the grounds and damn if I didn't find the Cobra right away. It was parked in front of a "cabin" near the entrance to the golf course. It must be his. These cars were so rare there couldn't be two of them here.

I looked for a place to park, but before I could find something, I came to a guard shack. The guard explained that the area was only for members and guests. If I was visiting he would get permission for me to drive in. That wouldn't work. I just played dumb and acted like I thought it was a public park and turned around and drove out. I drove along the road approaching the place for about a mile before I could find a spot where I could pull over.

I figured if he came out, I could follow him. Maybe he would drive into town for something. I settled down for another wait. At least I was getting paid for it.

As I sat there I noticed something on the floor. It was the logbook that I'd taken from the van the Iranians were using. I had forgotten all about it!

I leafed through it. Nothing interesting at all. Just dates, times, notes on people who came and went. I even saw my description and license number in there. Shit!

I wanted to end this now. Gunter was cornered, sort of. If luck would just cooperate I could serve him. I'd have no doubt about his identity with a car license number and his face in my memory. He couldn't weasel out of his service. I could go to court and identify him cold.

I waited. I was getting twenty bucks an hour. Plus expenses and travel at thirty-five cents a mile. I felt great, if slightly sore and a little put out that everyone seemed to know more about what he was doing than I. Than me. Whatever.

I heard him coming. Couldn't miss the roar coming down the road. I fired up the van and waited for him to pass. That didn't take long. He flashed by, the engine screaming. This was a guy who didn't care about being found! He certainly wasn't keeping a low profile.

I pulled out behind him. He was flying and far ahead already. I floored it, and wound the engine out in third unmercifully to get the most acceleration possible. I felt ridiculous.

However, within a couple of miles he was required to slow going into town and I caught up in time to see him turn down the main drag in Sonoma. It's a small town and I didn't think I'd lose him now. I trailed a couple cars back and when he turned right I slowed at the corner and peeked around. He was parking in front of a restaurant. Perfect!

I pulled up parallel to his car at the curb, and just a little in front, so he couldn't jump in and take off on me. I got out slowly, trying not to spook him and walked around the front of the van. He was telling the parking valet that the car stayed where it was. The valet did not argue. He just stared at the car and nodded. I walked over.

"Hey, wow, that's some car!" I called.

Gunter was predictable. No man owned a car like that who didn't love a compliment. He drove it to feed his ego and having other guys drool over it was like walking into a class reunion with a Playboy bunny for a date.

He stopped in mid-turn toward the restaurant entrance and flashed a practiced smile. "Thanks," was all he said and turned to go. But by then I was on top of him and reaching for the paper. He saw my hand going to my inside pocket and freaked, throwing himself to the side and diving to the door.

"Hey, whoa, whoa. I'm not gonna hurt you!" I yelled while at the same time I sprang forward to stay within range.

He was cowering on the sidewalk, hands over his head. "Don't!"

"Hey, Gunter, I ain't gonna shoot you. I have here an order to show cause issued in Federal District court with your name on it. You've been served."

He couldn't believe I wasn't shooting him for a second or so, then he pulled himself up. I was still holding the papers.

"I don't want those. I won't accept those. You need to see my attorney."

"Mr. Gunter," I sighed. I'd heard this rap before. "You don't have a choice. I've identified you. I have affected the personal delivery of these. And this order has to be served on you personally. Your attorney can't accept service for you, even if he wanted to. So just take it and call your attorney in the morning. It was inevitable." He took the papers, dejected.

I started to turn away, but he reached out and said, "Hey, wait a second."

"Yeah, what?" I was trying to get out of there before he decided to get violent.

"Well, you found me. Other people might find me too." Yeah, duh.

"So..." I led him forward.

"How'd you find me?"

I jerked a finger at the car. "Christ, how could I miss you?" and walked away.

I roared home in high spirits. I wanted to call Harry and tell him it was over. I was out of it now. I had done what I was supposed to do.

When I got home I was excited and high. So of course, I got higher. But after a while I was not satisfied:

 1. Sam was dead.

 2. I had been beat up and threatened. That has a tendency to piss a guy off.

 3. Even the Ice Queen's fate bothered me.

Too Many Spies Spoil the Case

But what could I do? I wasn't going to get any support from Harry and I didn't have any idea who'd whacked Sam, although the Iranian hotheads were in the running. If I only knew what the damn case was about.

I was in the office at the stroke of eight. I blew through the door and dropped the note card from the Gunter service on Van's desk.

He picked it up and looked at it with his red watery eyes wavering. Hard weekend for Van. Every weekend was a hard weekend for Van. His eyes drifted over to me, sitting in the chair at the side of his desk.

"You got Gunter." He'd forgotten I was working on it, I think.

"Yeah, Van. Caught up with him in Sonoma."

"Gee, the client's bill's gonna be big."

"Well, Van, I think they can afford it."

"Yeah, sure. Of course. So, you're ready to take your old stuff back and get back to work?"

Suddenly, I wasn't.

"Hey Van, you know, I'm gonna need some time off. Just a few days. I'm gettin' a little burned out, know what I mean?"

Van's head bobbed on his thin neck. "Sure, Doug. Sure. The rest of this week?"

"Yeah, I think so. I'll be back in action on Monday."

"Okay. Here's your check for last week."

Four hundred and thirty five bucks. By the time I deducted my costs for gas and parking, I was clear maybe three fifty. It's a living.

"I'm gonna chat with Harry for a sec then take off." Van nodded and went back to sorting out his papers.

Harry wasn't in until about half past eight. I waited in the front office, watching the girls work, said hello to Darrell the document subpoena manager when he walked by, and watched Barbara work the phones, type, take notes and call Van on the intercom all at the same time, it seemed. She was a whirlwind. She winked once and then was back in action.

Harry nodded to me when he arrived and motioned to follow him into his office. I closed the door while he sat, then I plopped into one of the armchairs.

"Got him."

"That's fine, Doug. I knew you would. I told Mr. Belli's office that I put my best man on it and that you would not let him down." He mixed his plural noun with the singular pronoun, but who cares. I smiled at the compliment.

"You want to hear about it?"

"Sure, sure. How'd you get him?"

I told Harry a condensed version of the events. I did not mention the Iranians in this version, just that I observed other people staking Gunter out as well. Harry nodded, complimented me on the follow up with the doorman. I gave him a typed accounting of my time, miles and expenses. He frowned at the twenty bucks for Jerome.

"Harry, there's just this." He looked up from his desk to see my face.

"Look, I had a little run in with some guys." I told him about how I sprung the Iranians' derelict van and the subsequent interview by Mr. Dark.

Harry fingered his lips and didn't speak. Then he picked up the phone and dialed a number. "Good morning, Meridithe. Is Mr. Belli available for a brief report? Thank you, of course I'll hold." He ignored my stare.

"Mel, Harry Silver. I just wanted to tell you we were successful in serving Mr. Gunter the OSC. Yesterday, in Sonoma. Yes, I did say that." He paused and listened for minute.

"Look Mel, I have a favor to ask of you. The young man we were talking about, he's here in my office. Yes, I will. I was just wondering, given that he has put a lot of time in on this case, and the unfortunate events, yes, that's right, well, I would like you to hear his full report." He listened for another half minute. "We'll both be there."

He hung up and talked at the same time. "Write up your report and have Barbara type it. Make three copies. Have it ready by two. Oh, by the way, Mr. Belli said thanks for the good work."

"Yes sir." I snapped to attention, almost, and went out. Borrowing a corner of Dixie's desk, I typed up my report, going in strictly chronological order. I did not clog it up with a lot of "the subject did this" and "I observed that" crap, but just outlined the events as they occurred and what I had seen, done and concluded.

I was finished by eleven thirty and gave it to Barbara for a retyping (naturally mine was rough) and she looked up at me once or twice while she read it. I walked out before she finished and went downstairs to the coffee shop for lunch. I lounged around until two thirty when Harry and I took a cab to Belli's office.

Harry didn't say anything to me except to clear up a couple of points in my report. "This is fine, but in the future, please put your conclusions at the end, not in the narrative."

"Yeah, sure. Of course." Okay, I was a putz.

Chapter Thirteen

The First Thing We Do Is Kill All the Lawyers

We walked into Belli's reception area and I gazed around like a kid. Everyone in old San Francisco knew the Belli legend and his office was a landmark for those following the political and legal affairs of the City. The receptionist greeted Harry as "Mr. Silver", she buzzed once and Belli's secretary, Meridithe, came out of a door in the side wall. She smiled at Harry and greeted him nicely. She was as ugly as a mud fence, but efficient and polite. It was kind of strange to go into an office where I was not being questioned or snarled at.

As we entered the lawyer's office the thick red velvet drapes closed, moving on a motorized track. This rendered the office totally private.

He waved us to seats in front of his black roccoco desk, shook my hand and looked in my eyes as Harry introduced me. I smiled and told him it was my pleasure to meet him.

"Good job, young man. Good job. I know he was slippery." Belli tilted his not inconsiderable bulk back in the massive leather chair. He looked like a judge on the bench.

"Well, actually sir, once I got a line on him he was as easy as pie."

"I see. Well, in that case Harry, my bill should be quite low." He laughed and Harry smiled softly.

"Oh no Mel, it will be quite large, actually."

"Hell, that's okay Harry. The Iranians have got plenty of money. Bill double!"

"I want you to review Doug's report with us." He handed Belli the document and he started reading right away, with his half glasses positioned on his nose.

He ran through the eight pages in three minutes. Then he pushed the glasses into his mane of white hair and looked at me, then Harry.

"And you would both like to know what this is about?" He was a smart man and didn't need crayon drawings.

Belli pushed back in the chair and sighed. "Okay, I know Harry, you won't repeat this. You, Mr. McCool, are going to exhibit your professional qualities as well, and your discretion will be absolute."

"I know how to keep my mouth shut." Don't patronize me, old man.

"Good. The wise man learns more with his silence than the fool with a thousand words." He was quoting a fortune cookie, I think.

"Here's a summation. Mr. Gunter contracted to deliver several containers of surplus aircraft parts he acquired through the Air Force salvage system. He then delivered those containers. They did not contain what he had represented they would contain. This was discovered after he had secured payment. Naturally, the Iranian government was unhappy with this turn of affairs, but Mr. Gunter was effectively out of their reach. They retained my services, upon recommendation from some mutual friends, and I proceeded to secure a judgment against Mr. Gunter and Midland Surplus. However, it was necessary to eventually secure the order to show cause why we should not obtain the assets. After much wrangling, that order was issued. Now that it has been served, we shall proceed to seize the assets immediately." He paused.

"However, you raise an interesting issue here. You have apparently discovered that the Iranians have been keeping a watchful eye on Gunter. You obviously crossed paths with them. They were a bit confused by the inevitable delays of our legal system. After all, this represents several years of procrastination and aggravation."

I had to interrupt. "Would their confusion extend to not thinking murder was illegal?"

"I believe it would be rash to assume that it is these men that are guilty of Mr. Feinstein's death."

I was surprised he knew or remembered Sammy's name.

He waited for us to absorb this. "Now, the fact is that certain other parties were involved in this affair. Mr. Gunter alleged that he had included the specified parts and that they were stolen by third parties. However, he could not make a claim against the insurer, since he could not prove that the parts had been in the shipment in the first place. The contract, however, had specified these parts and through some oversight they did not appear on a bill of lading."

"Rather sloppy work," I thought, but did not interrupt.

"Thus, I would suggest that it is possible that the 'marshals' who visited you were actually agents of another government."

"Ours." I offered.

"Well, I would assume so. It is highly likely that the item specified in the contract was actually something that was being secured without the express permission of the United States. And so, you see, Mr. Gunter and Midland were kind of in a bind. They aver that they included the item in the containers, but did not invoice them out of discretion. They allege that the Iranians actually received the parts but are trying not to pay for them. In any event, they have lost and we will secure their assets."

"What would happen if Gunter were to die?" I asked, as casually as I could.

"Well, that would slow the process down considerably. Complications with the estate, and trying to sort out personal and corporate assets. Not a disaster, but it would be more delay."

"So the Iranians wouldn't want him dead, necessarily."

"It would be rash and unwise. I believe the people I talk to understand that."

"So why was he afraid I was a hit man? And why would someone blow that receptionist's brains all over the office paneling?"

Belli winced at my graphic language. "I don't know. Of course, he could have other problems we are not fully aware of."

"Then his business practices were not always...reliable?" I was starting to talk like him.

"I'm getting the distinct impression, Mr. McCool, that you are *attempting* to interview me." His white eyebrows were raised, but he was smiling as he said it, and he glanced at Harry.

Harry flicked me a cautionary look. "Mel, quit fencing and skip the bull. Doug got the crap beat out of him and Sam is dead. Killed by a pro. I'm pretty fuckin' miffed over this and I want the straight story!"

I sat back, shocked. Harry! I waited for the explosion.

Belli's chin came to rest on his chest. "Okay. Here's the unvarnished version. The fuckin' ragheads were trying to buy a highly sophisticated radar system, DALTA, which stands for digitally assisted laser target...er, something or other, known by its code name - Kali, the Hindu goddess of destruction. We're pals with the Shah and all that, but this shit was too good for him and his camel jockeys."

"Gunter had been struggling in the surplus parts business and he was getting hard up for a good customer. The Iranians approached him to secure these items, unknown to the proper authorities, and include them in a shipment of regular aircraft spare parts. Deal is negotiated. The Iranians insist that it be in writing, it's so much money and all that. Millions. So the deal is consummated and I believe that Gunter did as he was hired to do. However, someone, some *organization* helped themselves to the parts in question, while they were being transshipped, and re-sealed the containers. It later turns out that the ship that carried the containers was registered to a front company for the Mossad, Israeli Intelligence." Like Harry and I wouldn't know who the Mossad was.

"It might be that they took the parts, it is most certain they must have, as they were also not able to obtain this technology. They may be cleaning up the back trail." Belli showed a remarkable familiarity with the terminology of intelligence work, like "back trail."

He explained that *if* Gunter were dead, the case might prove to be no longer worth pursuing. The Israelis would be trying to get the whole thing quieted down.

Everyone would gradually forget about it. Many times before the Israelis had pulled off intelligence coups that stirred up a hornet's nest, only to have the whole brouhaha fade into the twilight within six months. This deal was four years old now.

Belli paused. I took the opportunity to ask a question that seemed to have been skipped over. "Mr. Belli, if I may..." I began, not wanting to seem to be interrupting him. He waved a finger to continue. "...Isn't it a little unusual for a country to take what was an intelligence operation into open court? Weren't the Iranians concerned that their attempt to obtain this classified material would be exposed?"

"Well, yes, of course they were. However, through certain negotiations that we were able to conduct with various interested parties, we were able to have everyone stipulate to certain facts, and avoid the introduction of certain facts into evidence." He paused to consider his answer, then added, "Gunter had been in the surplus disposal office at the Pentagon. His career was stagnant and he could see no further route to promotion. When his retirement became optimal, he exited the service, and joining with two other partners, formed Midland Surplus."

"They were able, through their contacts still serving in that department, to arrange for certain items, that should not have been categorized as 'surplus-disposable' to be so categorized. Their contacts then informed them as to the lots that contained these valuable items and Midland would bid extraordinarily high prices for what was supposed to be generic aircraft parts. In fact, these were premium items that were worth hundreds of times what Midland obtained them for, and they were resold on the international market at huge profit. Not all the material was classified, but a good deal of it should not have been sold to the parties who ultimately obtained it."

He went on, summing up the whole caper: "Eventually, Midland became well known for being able to obtain material that others could not, and the Iranians approached them as I outlined. When Midland failed to deliver the items as promised, the Iranians were out $350 million, and were not going to stand for the loss. They had the temerity to try this means of recovery and we were able to help them prevail, although discreetly.

"So, now that you have successfully served Mr. Gunter, Midland Surplus, collectively and individually, must respond within three days and show cause why the assets previously awarded to my client should not be seized and distributed forthwith." He was back in lawyer mode.

I still thought it pretty odd that an attempt to steal US aircraft technology would result in a lawsuit but the law was strange no matter how you looked at it, and no doubt Mel was not giving us the whole story, but an edited version that suited his own purposes.

I leaned back. Eyes flicked from one to the other around the room. I spoke up once more: "So if you don't want Jim Gunter dead, you had better do something, 'cause this guy is walking around with a target on his back. In three days the only thing you're gonna be getting is lilies for the funeral."

Belli leaned forward and shot a look at Harry as if asking if my assessment was reliable.

Harry spoke up. "For God's sake Mel, he was tooling around the wine country in a classic sports car. My man tracked him without a great deal of trouble." Easy for him to say. "I'm sure organizations with more resources and less *limited* budgets would find the man easy pickings."

Mel thought this over for a moment. "Up until now I was not really worried about such a situation. But it's literally down to three days. By Wednesday at five PM, if Gunter's counsel hasn't come up with some sort of stall, the assets will, for all intents and purposes, be ours. Gunter's elimination could delay the whole process for another year or perhaps two. It's possible that whoever would benefit from that kind of delay, and perhaps a loss of interest by my clients and others in the meantime, would see that removing Gunter from this mortal coil could be expedient in several venues." Oh God, a lawyer talks and you need to sort out the clauses and phrases for five minutes to figure it out. In other words, Gunter could very well be dead meat when word got out that he'd been served.

"I suggest you get him put away somewhere safe for three days, or rather," I checked my watch, "two days and fourteen hours, more or less."

Belli appeared to be thinking hard. His eyes were narrow and brow knit. His cherubic face was stern and unmoving. He drew a large breath, as though preparing to dive into deep water. He looked at Harry closely.

"Harry, I know this is not your regular type of operation. But given that the situation is urgent, from my perspective anyway, could you be induced to arrange for Mr. McCool to make himself available for a special assignment?"

Harry did not answer, but gave a little shrug that indicated Belli could go on. "Mr. McCool, would you be interested in, well, keeping watch over Gunter for the next forty eight plus hours?"

"You mean be his bodyguard?"

"More or less a guardian angel, so to speak."

Harry was shaking his head no. "Mel, you can hire security firms for that. It's not even close to our line of work."

Belli disagreed. "I cannot force Mr. Gunter to accept our assistance. A security team or pressuring him to lay low would possibly backfire."

"So how do you guard a man who doesn't want your help?" Harry was thinking out loud now.

"Well, that's an interesting problem. You see, in this case, we have an abiding interest in keeping him safe and sound. He would have the same interest, one would think, but may resist the suggestion, coming, as it does, from a source he regards as an adversary, and a successful adversary at that. He might even think that we were threatening or trying to frighten him." Belli paused for breath. "What I would suggest is that you continue to shadow him, now that you have a fair idea of where to find him. And, well, discreetly look after his safety. Should you see anything threatening, you could alert the police."

"Mr. Belli, if the Mossad wants Gunter dead, you might as well buy a sympathy card now, while it's on sale. They'll whack him before I could find a phone."

"Well, yes. However, I did not intend for you to be alone in this matter. In fact, my clients have made it known that some of their, uh, *employees* have already developed a healthy respect for your abilities, and I think once I make it clear to them how Gunter's survival is in their interest, they could provide assistance with additional manpower. Of course, their resources are somewhat reduced. Apparently two of their number are no longer able to continue their duties. One of them was returned to hospital in Tehran with a subdural hematoma and fractured skull, and the other unfortunate gentlemen apparently died of a sudden onset of respiratory arrest."

Oops. That made two guys I'd killed, albeit inadvertently, within less than two weeks. And put another in the hospital. I was getting to be a hazard to other people's health.

"Let me assure you that my clients' staff do not hold a grudge in this regard, these incidents being regarded as the normal consequences of their official duties." He took a beat and then looked at Harry. "We would offer your firm a flat fee of one percent of the settlement amount for the two days."

Harry blinked once or twice. That was a lot of money in anyone's accounting, and Harry was well off, but not that well off. As for me, well I was fairly drooling. It didn't take *me* long to calculate one per cent of three hundred and fifty million.

Belli continued as though everyone was in agreement with the idea. "You have experience with weapons. You obviously are a capable man in other regards as well. You have a firearm and the necessary permit to carry one?" Belli had apparently received a short resume of my experience from Harry.

"No permit. No weapon. Not my regular line of work, you see." Actually, a service .45 resided in a shoebox in my closet, but I saw no need to tell Belli and Harry everything about my personal life.

Too Many Spies Spoil the Case

Harry and Mel looked at each other. A silent agreement seemed to pass between them. Harry let out a long sigh as Belli waved a hand dismissively, "I will arrange for the permit to be issued today. You can pick it up by four. I will call and tell you whom to see."

Harry sighed again. He fixed me with a hard look. "Doug, you want to do this." It was not a question and needed no answer. "When we leave here, you can go to a friend of mine. He will give you whatever you need."

That was it. Suddenly, Belli stood up, we were all shaking hands and Meridithe took us to the main reception area and called goodbye to our backs.

Magically, a cab was waiting. Belli must have signaled her to call one. We rode back downtown.

"Now look, Doug. My boy, I can call you that, I'm old enough, you are not to be foolish. No unnecessary risks. Go to the San Francisco Gun Exchange and ask for Nate Posner. I'll call him as soon as I get back to the office and tell him you will be arriving. He will provide you what weapons you need and send the bill to me. Get whatever you think necessary. Come back here after and I will brief you further."

So Harry was dropped at the office and the cab took me to the gun store.

Chapter Fourteen

When the Going Gets Tough, The Tough Go Shopping

San Francisco Gun Exchange is a perfect cube of a building on Second Street, large windows with great iron bars and the name in big steel letters on the front.

I walked in. The place was a temple, a cornucopia, a smorgasbord of weaponry. I found my way to a counter where a surprisingly young girl was busy arranging pistols in a case. She greeted me when I approached.

"Nate Posner, please. Tell him Doug McCool from AAA is here."

She looked a little surprised, but turned and walked down to the back of the store, opened a door, entered and closed it behind her. A minute later she came out.

"Mr. McCool, my father said I was to assist you with whatever you might need. My name is Naomi Posner." She looked at me steadily, but curiously. She had large brown eyes and wavy dark hair, freckles and soft full lips. She looked like a candidate for Playboy's "Girls of-" series

"Okay, great. Let's see. I need a large caliber revolver, .357 with at least a six inch barrel." I had been thinking about what I wanted on the way over.

She motioned me to follow her and she led me to a case twenty feet away. There were at least fifty pistols on display, all large caliber revolvers in stainless, nickel and blued finishes. She withdrew a Smith and Wesson .357 Model 19 Combat Magnum and laid it on the soft pad on the counter. I picked it up and examined its balance, weight and the comfort of the grip. It seemed adequate. While I was playing with this gun, she reached into the case and took out another. This one was larger, an eight inch barrel, Ruger .44 Magnum Super Blackhawk.

"I think this is the best damn gun made. That is, if you want what you hit to stay down. It's very accurate and extremely light for its size. We have a shoulder holster that will accommodate it easily. It's big, but unless concealment is your most important requirement, this is the best gun on the market today."

I took it up. It was huge, a great cannon of a gun, but perfectly balanced.

"I don't care for this grip."

"We have a very nice Bulldog grip that will suit your hand well. Would you like to try it?"

"Here?"

"We have a range in the basement."

"Yes."

"Let me find you the grips you need and change them. While I'm doing that, is there anything else?"

"Yes, I want two hideouts. One for an ankle holster, one for inside my waistband. I'll look around."

She went off with the Blackhawk and I wandered from case to case. There was every sort of gun imaginable on display. I found a lovely Walther PPK in 9 millimeter, only four inches over all, a flat little square spud of a gun. A Model 10 Browning nine millimeter caught my eye. Perfect for tucking inside the waistband and shared the same ammunition as the PPK.

Naomi returned with the modified Blackhawk. She nodded her approval of my choices and we gathered up the arsenal, several boxes of ammunition in appropriate calibers and I followed her downstairs. There was a thirty-yard range in the basement, well soundproofed, with tables, sand bags and tools for adjusting sights.

I loaded and unloaded all three guns twice, and Naomi showed me their disassembly and assembly. She handed me a set of ear protectors and we were ready to rock. I took a solid basic standing position and let the silhouette target have it.

My first six shots with the Ruger were pretty miserable. But the next six were better, and once I got over the tremendous roar the thing gave when fired, I was able to group four of six in the chest or head twice in a row.

I fired two groups from the table, bracing the gun on a sandbag. It seemed to be favoring the right, but Naomi adjusted the sights and after that, I was dead on.

I moved to seven yards to practice with the two automatics. I didn't so much care about being accurate as I did about being able to instinctively shoot, and I was pleased with the PPK. It was just like pointing a finger, and I could group six shots in the kill zone every time. The Browning was a little harder, but I felt okay with it.

Naomi had brought down a selection of holsters for me to try. The Ruger was huge and hung under my left arm like a third limb. She helped me adjust the rig that carried the gun vertically, with a strap that fastened to my belt. Once I got it on I practiced drawing a few times. It was not the gun for a quick draw contest, but once the thing was out, the intimidation factor was tremendous, the killing power overwhelming.

"Here." Naomi handed me two speed loaders already filled for the Blackhawk, and two spare clips each for the autos. She even helped me load the clips. She was quietly efficient about it and revealed a practiced skill with the firearms that was incongruous with her college-student looks.

I put the Browning into a small waistband holster that clipped inside my pants, and the PPK fit nicely into an ankle holster. When I was done, I felt like I'd gained fifty pounds, and was very conscious of the bulge under my arm, in my waist and on the outside of my right ankle, but my confidence factor was ten times higher than when I had entered. I was armed to the teeth. I pulled my jacket on over the arsenal and checked my appearance in a mirror. Unless you knew where to look, I didn't think I looked so obvious.

I returned to the office and was very self-conscious of my bulging armament, but Barbara just waved me to Harry's office, the other women looked up quickly and then returned to their typing. There was a subdued air about the place.

Harry's brief was simple. I was to meet up with the Iranians in an hour at the Mark Hopkins, near Gunter's digs and have a pow wow. A messenger from our office had already picked up a concealed weapons permit, all filled out and ready to go. I marveled that Belli could arrange for such a rare item in such short order, but I figured the San Francisco PD probably owed him a favor or two over the years. Harry arranged for credentials identifying me as an operative in his employ. This allowed me to function as a private investigator under Harry's license. Cool. Things were moving so fast I didn't have time to think about it. The last thing Harry handed me was a letter for me to sign. It said that any remuneration received from Belli in this case would be split sixty-forty and I was getting the fat half. Harry was being generous. I signed in a daze.

Chapter Fifteen

Happiness is a Warm Gun

I called the room number at the Mark Hopkins given to me. A familiar voice answered. I answered back.

"Doug McCool here."

"Ah, yes, Mr. McCool, please come on up." Mr. Dark, the ferret.

"No. Frankly, our private conversations have been unpleasant. You can meet me in the bar. The Top of the Mark. We can talk there just fine."

"I don't think we want to talk about these things in public."

"Try not to shout and we'll be okay. The bar won't be very crowded at this hour and there's no way I'm gonna be in a room alone with you guys."

"Very well. I will be there in ten minutes."

"Okay."

I took the outside glass elevator to the bar at the top of the hotel. The view is majestic, San Francisco laid out before me like a little architectural model, and beyond you could see the Bay riffling in the wind, the bridges delicately arching over the green water. The East Bay was a smudge of brown through the smog.

I took a table in one corner. It was five fifteen and the bar was not particularly busy yet. The business drinkers who would be entertaining customers at the hotel weren't finished with their day, and it was too early for couples going out for the evening. Two suits were at the bar, getting an early start on their evening high, and one table held a group of men and women laughing and talking. Looked okay for a quiet chat with the ferret.

He showed up about five minutes after me, looked around for a second, then walked over. I stood up when he got to the table, we shook hands formally and sat, cautiously. He gave me a name, David Farrar. I doubted that it was his real name, but it was something to call him. We adjusted our chairs so we could partially face each other, with both our backs to the view out the windows, allowing us to keep one eye on the entrance to the bar. We were just not the view-admiring types.

He looked the same, dressed in a slimly cut black suit, white shirt, old-school striped tie. He eyed me closely. He was a composed person; he did not fidget. The waitress sauntered over. We ordered Cokes and chatted idly about the weather. We turned once to give the view an obligatory gaze and comment. When we had our drinks and were alone again, Farrar began:

"First, I want you know we made a mistake in dealing with you the way we did. A mistake that we have paid dearly for, as you are aware. We acted impetuously and I have been disciplined by my superiors. I hope that at this point, since our interests have for the moment converged, we can forget the past and work together."

"One thing first. Was it one of your guys that croaked Sammy?" I wanted to know.

"Croaked?" He looked confused.

"Our man outside Gunter's."

"The old man with the big car?" He seemed honestly confused.

"That's right."

"It was not one of us. I promise you. You know there is another team."

"Yeah, I spotted them once."

"Israelis."

"No shit? What's their beef?"

"Beef? You mean why are they involved?" I nodded. Have to remember to use standard English with this guy.

"The theory at this point is that if they eliminate Mr. Gunter they accomplish two things: one, they delay the case and perhaps it just fades away; two, they eliminate a trail that leads to them. Mr. Gunter could not be questioned very effectively dead, could he?"

"Fair enough." I was a reasonable man. I decided to accept his version of things, for now. Besides, I felt a little bad about the amount of damage I'd inflicted on his team. Not that they didn't have it coming, but they were the worse for wear.

We spent a few minutes comparing notes. Farrar told me his team now consisted of himself and the driver, whose name he gave as Peter. They would defer to my priorities in working out assignments. He outlined the resources available: they had a rental car, radios for the three of us, pistols and two silenced Uzi's available. Goodness, the toys these guys play with. They were supposed to be very discreet, however, and were concerned about any contact with American authorities.

We decided we would try to locate Gunter first, then work in teams of two, twelve hours on, six off, staggering the relief so that one member of the stakeout team would be fresh and the other would have gotten some rest within the 24 hour cycle. We both knew that fatigue is the critical factor in high stress situations. A man who was over-tired made mistakes in judgment and his reflexes were unavoidably slowed. The human body can be trained to sustain long periods of combat stress, but that level of fitness and preparation requires constant training. I wasn't in that kind of shape, and Farrar, I began to realize, was one level removed from a regular operations type guy. I had disabled the two field ops available, and to send in more on short notice wasn't possible.

Farrar returned to his room to collect "Peter" and we met in front of the hotel. I recovered my van from the valet and within a few minutes they were loaded up. We drove the two blocks to Gunter's building. They waited while I parked and went in to see what Jerome might be able to tell me.

He was at his little desk in the lobby, reading a book. He smiled when he saw me. We shook hands warmly. He seemed to be a stand-up guy.

"He came back Sunday evening," he answered in response to my question, "and then went out again. Took a cab. I don't know where he went."

"Jerome," I added. "Anyone else been around lately, asking about Gunter?"

"No sir, no one since them two I tol' you about."

"Anybody come around asking questions about anything?"

"Yessir. First thing this morning, two gen'lmen showed up. Real estate men, they said. Gave me their card, here somewhere." He pulled open a drawer in the desk and pulled out the card of a large commercial real estate company. The card proved nothing. You can get a business card printed in two hours with anything you want on it.

"What did they say?"

"Said they was looking over the building for a buyer they's representin'. I let 'em look over the building and I called the management company while they was lookin'. But Mr. Seinfield, the building manager, he said the building weren't for sale and to tell them to take off. So I told 'em that and they said 'okay' maybe they had got it wrong, and took off."

"What'd they look like? You remember?"

"Oh, well, they didn't look too special. They was both pretty big men, tall, about six-two, six-three, wearing suits and carried briefcases. Brown hair, both of them, 'cept one had more gray in his. They was nice enough fellas, I guess. They asked me if any of the tenants was there that they could ask to see an apartment, but I says that they couldn't go disturbin' anyone without my boss sayin' it was okay, so they left."

"Seen them since this morning, or anybody else hanging around?"

"Well, ain't nobody come in here 'cept the usual, you know, the mailman, phone man."

"A phone man came in?"

"Yeah, about 12:30. Said there was a problem with the line."

"Where'd he go?"

"Into the garage. I asked him if he needed me to show him where the box was, but he said no." Jerome thought for a moment. "You sayin' maybe he weren't no phone man? And them real estate fellas weren't no real estate fellas, were they?"

"No, probably not. Look Jerome. Gunter's in a lot of hot water right now. Don't go stickin' your neck out. If he comes back here I need you to do me a favor."

He nodded. "Okay."

"Call this number, day or night. Just tell the person who answers 'he's here.' You don't have to say anything more than that. Anything else happens, you call the cops right away. Then you get in that little closet of yours and close the damn door. You got that?"

"Oh yeah." He looked serious but not very frightened. I gave him a card with Harry's name on it. Harry was going to be the liaison for us. He would page me for anything important. We worked out a little number code. The Iranians only had the three radios and we needed them. It was clumsy, but would work.

I slipped a wad of cash into Jerome's hand. He started to protest, but I just put my finger on my lips. "I hope you don't earn it, Jerome. I hope you don't earn a penny of it." He relented.

I went back outside and consulted with my new allies.

Farrar thought about what I told them and then looked at Peter for a moment. "Bomb?"

Peter shrugged. "I'd put them in the two cars and figure that was the easiest way to squash him."

"You guys know how to defuse a car bomb?"

Peter allowed as how he probably could, but he didn't look happy about it. I don't blame him. One mistake and you would cease to exist. Or be mangled horribly. I was glad I didn't know anything about bombs.

I took Peter across to the building. He took a small box of tools. I explained to Jerome that Peter needed to check on the phone man's work. Jerome nodded okay and pointed to the door into the garage.

"You need a hand?" I foolishly volunteered.

"No, it's better you don't accompany me. We can't afford to lose two more people on this job. I will be okay."

I told Jerome to wait in his little cubbyhole office, with the door pulled to, just in case, and I went back across the street. I doubted they would blow up the whole building just to get Gunter, but why hang around to find out.

Farrar and I went through three cigarettes each, one after the other, before Peter came out, looked up and down the street and then came over to where we were waiting. He carried two small boxes dangling from wires in one hand and his tool kit in the other.

Too Many Spies Spoil the Case

He gingerly laid the boxes in the trunk and replaced the tools. "Yes, both cars were rigged. Wired into the ignition and placed under the seats. Fortunately, not sophisticated, a quick job. However, at our first opportunity, we should dispose of those boxes. They would certainly destroy the car and everyone in it if they were to go off." He added as we looked alarmed. "They shouldn't go off. But we don't need to carry high explosives around, do we?"

Farrar and I agreed with that. We decided how to divide up. I was fairly certain that Gunter had gone to his boat. He didn't seem smart enough to check into a hotel under a false name and lay low. So we left Peter with the sedan at Gunter's and Farrar and I drove over to the marina. We divied up the gear so Peter and Farrar each had an Uzi. Of course, I carried my own arsenal.

On the way there Farrar asked about my background, specifically my training and military service. I answered in generalities but told him basically what he wanted to know. He shared with me that he was a captain in the SAVAK, the Shah's counter-intelligence and general security outfit. I'd heard that the SAVAK guys were pretty fierce. CIA-trained and equipped, they were known for torture, murder, kidnapping and the like. I asked Farrar about that.

"Yes," he said, "we are very aggressive in defense of our country. You must understand, there are many forces that oppose us. Fundamentalist Muslim, the Soviets who covet our oil, the Israelis, our traditional enmity with Iraq, revolutionaries and counterrevolutionary groups, terrorists of all kinds...we are a constitutional monarchy, but I admit, sometimes the constitution is a little vague in how these threats may be dealt with. The same is true for your security services, no?"

I nodded. The Constitution seemed to be a pretty thin shield against the FBI, CIA, NSA and the various military intelligence and counterintelligence groups. Not to mention anti-Castro and anti-Communist free lancers of various kinds and our own police departments' intelligence units.

We parked across the street. Nothing looked out of the ordinary at first glance. There was an assortment of cars and trucks in the lot, some of them I recognized, some I didn't, but that didn't mean anything. Sitting in the Microbus, Farrar and I debated how we would proceed. We wanted to make sure we were sitting on Gunter and not just an empty boat. But we didn't want to spook him or anyone who might be watching. It was nearly seven, so we decided to wait until dark and see what developed. I walked to the cafe two blocks away and got us sandwiches and coffee. We ate silently. Farrar laid the Uzi on the floor between us and threw his jacket over it. We discussed guns and sports for while, then settled silently to wait.

Twilight drifted over the scene by eight thirty and we watched for a light onboard the boat. For a while there was nothing, but then we could see a faint light coming from one of the portholes near the bow. What an idiot! He didn't have enough brains to hide out somewhere he couldn't be found.

Farrar radioed Peter to tell him we'd had Gunter in the bag and to go ahead and get some rest. Peter would catch some sleep and relieve me. Farrar would get a cab, rent another car and return. I would relieve Farrar in the morning.

We saw a light go on in the main cabin. The curtains were drawn but we could make out shadows behind them. The boat then tilted slightly to one side and we saw a figure climb over to the dock with the assistance of another figure that stayed on board. The departing figure walked up the dock, pretty unsteadily on the bobbing planks, then came up the ramp. As she drew closer we could see she was a young black girl, wearing a long blonde wig. She walked more assuredly once she got her feet on land. We were both amazed when she walked over to the bushes, hiked up her skirt, aimed a penis at the ground and peed a large puddle.

Farrar looked at me with an amazed expression. "She's... he..." I felt sorry for him. The first time you see a transvestite can be like that. I nodded silently. He closed his mouth and nodded too. The TV finished his piss and waited near the street. I wondered if Gunter knew what he had been getting. I've heard about guys that were fooled for years.

In about ten minutes a Yellow cab pulled up, she signaled the driver with a wave, popped in and took off. That damn Gunter certainly indulged himself. Here we were sitting in a cold, uncomfortable VW van eating sandwiches and drinking cold coffee while that son of a bitch was on a warm comfortable yacht fucking his brains out. And we were keeping him alive! If that shithead had gone home and started a car, he would have been bird food in a millisecond. It makes you wonder. Farrar and I just looked at each other.

Farrar decided that he would walk to cafe before it closed and call a cab. He wanted to make sure he could get another car before it became any later. I told him to pick up some cigarettes for me on his way back.

I sat in the bus. This spy stuff seemed to involve a lot of sitting. I had to watch my cigarette supply, I'd forgotten to bring more than one pack. I shouldn't have been smoking at all, it kills your night vision, but my God, how long can a nicotine addict sit and stare at nothing? I cupped the butt to keep the glow from revealing me.

I started to nod off about one. Farrar hadn't returned, I couldn't figure out what was keeping him. I tried the radio but got no answer from either him or Peter. Maybe he'd run into trouble getting another car that late and called Peter for a ride. I was tired. I thought about this situation. Was this really possible? I found myself having gone from a directionless guy humping process for three hundred a week to some sort of half-assed body guard working on a case that would net me,

Too Many Spies Spoil the Case

I had plenty of time to do the math, about a two million dollar fee. I was able to amuse myself for a while contemplating what I would do with that much money. I couldn't comprehend that kind of wealth. Of course, if I got killed, I'd be the richest corpse around.

My eyes were half closed, the sockets were burning I was so tired. It felt ecstatic to close them. My head bobbed up and down, jerking me awake, then falling to my chest. I smoked so many cigarettes that my lungs creaked in protest. The coffee was long gone and my pee jar was full. I jerked awake for about the tenth time when I thought I saw something.

The lights in Gunter's boat were out. He was sleeping in a warm comfortable bunk. I was sitting here, cold, stiff, bored and wretched.

I stared into the blackness of the water in the slough. After a minute or so I saw a wet glint. The glint changed position, coming up the slough from the Bay end, toward the marina. A rubber boat. One of those Avons, with the inflatable rubber hull. I could see motion. Two figures, paddling slowly and silently. At least, from where I was, there was nothing to be heard. I glanced at my watch. Two thirty. That's the time I would choose. The time of night when most people died. When the metabolism was at low ebb. I felt a little squirt of adrenaline bring me up to full alert. I cursed the missing Farrar and tried to get him on the radio. I depressed the send button and called softly.

"Darkman, this Iceman. Darkman, this is Iceman." Sounds silly now.

After a few seconds Farrar's voice crackled back. I turned the volume down.

"Darkman here. Go."

"We have visitors. Two by water. Get your ass over here. I'm going to cover the cork." 'Cork' was our code word for the boat.

"Roger that. We've had some problems here. On my way." I slipped the radio into my outside pocket, reached up and turned off the dome light. I wondered what Farrar and Peter's *problem* was.

I pushed the car door closed with a little click. It sounded like too much noise in the stillness, but I didn't think the boatmen could hear it. There was a street light across from the marina parking lot, and a couple of bright area lights, at the gate and where the gangplank met the dock. After that there were just some dim incandescent lights that made yellow splashes, lighting the wooden planks and not much else. I ran across the street, angling toward the bushes at the south end, the end away from Gunter's boat. I was worried about trying to get closer without being seen. I hadn't seen other observers, but they could be anywhere.

I couldn't see the boat from where I was crouched in the foliage, but judging by their speed they would be very close to Gunter's slip. Once they were on board, Gunter was dead meat. I took a chance and ran across the lot, dodging among the various vehicles for cover, staying low. I could see the rubber raft clearly now, with the extra light around the marina. They emerged from the shadows approaching their goal.

Sliding the Blackhawk cannon out, I held it by my side, then scrambled around the back of the last car that offered cover and crab-walked to get even with the boat. When I drew even, I lay prone.

The boatmen drew even with the stern and started angling in. They apparently intended to board over the stern and rush the cabin. I figured they would pop the cabin door as quietly as they could and shoot Gunter while he slept.

This wasn't a good position. I was at least thirty yards away. The bank, a little strip of water and then the dock were between me and them. There was no way I could get to the dock without being seen and heard. I didn't have a key to the gate, and besides, the gate was brightly lit anyway. I would have been revealed there clearly.

I decided my only chance was to get an angle that would let me cover the stern from the bank, and when the first guy climbed over, try to pop him. I reasoned that it wouldn't really matter if I hit him or not. The roar of the Ruger going off would wake everyone up anyway, and I assumed it would scare them away. Or not. They might just rush the cabin and shoot Gunter anyway. I decided it would be best if I could hit one of them. Great. Another life to add to my count.

I eased to the left to get a better angle on the stern. It put me farther away, but with a wider field of fire. I intended to blast everything near the stern. With the .44 roaring away, they wouldn't be inclined to see how many guns there were. I would have to change position quickly, before the muzzle flash let them zero in on me. I figured six shots, roll to the right to get the opposite angle, speed load and blast away again. I was not able to sustain a long exchange but I did have the advantage of elevation and surprise.

The rubber boat was now next to Gunter's. It was actually so low in the water that I couldn't really see it, but I watched it disappear behind the stern. I cocked the revolver and aimed about four feet above the dark stern against the slightly brighter water. I tightened my two-handed grip.

Water reflects light. Can't be helped. His black neoprene suit was wet, of course, and it glinted in the glow. I watched the glint come up...

...and squeezed. I wasn't ready for the explosion that followed. I jumped with surprise. The night was gone and I was blinded from the flash. I brought the barrel down to the general vicinity of the target and pulled again. Another tremendous roar in the stillness, the echoes magnifying as the sound waves bounced off the office buildings nearby.

I fired four times then the earth on my left erupted. No sound, just a shower of dirt next to me. I leapt to the right like I had grabbed a live wire. I just levitated straight up and was two feet away before I put the things together.

Fuck! That was a bullet. They found me quickly and were returning fire! I rolled furiously to the right some more, to bring me on the south side of the boat, angling toward the stern from the opposite side.

I reached that position when the dirt exploded again, this time on my left. Had they anticipated me? And found me in the dark? This miss was too close to be random.

All of sudden I realized, while rolling back the other way, then stopping partway and rolling to the right again, just to confuse them, that these shots were coming from behind me! As soon as the synapses that formed the thought clicked, I rolled toward the bank and over the edge, toward the water and Gunter's boat. A third silent shot wished me farewell.

I log-rolled all the way over and picked up speed with the slope, splashing into the water in a couple seconds. The cold slap shook me. I lay in the muck, my face a centimeter away from the water, getting the greasy salty stuff in my eyes and nose with each wavelet.

I paused to work out my situation. Strategically, I could be in a shitload of trouble here. There were hostile parties in an elevated position with a clear field of fire across the whole parking lot and two hostiles on the opposite side, with only the dock, some shallow water and muck and the length of the boat separating us. They had the raft, and wet suits. I was freezing already. Survival time in fifty-two degree water was about forty-five minutes, at best. After that, hypothermia, unconsciousness and death. Time was not on my side, although reinforcements were on the way. I figured without any traffic, Farrar was maybe twenty, twenty-five minutes from here. He could drive quickly, but if he got too crazy, he risked being stopped. I didn't think the Uzi would help him with the cops. And a speeding car at three in the morning was too suspicious. Farrar would get here when he got here, but it was going to be close. Time was definitely not on my side.

I looked behind me at the boat. That was where the nearest threat lay and was the best position. While the guy with control of the lot was in a commanding position, by the same token, he was pinned down. He couldn't leave it to rush me. Unless there were more guys at ground level. In which case I was fucked.

I slipped deeper into the water and checked the Ruger's load. I kept it up out of the water as best I could. "I hope this ammo is water proof," I remember thinking.

I worked over to the bow, swimming under the floating dock to get to the other side. If the Ruger wasn't wet before, it was now. Guns are supposed to be able to fire wet, but I have had them fail. There is no sillier feeling than pulling the trigger and having the gun click impotently. All of sudden your firepower has been reduced to that of a club. And not a very big club at that.

I listened closely. There was no sound. I didn't hear moaning or whispering. That meant that either my four shots had killed one or both, or that I had missed. They would be in the water, wondering where I was, listening. Would they have radio contact with the sniper? I would suppose so. Great. They knew where I was, but I didn't know where they were. How I longed for X-ray vision about then. I held onto the dock with one hand, the other holding the Ruger. It wasn't a good gun for close quarters, taking much too long to swing the barrel compared to a short gun, but I couldn't afford to take the time to replace it with the Browning. I assumed that the Walther was now filled with mud and would likely be useless.

I had to do *something*. The water was so cold I was getting weak and my arms felt like lead. It wouldn't be long before I would be nearly helpless. Eeny, meeny, minie, moe - I chose the south side. I don't know why. It felt better.

I eased down the length of the slip toward the stern. I pushed against the boat hull to move it over so I could pass. It floated away slowly, leaving me about eighteen inches to get by. I pointed the Ruger forward as best I could. Christ, it was heavy. What had seemed a beautiful weapon a few minutes ago now felt like a sledgehammer.

I could only hear little wavelets slap against the hull and the dock. Either these guys were very, very quiet and disciplined, or they were dead.

I finally reached the end of the boat. I would be revealed in another two feet. I took a deep breath and pushed myself around the stern in one move.

What I saw there was a shock, even though I had caused it. Floating in the water was a headless corpse, it's gaping neck facing me. I gasped and inhaled a bunch of water, then choked and coughed. It didn't matter, because in the rubber raft was another corpse, this one with its left shoulder gaping from the back, where the slug shattered bone, sheared arteries and exploded out the rear, carrying tissue in a spray that covered the side of the raft. He had gone into shock immediately, and bled to death in minutes. The blood had pumped all over the boat and floated in globs on the water. I recognized him. One of the "marshals" from Harry's office. The other guy was unrecognizable, since he had no head, but I assumed he was the other one.

I had to get out of the water. I could hear voices, and sirens in the distance. I threw the pistol onto the dock and climbed up on the north side, with most of the boat between me and the sniper. Nonetheless, the boat railing disintegrated about three feet away from me, showering me with splinters. I slid over the side and into the cockpit. Just as I did, the light in the pilothouse came on and Gunter flung the door open, yelling something.

He fell across my outstretched body, and I helped him the rest of the way by grabbing his shirt and pulling. His head smacked into the wood floor of the cockpit, making a sound like a dropped melon. He started swearing. I swore back at him.

"Shut the fuck up, you idiot. They're trying to kill us you dumb shithead," I was not feeling very kindly right now. This was too much like earning my money.

Gunter was so shook up he just looked at me and nodded. I signaled for him to crawl into the wheelhouse and shut off the light. I couldn't believe he was that stupid.

"Now just stay where you are," I whispered hoarsely, trying to make my voice loud enough for him without advertising my location to the world. "We have got to get the fuck out of here, now! There's cops coming, I just killed two guys, and we have a sniper pinning us down." Gunter seemed to appreciate the position we were in. He slid up to the wheel area, reached up with his hand and found the ignition key in the lock. He turned it and a starter ground noisily. With a roar and a clatter the diesel started. It would need time to warm up, and we were almost out of time. Plus we had to cast off with the damn sniper watching.

I slipped back over the railing on the far side of the boat and unfastened the lines on that side. I just stuck my hand up over the rail and pulled them loose. But I would have to reach the one on the south side of the bow. The south side stern line I could reach from inside the cockpit, but the bow line was in the open.

Gauging the increase in loudness of the sirens I figured we had about three minutes. I went to the extreme end of the bow on the safe side, dashed out into the open, dodging back and forth, and snatched the line off the cleat. For a horrible two or three seconds, my back was totally exposed. I waited for the blow. The line was off and I was back in cover.

I returned to the cockpit as quickly as I could, staying low, and pulled the other line free. Still no shots. I motioned to Gunter to back the Hell up and get us out of there. The diesel clattered in protest, but we started moving. I have to hand it to him, he stood up and steered with only a slight hesitation. When we were clear of the slip he pointed us toward the Bay and we slowly gathered speed. Just as the cop cars were crossing the Third Street Bridge over the slough, we were passing under it. Gunter nosed us into the side of a pier and held us there, still next to the bridge. Only someone looking straight down would see us.

We waited for a minute, then he took us down the slough, which was much wider here as it approached the Bay, and suddenly, we were in open water.

I joined him in the wheelhouse, the pistol put away. I must have looked a sight, covered with mud, wet, my clothes smeared with blood where they picked up gore from the stern.

Gunter looked at me in the dark. "You're the guy that served me those papers."

"Yeah." I was not feeling too verbal. I was so exhausted from the effort and tension I was shaking. "You have a guardian angel. You owe people money, Gunter, and that's the best life insurance you can have."

He nodded. He was worth a lot alive to certain people, and dead to others.

"Where are you heading?" I wanted to know if he had a plan.

"We're heading for the Gate, at the moment. What do you think we should do? The cops are going to find out about the boat from my neighbors and they'll call the Harbor Patrol and the Coast Guard."

I realized that we were sitting ducks. By the time we got half way to the exit from the Bay they would have us. They had radar, radios, helicopters and a double homicide. That would get their attention.

"You're gonna have to abandon this boat. We need to pull into one of those piers and get the Hell off right away."

Gunter moaned when he heard me say abandon the boat. "Oh well, I wouldn't have owned her for more than another day or two. The Iranians will get her anyway."

He angled us toward the huge black commercial wharves and pulled us in between two docked freighters. They looked like skyscrapers next to the teak yacht. We saw a rough ladder that led to the top of the wharf and nosed up to it. I went forward, tied us up and we crawled to the top, peeking over the side to see if there was anyone around.

There was not. Hunched over, trying to look like a couple of early rising workers we started across the Embarcadero, that wide desert of pavement the runs along the San Francisco waterfront like an asphalt scimitar, from the east side of the docks all the way to Fisherman's Wharf, Tourist Hell.

I slid into the first phone booth we ran across, at the Hyatt Regency Hotel. We went in the back way and found some phones that were isolated from the lobby. It was three forty five. I tracked mud and water across the lovely carpet. Called Harry. "Come get us. Outside the Hyatt Regency, across Market Street on the other side. Hurry."

We backtracked out of the hotel without being seen and crossed the street. Then withdrew into a dark doorway and waited. It seemed like a long time to stand there, shivering and worrying about police cars and long stories. Gunter stood there, silent. My cigarettes were ruined, of course, and when I asked him if he had any he shook his head no.

Cars passed by regularly, but none slowed. A police cruiser passed, and my heart stopped, but it went on by without taking any notice. Finally, a tan Buick slowed down when it reached the corner where we were hiding, the inside light flicked on and I recognized Harry. I pulled at Gunter's sleeve and stepped out. I opened the back door and half pushed Gunter in, then climbed in the front.

Harry looked at the soaking bundle of clothes that represented me and said, "Okay?"

"Just get me some coffee and cigarettes. And get us the fuck out of here."

Harry eased the big car away from the curb and headed for his place in the Avenues. He stopped at a corner market and got us coffee and a pack of smokes for me. I held the cup with both hands until the feeling in them returned, then held it between my legs while I lit a cigarette, took a long drag, coughed a bit, and exhaled the smoke out the window. I said nothing, but drank the coffee as fast as I could and smoked three cigarettes, one after the other.

After he'd taken some coffee, Gunter spoke up. "Where are you taking me? Who are you?" he paused. "I guess I should thank you, those guys were gonna kill me." His voice kind of trailed off at the end, like he had just realized that.

We ignored his other questions, but I mumbled, "Your welcome," to his thanks. Harry looked at him in the mirror.

"You are safe with us, Mr. Gunter. Please just relax. Do not attempt to leave, however, or we will be forced to restrain you. Is that clear?"

Gunter didn't say anything, but he must have nodded his assent. After about twenty minutes we were at Harry's. The door opened as we pulled into the driveway and the car slid into the garage. The door closed behind us and I finally relaxed.

Chapter Sixteen
Gunter's Apologia

When we walked in the house Dorothy took one look and went to get a towel and a blanket for me. Harry started more coffee. "Dorothy will make you something to eat, Doug. Go down the hall there and take a shower. We'll find you some clothes."

Dorothy met me in the hall with the towel and blanket, pointed me to the bathroom. "Just leave everything in there," she mothered. "I'll take care of your clothes. Now get a nice hot shower while I cook."

Suddenly I was so hungry I thought I'd pass out. "Yes, breakfast. Lots of it. And coffee," I ordered and began to pull off my jacket. Dorothy stared at the cannon strapped under my arm, but said nothing else and closed the door behind her.

I struggled to peel off the shoulder rig, my shirt, my other two guns, and the rest of my clothes. I was right about the automatics, they were both filled with mud. The Ruger didn't look very good either, and I wondered idly if the thing would have fired or not. Oh well, no matter. I stepped into the hot stream and surrendered to the sheer delight of heat and cleanliness. I just let the water pour over my head and aching shoulders. My arms felt like I had been lifting weights all night. I almost fell asleep standing up.

After running up the Silvers' water bill, I got out, dried off slowly and then wrapped the blanket around me. When I wandered down the hall Harry spotted me and took me into their bedroom where he handed over a robe. I turned discreetly and dropped the blanket on the bed, putting on the robe, then wrapped the blanket back around me. I followed him to the kitchen.

Gunter was sitting at the dinette drinking coffee. Dorothy was at the stove with pans going on three burners, the toaster working and the table set. Soon we were eating eggs, hash browns, bacon and toast with juice and coffee to wash it down. I was surprised about the bacon, since I thought they kept kosher, but it turned out to the kind made from beef. I didn't care if it came from dog, I ate everything put in front of me.

After the meal I filled them in on the night's events. I still had the radio in the pocket of my jacket, but of course it was ruined. Harry called the Iranians' room at the hotel and Farrar answered. Harry told him that we were safely hidden.

Farrar told Harry what happened on his end. He arrived as I began my attack, saw the sniper in the office window across the street. I hadn't heard it, but he took the sniper out with the Uzi and then tried to find me. He saw me just as the boat started to take off, but by that time, the police were getting close and he beat it.

His delay was caused by trouble at their end as well. While Farrar was rounding up another rental car, Gunter's building was attacked. Two men ran into the lobby, just after one o'clock. Apparently Peter dashed across the street right behind them. The two men ran up the stairs and kicked in Gunter's door, firing wildly. As they came down the stairs they met Peter, with fatal results. When Farrar got there with the car, there were cops all over the place. Farrar saw Peter's bullet-riddled body being carried out, told the cops he had a friend living there and got a condensed version of what happened. Jerome's body was found behind the desk. Poor Jerome. I felt guilty, although I didn't think I could have prevented it.

Dorothy put on the morning news at six; they were talking about the firefight at the marina and at Gunter's building. There weren't very many facts: four bodies, missing boat found abandoned, whereabouts of owner unknown, reasons for the gun fight unknown. Same story at the apartment. There was no mention of the sniper's body being found or anything about Gunter other than being named as the owner of the boat. There were television pictures of the dingy, the boat and the area, an interview with the hippy couple, who were clueless, of course, and the police lieutenant in charge of the investigation who was pretty clueless himself. Then they showed the outside of Gunter's building and blathered some nonsense about it as well.

Gunter kept quiet, surrounded by strangers. Harry said he would call Belli later in the morning and told me to go to bed. Despite the coffee I was asleep within ten minutes of lying down. No dreams.

By the time I woke up, bleary and aching, Harry had touched base with Belli, Farrar was outside on point in a car, Dorothy was in the office watching the store, Gunter was crashed in another bedroom. I found my clean clothes draped over a chair. The jacket was ruined. I put on the rest and stumbled out to the living room.

Harry brought me up to speed with coffee and information. No one knew who the five gunmen were with, our assumption: Mossad agents attempting to muddy the water and put the whole affair into deep freeze. I didn't think the Israelis would be so violent, especially in the United States, but what the Hell did I know? International espionage was not exactly my province - everything I knew about it was from newspapers or magazines. Since the Black September Olympic massacre last year the Israelis had gotten pretty tough. There were newspaper stories of Palestinian terrorists dropping dead all over Europe.

I didn't waste a lot of time speculating. I planned to brace Gunter when he woke up and see how his story compared to the version Belli had fed us.

Harry's plan was to simply keep Gunter holed up at his place. We had about twenty-four hours to go and then we didn't care what happened to Gunter. His survival was not, uh, germane to our goal, which was to see that Belli and the Iranians got their money and we got our cut. Cold, but true. We didn't intend to throw Gunter to the wolves, exactly. He was probably safe once the seizure of the assets was complete, as killing him would only accomplish a small goal- he wouldn't be around to squawk his version of events. That wasn't enough, in my opinion, to motivate his liquidation- unless he knew more about the disappearing parts than he let on.

Gunter wandered out of the bedroom where he was sleeping, rubbing his face and looking bleary. We pointed him to the coffee and Harry fixed him a sandwich. When he was back among the living we sat around the kitchen table. As a reward for my valor, Harry even relented about smoking in the house, although the windows and sliding door were all open. I offered to smoke outside, really.

"Gunter, you go by James, Jimmy, Jim...?" I started off. "I figure we can be on a first name basis now. I'm Doug McCool." I stuck my hand out. We hadn't the opportunity to indulge in social graces earlier.

"Jim is fine," he answered, taking my hand in a good handshake. He didn't try to squash it, but I didn't feel like we were holding hands, either. "Let me tell you again, I do really appreciate what you did. What I don't get is where you guys fit into this."

Well, that was understandable. Were we adversaries strangely drawn into temporary alliance or could we somehow be a saving grace for his growing bundle of problems? I'm not sure myself.

Harry started pumping him first. As he was doing a lovely job of building Gunter's confidence, I sat back and let the two older men bond. They were of a common age.

They started off comparing service histories. I hadn't known that Harry was in the Marines during World War Two. After learning about the camps, he admitted to having taken a malicious pleasure in killing as many Germans as opportunity presented.

I wish I could have fought in that war. I wanted a clear moral conflict, where I was fighting for my home, family and beliefs. Vietnam weighed on me because of its moral ambiguity. Hell, after having been there, I could only see us as having been the oppressors, fighting on the side of corrupt allies. The tangled web of bad political decisions went all the way back to Dean Acheson and the Domino Theory. Politicians...don't get me started.

At his age Gunter saw service in Vietnam, but his specialty was supply. If the Army would have let *me* choose, I'd have taken supply, too.

By demonstration from his superiors, Gunter learned that there were certain officers who managed to retire into extremely lucrative careers. Thus inspired, Gunter learned all he could about the international arms market and how to get involved. After all, countries don't buy fighter airplanes from a guy in a plaid sport coat named Smilin' Honest Al. It was more, 'Have your generals call my generals, we'll work out a deal.'

He found an opportunity in the surplus spare parts business. It may surprise you to learn this: the military is very wasteful. Oh, you've heard. Well, this results in lots of stuff, frequently perfectly good stuff, getting stored somewhere until the military doesn't want it or need it anymore. So they destroy it or they sell it for a tenth of what its worth. You have to sort through a lot of dreck, but you can get some pretty cool goodies if you know where and when to look.

So naturally, it was a big help if someone whose job it was to prepare all this stuff for sale were to let you know well in advance what was coming up. You might find a customer for it before you even bought it. You would have time to research the market and find out the best price.

Then, Gunter and his partners added a new wrinkle. If that stuff were to be combined with a bunch of junk, and were to be described as junk, but you knew that lot number 'such-and-such' was the real deal, you would pay a higher price than anyone else would bid, but nowhere near what the real items were worth. This was tantamount to bid rigging, but with a slight twist. Naturally, his co-conspirators were anonymously rewarded in foreign accounts each month.

Neither Harry or I said anything. We just nodded and smiled. We were grownups and the scheme was hardly that original. We were kind of surprised that no one thought of it before Gunter.

Business was good. They started taking requests for certain items. So the scheme then enlarged to include the officers responsible for declaring certain items surplus in the first place. This made it a lot easier to fill custom orders.

The Iranian deal was Jim's swan song, however. The order was so outrageous and the price so compelling, that he and his two European partners could retire rich. They would get five hundred million dollars. Half a billion! Three hundred and fifty million for ten items, and one hundred fifty for various spare parts to fill a container or two. All they had to do was find ten computer-controlled, laser-guided targeting systems for the F-15, aka DALTA, code-named *Kali*. Easy!

These were not supposed to be exported, of course. But that was a small problem. If they were just electronic parts- if say, the housings were removed and then lost. And they sat around in a warehouse and aged for a while, and then the right guy inventoried them and called them parts for radar systems, well, voilà, there you go. Just dust 'em off, bolt these surplus housings back on and you're ready to rock and roll. It took the right guys in the right places, but it was meant to be. The scheme worked just like it was supposed to, and except for a few little logistical problems that every operation might run into, the stuff was packed up, containerized and sent on a long sea voyage.

Well, the Iranians should have specified airfreight and popped for the extra bucks. But they didn't think of it, and while the containers were on the ship, they were unsealed, the special goodies were taken, and the containers resealed. When they were finally opened at some Iranian AFB, oops, what crates?

There were many acrimonious conversations. Threats were made and counter threats made. Reputations were slandered throughout the arms business. If you can't trust an international arms smuggler, then by God, whom *can you* trust?

The rest progressed more or less as Belli outlined earlier, except that Gunter said that it was a set up all along and that the Iranians were fucking with him. There had been some previous deals that were billed a little higher than perhaps was completely honest. Having been taken advantage of before, they concluded that they'd been had and that Gunter bluffed, thinking that written contract or not, the Iranians wouldn't have the guts to take him to court. The Iranians were intent on calling his bluff by actually suing. It went down hill from there like the whole mess was on skis and the road to Hell was ice. Midland hired good attorneys, or so he said, but they lost anyway. Now he was screwed and the Iranians were going to get everything Midland and its partners owned. I couldn't seem to dredge up much sympathy.

Harry and I listened patiently to this whole tale, which I have edited for self-justifications and minimizations, blame-spreading and finger-pointing. Why should anyone else have to suffer through it? At the end Harry leaned forward, took Jim's shoulder in one hand, and said cordially, "Jim. That's a great story. But you don't mean to tell us that you didn't squirrel that money away somewhere safe offshore the same day you got it?"

Well, they had and they hadn't. When they sought advice on this type of banking transaction, it was found to be difficult and expensive. All those lawyers and accountants and dummy corporations and shell companies- so they scrimped a little on covering the paper trail. That was foolish, because Mel's financial investigators succeeded in proving where the assets lay- three hundred and twenty five million in bearer bonds in a vault in Zurich. Where Iran keeps a lot of money. The bank was interested in keeping the Iranians' business, was it not? Miraculously, certain banking laws were found to be inapplicable, the loot revealed and the account frozen. Midlands partners couldn't have cashed a check for five bucks at that bank. The same held true for his US assets as well. It was a sad story, no doubt.

We found a baseball game for Gunter to sleep through for a hour or so. Harry and I repaired to the back deck and compared notes.

We decided that Gunter was too composed when he told this story and probably had forgotten to mention a few million tucked away somewhere. We were pretty sure he wasn't going to starve. Other than that, we weren't able to arrive at a conclusion about who all the players might be, or why they were so violently intent on turning Gunter into a corpse.

I told Harry I would baby sit Gunter if he liked, but he allowed as how he and Farrar could keep Gunter alive. I realized I needed to collect my van before it disappeared or collected a bunch of tickets. I put the Blackhawk along with the shoulder rig in a gym bag that Harry provided. He had cleaned up the guns, although he didn't have a kit for the Ruger cannon, but he had done what he could. I loaded them all with fresh ammunition and tucked the two hideout guns in their proper positions. I resolved to drop by the Gun Exchange as soon as possible and have them disassembled and cleaned by a pro. I could get cleaning kits at the same time, an oversight caused by urgency the previous day.

Farrar ferried me to my car, which was unharmed except for two parking tickets. There was still crime scene tape everywhere, including the office window in the building. I guess the cops noticed the shattered glass and bullet holes from Farrar's Uzi concert. I didn't stick around, hopped in the bus and headed for home.

Walking into my cave-like apartment was like entering into a world of normalcy and familiarity. I took off my clothes and sat around nude. Turned up the heat to take the chill off, poured a big tequila, but threw away the remains of the lime in the fridge since it was green in the wrong places, and rolled a big joint. In fifteen minutes I was mellow. I flipped on the TV just for noise. It was eight o'clock and ABC was rerunning *Maude*, the one about abortion. The first time it had aired the Catholic "Stop Immorality on Television" crowd screamed like stuck pigs. Looks like ABC was thumbing their nose by rerunning it. Three cheers for ABC.

It suddenly dawned on me that with the next setting of the sun I would be rich. Rich! Two mil was a lot of money for a lad of my tender years and I could think of a lot of ways to spend it. The evening passed pleasantly: mentally counted my money, making a list of things I would buy. Cars, homes, gadgets of all kinds, clothes from Wilkes-Bashford just like Willie Brown, the Speaker of the California Assembly. I tried to speculate on a future for myself. I certainly didn't intend to be a process server - not with that kind of money in the bank.

Chapter Seventeen
Sweet Dreams Are Made of These

Wednesday dawned bright. In ten hours and forty-three minutes I would be rich! Well, sort of. Who knew how long it would take to actually get my grubby little paws on all that filthy loot. I thought about getting it all in hundreds and rolling in it naked. It was such a compelling image I could smell the powerful odor of such a huge pile of money. Imagine what two million dollars would smell like?

I called Harry and arranged to baby sit Gunter. We figured that an Iranian secret agent would not make Gunter a good companion, so Farrar was stuck outside.

We spent a quiet day. I read the *Chronicle* from front to back, especially Herb Caen nattering on about Trader Joe Bergeron and Willie Brown's latest sartorial adventures. I figured old Herb hadn't bought a drink, a meal or a suit in twenty years. He got invited to every SF social event in return for which he plugged it in his column. You were cool if your name got in Herb Caen. I looked over at Gunter.

"So Jim, what are you going to do when this is over? You got any plans?"

He looked up from the Sports Illustrated. "Hmmm? Oh, I've heard there are some good opportunities in Central America these days. Lot of demand for cargo aircraft in South America. Argentina has a pretty big defense budget. I'll poke around there and see what I can scare up." His tone was casual. I thought, "Bet we can expect a war with Argentina some day." But I just nodded and said nothing. Jim Gunter was a guy that seemed to land in shit and come up smelling like a rose. You know the expression "If life hands you lemons, make lemonade"? With Gunter, he'd get the lemons during a heat wave.

That was it. This is the way the world ends, not with bang, but a whimper. Belli called Harry about three thirty, said that he had confirmed with Gunter's now ex-lawyers that they were not filing a counter motion. Cool. It was a done deal. Very cool.

The newspapers were full of stories about that little affair at the marina. Five dead guys were a little too much to just blow over. As soon as we turned Gunter loose his local attorney arranged for him to go to headquarters and be questioned. Gunter's story—I had helped him work on it—was that these guys must have gotten the wrong boat, or the wrong marina or something, and in the course of who knows what, there had been the shootout. He had, reasonably enough, gotten the Hell out of there when the shooting started. He left my name out of it. I had pointed out to him that I could fabricate a version of events that would have gotten him thirty years. Belli even consulted with Gunter's counsel to help smooth everything over, and the police were ultimately assured that the bad guys had gotten their due. A drug deal gone bad. They weren't satisfied by any means, but they couldn't make any kind of case against Gunter.

 Belli told us that the three corpses turned out to be mystery men. No ID, no one claiming the bodies, fingerprints now being checked by the FBI. No word from them yet. More questions than answers were raised.

Chapter Eighteen

Unhatched Chickens

My life returned disgustingly back to normal. Van handed me a big stack of subpoenas, summons, divorce papers, bill collectors' suits, eviction notices and three notices to vacate. Time to return to reality. I stored the arsenal in the apartment. There was no way I was walking around with even one gun, let alone three. To everything there is a season. In my experience, people who carry guns frequently get shot.

Sadly, as cool as being a *private detective* sounded, there really wasn't much to the regular work. It was mostly taking pictures, doing research, knowing how to access the public databases, interviewing witnesses for the tenth time to try to shed some light on the case from your clients' point of view. Trying to find someone who would say your guy was okay, it was the other guy that was the bum. It's a job, but you wouldn't get all dewy eyed about it. I'd had my taste of cake, now it was time to eat bread again.

Monday I came into the office after doing my AM serves, like I always did. I had given Barbara a casual version of events, with a lot of the bullets-flying-and-body-parts-floating stuff edited out. Everyone else, except Dorothy and Harry, of course, knew nothing about the previous week's events.

Harry called for me on the phone intercom. I fairly sprinted to his office. News? He looked serious. And unhappy. I was instantly the same. He waved me to the chair.

"Mel has some bad news. A very odd turn of affairs. The money, the assets in Switzerland, has been transferred, but not to the proper account. The bonds were to be converted to cash, and the amount credited to a special escrow account with Bank of America here in San Francisco.

"Apparently someone obtained the proper authorization codes and delivered instructions at bank opening for an account number in New York instead. The trail of funds simply vanishes, for the moment. The New York account has been closed and the records are currently being examined by the Federal Reserve and the bank examiners for New York State. Who the Hell knows what they'll turn up, but for now, the money is gone."

I just sat there with a stupid look on my face. Easy come, easy go? I was too surprised and pissed off to even speak.

When I finally became a rational human again Harry and I talked around the facts as he knew them but nothing was concluded. The only fact we knew for sure was our money had just evaporated. I staggered out of his office, past Barbara's worried look, and down to *The Office* in a numb fog, sat in a booth alone and waved to Sharon at the bar. She popped over in a flash.

"What'll ya have, Doug?" What a life, bartenders know me by my first name.

"Long Island ice tea, Sharon. I'm in mourning."

"Oh yeah? Who died?"

"My future."

Sharon patted my cheek. "Oh anybody as cute as you don't have anything to worry about. Get some older woman to take care of you. Like me." Sharon was sixty, with white blond hair down to her waist, wore her blouses low and had the equipment to make it interesting, stretch pants that never showed a panty line and she owned the place. I should be so lucky.

"Anytime." I kidded her back. At least, I took it as though she were kidding.

She walked slowly back to the bar, letting me appreciate her ass and returned with my drink. "You want to talk, you gotta sit at the bar. So since you're here, I figure you need some time to think." I nodded that she was right.

Two "ice teas" later I was on autopilot. My brain just barely ticking over. I glanced at my watch. It wasn't yet noon and I was drunk. Not good.

Bill showed up about twelve thirty and slid in across from me. I was picking at the sandwich in front of me.

"You don't look happy," he assessed.

"You're right, I'm not."

"Want to talk about it?"

"No."

"Fine with me," he agreed nonchalantly. "Did you ever have a chance to talk with Barbara about our idea?"

Suddenly it was *our* idea. I had completely forgotten about the discussion only ten days ago. I'd had other things on my mind. But of course Bill didn't know that.

"Uh, gee Bill. No I haven't had a good chance."

"From what I hear, you haven't been doing much talking together at all."

I didn't answer, but probably looked guilty enough.

"Hey, a funny thing. I went to this apartment in the Western Addition the other night. The door to the subject's apartment was all sealed up with crime scene tape and a neighbor told me the guy was killed a couple weeks ago. Guess Dixie won't have to skip trace him."

I gave him a half-hearted smile.

He began telling me a story about another serve. "I go up to this place, nice apartment house, kind of near the Tenderloin, but more toward Van Ness, you know, on Pierce." I nodded that I knew the area he meant.

"So it's up three flights of stairs, no elevator. I'm out of breath when I get there. Knock on the door and guess what opens?"

"Either a guy eight feet tall or a naked woman."

"You're almost right. It was this girl. Wearing a nightgown and, what's that fancy robe thing called?"

"Peignoir?" I supplied.

"Yeah, that thing. She was *nice*. She is just like standing there, with the door wide open, looking at me and for a second, I didn't know what to say. I must have stuttered I was so surprised." Usually Bill is making himself out to be cool, so this was a surprising confession coming from him.

"I held out the summons and stammered out the name. She says that's her, and what did I have for her, so I give it over, she opens it and starts to read it, and she asks me what it is. I tell her 'It's a summons,' and she goes 'What's that?' and gets all worried looking and then she sees what it is and son of a bitch, she starts cryin'." He stops to shake his head mournfully about how unfair crying women are.

"So I say, 'Look, it's not that big a deal' and offer to look at it and I tell her, you know, I can't give you legal advice but get a lawyer and all that stuff and she starts tryin' to tell me about why Macys is suin' her for a bill she can't pay and..." He drifted off and waved a hand in the air.

"So you went in?" I knew he had. I would of.

"Yeah, so she offers me a drink and we sit on the couch and I read the complaint, and it's just one of those standard unpaid bill things, you know, no big deal and I talk to her about it and she calms down and well..."

"I'm getting the picture..."

"So anyway," his voice dropped to a loud whisper. "Next thing you know, she's in my lap and we're kissing and she's moaning, then she slides down to the floor and opens my pants and starts sucking my cock like it's the end of the world and she's got to finish before we die. She pushed me back on the couch and is giving me head like I can't believe."

"How nice. Just for being you." Bill was a good looking guy, if I haven't mentioned that before.

"So anyway, I like have to pull her off, so I don't, you know, come right away and then I figure I can do the same for her only she won't let me. Doesn't want her panties off at all. Just wants to get back on the knob. So I lay back again and she just goes for it until I shoot the moon. I thought I'd break something I came so hard." He rolled his eyes for emphasis.

"I have to say Bill, in three years of process serving, that's never happened to me, and I've never heard of it happening to anybody else." This was a fantasy that ever man has, but few ever realize. But I believed Bill. He might be a bullshitter in many ways, but this story sounded like it might actually have happened. Besides, it was beginning to look like Bill and I might wind up partners. With my two mil gone, I had gotten the bug. I wanted to make some serious money. So I wasn't going to call my future partner a liar, even if I thought he was.

"No, honest, we have a date for Friday night."

"A date?"

"Yeah, I'm takin' her out to a movie and dinner. You know, a date."

"Cool. This cocksucking champion got a name?"

"Oh yeah, Carol."

"Great. Carol the Cocksucker," I kidded him.

"Carol...something. I forget. I'll remember or look at the mailbox or something. Anyway, she's real nice. Slim, nice little tits, very firm. 'The closer to the bone, the sweeter the meat'," he quoted that old saw.

"Spare me!" I was starting to sober up, having eaten my sandwich while listening to Bill. "Bring her by here Friday after work, before you guys go out so the gang can meet her."

"Okay, maybe. I'll ask her. You guys can be a little bit too much for a stranger. She might be shy. And for Christ's sake, don't tell anybody else that story!"

I frowned. "Of course not. You know me. The soul of discretion." I was planning on telling Barbara and the rest of the gang as soon as I could. She would be known to us all as Carol the Cocksucker forever.

Chapter Nineteen
Obla Dee, Obla Da, Life Goes On

My life slid into its old routine. Well, its new old routine, which now included seeing Barbara pretty regularly. While we were crazy about each other, there was this thing about the age difference, sixteen years to be exact. We talked about that, and other things that separated us, by history and inclination. I liked to spend a day reading, she would rather be doing. She was much more into partying than I, and we went to dance clubs a lot. She and Rick were pals immediately. Rick allowed as how if he were inclined that way, he'd have her in a heartbeat.

"You know, if that *nasty pussy* stuff was my thing," he sniffed. That became was his nickname for her: Nasty Pussy. Barbara loved it and he used it all the time. People would look around and the two of them would laugh. I admit I was a little embarrassed, but it was their joke and they loved pulling it.

Harry paid me a grand and half for the week's work on the Gunter case. Barbara insisted on a burgundy leisure suit for me, but I balked firmly on platform shoes. I wore my black cowboy boots, and that was that. Barbara took to calling me Leroy, as in *Bad Bad Leroy Brown*. I told her I didn't want to get into any fights and to stop.

On the first Friday of October, when I came in to AAA there was a message to call Mel Belli's office. Barbara handed it to me and looked impressed. "They asked for you by name," she said. "You're a star!"

I couldn't imagine why Belli or anyone in his office would call me. I pushed Dixie out of her desk and called back.

I was told Himself was on the phone, but Meredithe picked up and arranged an appointment. He was booked all day, so we settled on Saturday afternoon. "One half hour is all he can spare, but I'm to understand that this won't take long." She declined to tell me what the interview was about.

When I arrived the following afternoon Meridithe ushered me into the *presence*. The great man was on the phone, but waved me to one of the chairs facing his desk. We were in his office, the drapes open, and it was a strange to have people passing by on the street outside, looking in curiously, unable to hear through the double glazing.

Belli finished his conversation and then rose, came around the desk and sat in one of the chairs next to me. He reached over with his great pink paw and took my hand in it.

"You did well, Mr. McCool. Very well. And I am glad to see no permanent harm befell you." He rose and returned to his side of the desk and sat again. "I am flummoxed regarding this latest turn of affairs. How this other party obtained the code that released those funds is unknown. Only two people, besides myself, knew the proper code. Those parties have all been questioned relentlessly to no avail. Tracing the funds themselves has reached a dead end. The wire transfer from New York was to a bank in Panama, which when checked was found to be no longer in existence: the offices empty and the parties named in the corporate papers vanished. Along with the assets, of course. Apparently a dummy corporation established just for the purpose of receiving the transfer. A nice bit of sleight of hand."

"Midland?"

"Hardly. They botched the attempt to hide the funds in the first place. Besides, how would they have obtained the release code?"

I sat there, depressed. My money, gone in the twitch of a eye. I looked out Belli's window, stared at the building across the street. There was a For Rent sign in the window of the second floor offices. Something occurred to me. Offices. Now vacant. Sitting across from his windows.

"You gave them the code, Mr. Belli."

He looked like I had accused him of malfeasance. "I gave it to them? What do you mean?"

"Your windows. Someone sat in that office across the street. They aimed a special directional microphone at your windows. Even through the double panes, they could pick up your voice from the vibrations on the glass. You read the code aloud, they picked it up. Probably took some considerable technical skill to filter out all the ambient noise, but it can be done." I had read about just such a device a few months ago in *Popular Science*, but I didn't bother to tell Belli that.

He looked at the window and then at me. "Son of a bitch, son of a bitch," he muttered. "That was good. Who do you think?"

"I would expect technical expertise like that to come from an intelligence outfit. Maybe the Israelis. Maybe the damn Iranians themselves, just to cut you out of the deal. Or maybe there's someone else playing in this game that we haven't discovered yet."

He snorted, disgusted with himself and the world. "Well, in any event, I called you here to tell you some good news. You know that among Midland's and Gunter's personal assets were the boat and the two cars, of course. They are now the property of the Iranian government. They don't really care about the small amount of money that these items represent. In the face of your extraordinary efforts, I have successfully negotiated a reward for you. Harry is content that you should have it."

"And that would be...?"

"Would you be interested in that little boat of Gunter's perhaps? And I'm sure you could make some use of the Cobra." He smiled slyly.

They were giving me a fifty thousand dollar boat and a twenty thousand dollar car? Hell yes I could make some use of them.

I choked out a "Sure. Thanks," which seemed a little inadequate. "I mean, that's great. Really, I don't know exactly what to say."

"These items represent such a paltry amount of value that it's not worth their trouble. You may pick up the paper work from my receptionist. The boat is under seal at the police wharf and the car is being held at the Federal Building parking garage. The Federal marshals will help you with the arrangements. And, by the way, the local authorities appear convinced that the incident at the marina is a closed book. They will not be pursuing the matter further. The press was told it was a drug deal gone bad, which was what they wanted to hear."

"Doug, I may call you Doug? Yes, well, Doug, I hope you can be available for any future needs my office might have. You are a man of nice judgment and many resources."

I assured Belli I was at his service and left in a daze, clutching a manila envelope fat with legal forms. A boat and a fabulous sports car for two weeks work! I didn't feel so awful about the two million. A little wistful, perhaps. But still.

The next day the Arabs struck in a coordinated attack on Israel. It was, Sunday, October seventh, 1973, Yom Kippur, one of the two holiest Jewish holidays.

For nearly a week, the battle hung in the balance. Inexorably, the Israeli air force gained domination of the skies, and ultimately pushed the Arab forces back. In some cases the Israeli pilots had shown inordinately accurate fire from their aircraft. I expected the Iranians to ask for their stuff back.

On October 10 Spiro Agnew, Vice President of the United States pleaded no contest to income tax evasion in a highway paving contract kickback scheme. The next day Priscilla Presley's divorce from Elvis became final. Was nothing sacred?

Chapter Twenty

Yo Ho Ho, and a Bottle of Rum

I arranged for Jan to pick me up the on Monday and ferry me over to the Federal Building. I didn't bother to tell him why.

I was expecting hours of bureaucratic hassles and such, but actually it went pretty quick. An assistant prosecutor looked over the papers, had me sign here and there then directed me to the garage. He even called down to tell them I was coming. I went to the secured area where a guard checked my papers again, let me in the gate and pointed to my new toy.

The Cobra was metallic blue, with a broad white stripe down the middle. Low and wide, fenders flaring over fat black tires, two big black exhaust pipes exiting from just behind the front wheel wells and terminating just in front of the rear wheels- my eyes ran over the muscular curves of the car with lust. I loved this chunk of iron instantly. I could sympathize with Gunter for losing it, and at the same time exult that it was now mine.

I opened one of the tiny doors and slid behind the wheel. It was a tight fit for me, being about four inches taller than Gunter. I slid the seat back as far as it would go. My hands came to rest naturally on the wood rimmed wheel and the black ball of the shifter, the lever oddly cocked forward, an idiosyncrasy of these cars. I inserted the key and slowly, like touching a woman for the first time, I turned on the ignition, depressed the clutch and blipped the gas while I cranked the starter over. The engine spun for a moment until the carburetor float bowls were full, then with a tremendous roar, echoing off the concrete confines, the creature burst into life.

I eased it slowly forward, struggling with the clutch and gas to not kill the engine. The guard rolled the chain link barrier back to let me pass. He looked at the car with raw desire. For the first time I owned a car that other men looked at with lust. I killed it once, but managed to exit without further embarrassment.

I left the garage and drove up Van Ness, made my way north to the Golden Gate Bridge. After passing the toll plaza I headed across the span and into Marin County where I could cut over to the Coast Highway, State Highway 1.

The Cobra was lightning quick. This model was the older 289 cubic inch V8, not the monster 427, but the car was so fast I couldn't imagine driving the bigger brute. My butt was eighteen inches off the pavement, the wind whipped over the windscreen, the needles in the gauges trembled with life, the tach needle dipping and rising with each shift. I had to concentrate to keep the speed to within reason. With the slightest pressure on the gas in the lower gears the car would leap forward, tires chirping. In third or fourth gear the car would accelerate in perfect synchronization with my pressure on the gas pedal. It was the like the road just reeled in before me.

I turned off the freeway and wound through the brown hills until I reached the Coast Highway. I breezed along in the sun, feeling the temperature dip as I got closer to the ocean. Even though it was nearly the middle of November, the weather was mild. Suddenly, as I swept through a turn, there was the Pacific, that endless blue expanse beneath me. I felt like I was flying.

Highway 1, following the undulations of the rugged Marin coast, was perfect for this car. I could control it with light touches of throttle, brake and steering. It responded to my thoughts, it seemed. Just point into the corner and like magic, you were through it and on the other side, banking out of the turn and leaping into the next straight. In convoluted ess curves and decreasing radius corners the car would dive into the turn, could be aimed precisely with slight changes in speed and direction, and spit out of the far end like a watermelon seed.

More than once I had to slow down when the speedometer touched ninety. I would lose my license if not careful. I wondered how much it was going to bleed me to insure the damn thing.

After lunch I headed back. At one point a California Highway Patrol car pulled alongside me. I quickly glanced at the speedometer but I was okay. He saw me checking and just gave me a thumbs-up, smiling at the car. Even cops liked it.

I parked in my driveway. Rick was home and I yelled for him to come down. When he saw the Cobra, with me smiling next to it, he laughed.

"Oh dear, oh dear," he camped, "Dougie's got himself a real pussy mobile now. You won't be able to fight them off with a stick." He walked around the car, admiring it from every angle. We opened the hood to check out the engine, which I hadn't done until now. It was beautiful as well, four pairs of Weber downdraft carbs with chrome velocity stacks, the engine bay was wall-to-wall motor, every wire and hose fastened down and led neatly from its origin to its destination. Someone spent hours of careful work that showed in every detail.

Rick agreed that this creature earned the rights to the garage. "Don't be silly," he threw one arm around me. "Leave our crates out and put this honey away. Just one thing you have to do for me..." he gave me a wicked look.

"Oh no!" I pretended shock.

Rick laughed loudly. "Oh no, honey, not that. Just you've got to promise to take me for a ride once in a while."

"Let's go now." So Rick and I hopped in and went for a tear down the Peninsula, finding twisty roads and generally having a good time. I turned the wheel over to him, despite his protests that sharing this car was a nobler act than sharing my woman, and he was soon playing race driver too.

I have to admit that driving the bus the next morning for work was a let down. It was slow and clumsy, even at its best, and compared to the Cobra...well, there is no simile that is not trite: black and white, night and day, yin and yang...whatever. But the van had its virtues too, although speed and grace were not among them. But comfort and versatility had a lot to say for themselves too.

I called my insurance man. The first number he quoted me was incredible, but when I threatened to take my business elsewhere he came up with coverage that allowed me to call the car a "part-time, limited use" vehicle and the rate was bearable. Although I would have to make some sacrifices or work a little more to keep the thing. It was a high maintenance girlfriend.

The day after that I went down to police headquarters to claim the boat. In contrast to the Feds efficiency, the PD took two hours of hemming and hawing and checking and waiting for "word" and signing releases and receipts. I told them I wasn't signing anything until I saw the condition of the vessel, so that took another half hour and then they agreed that I could sign at the police dock after seeing the boat.

At the dock it was almost the same rigamoral over again. But eventually I got the right to what was now my property given back to me, and I looked the boat over.

This was the first time I had to inspect it in a leisurely way. In spite of a few marks and small gouges on the hull, the shattered railing and some other bullet damage here and there, it was in perfect shape. In fact the damage only served to highlight how nice the rest was.

I stepped into the cockpit well, captivated by the way the boat seemed to respond by rocking with pleasure. Naturally, the cabin was a bit messy and disorganized, and there were a lot of drawers dumped on the bunk and stuff left lying around by the cops when they searched, but it was devoid of any real malicious damage. I touched the brass wheel in the pilothouse. There was a raised seat for the pilot, and the rest of the wheelhouse area was a tidy little salon that would seat three or four without crowding.

Down a couple of steps, in the forward cabin, was the galley on the right and a toilet (*head*, in boat talk) on the left. The head included a shower/toilet area and looked adequate for one person. Brass fittings and varnished mahogany set an opulent tone.

In the bow was a double bunk as wide as a queen-size bed. The foredeck was close overhead, so I could only sit or kneel on it. More varnished wood gave a cozy feeling, with storage drawers and shelves cleverly placed. All the drawers and doors had positive latches so they would not open when the boat rolled.

I knew a little about operating a vessel of this size, only forty-two feet long, but I was by no means a real sailor. I had sailed with a friend or two before, and operated motor vessels as well, so understood the basics. But I would have a lot to learn.

A high school pal of mine, John Anderson, had been born with the soul of Sir Francis Drake. He was going to love this toy. He was the kind of compulsive workman that couldn't stand to see anything that wasn't perfect, even if the boat belonged to someone else. This trait made him one of the most successful boat yard operators in the Bay Area. Yacht owners begged him to take on their work and waited weeks or months if need be, but when it was done, it was done right. And if John couldn't do it right, he wouldn't do it at all. He was a fanatic when it came to boats.

My phone call released his pent up enthusiasm. "I'll meet you there at six!" he shouted.

"Let's make it eight." I was excited, but not that excited.

We met at the police dock. I had the foresight to acquire an armload of coffee and goodies from the *Nice Buns* boys. I handed it around to the cops in the area then John and I climbed aboard.

He started babbling the moment he walked up.

"Holy Cow! It *is* a teak lady. Built in Hong Kong, you know and worth three times what they sell for." He seemed determined to tell me everything he knew about the craft in the first five minutes. "The labor and materials are so much cheaper over there." He went on: "Hereshoff designed them for long distance cruising."

"You have to live on it, Doug." He pushed his ski-jump Swedish nose into my face. "You live on a boat like this, man." His bright blue eyes were fixed on mine earnestly. "You live here. It's great."

Then he regaled me with stories of marina life. He lived aboard a sixty year old classic motorboat, a narrow long greyhound that once ran rum into coves along the California coast.

"I'll think about it." John looked at me like the question had already been settled. He clucked his tongue in outrage when he saw the damage from the bullets. It didn't seem to bother him that a person might have been the intended target- just that it was sinful to have damaged such a fine piece of work. Then he was examining the engine, giving a running dissection of the good and bad points of its installation. He turned the key and started the diesel.

"Oh, I guess I should have let you start her up the first time."

"That's okay, John. I'll get lots of chances. You can be captain on the maiden voyage." He took this role seriously, ordering lines released and such and generally having a ball. I was happy to serve as crew.

We pulled out into the Bay and John eventually, reluctantly, gave me the wheel, then stood at my elbow supervising. We angled out away from the shipping docks and headed south, back to the Slough. We briefly consulted about trying the sails, but decided, or I should say John insisted, that he check out the rigging and masts before testing. So we chugged along, the boat rocking through the slight chop gently, John and I chattering and grinning about trips we would make. He developed a list of projects that would have me bankrupt in no time.

The light fog burned off, whisked away by the morning breeze, leaving a sharp, clear San Francisco day. We were on a boat in the Bay in the sunshine while those poor landlocked drones in the offices on shore were slaving away. We felt free of normal human bounds. I understood instantly why boats are referred to as female- they are as entrancing and capricious as an intoxicating woman, beautiful and dangerous all at once. They could lure you to your death or the joys of Valhalla, you never knew which lay in store. John saw my intoxication.

"You know the definition of a boat?"

"No, I'll bite."

He grinned. "It's a wood-lined hole in the water, into which you pour money." I took that as a warning. I could feel the addiction already.

We docked at Third Street. John looked around and declared, "You will have to move. Shit Slough is no place for this beauty."

I tried to shut up him by agreeing, before he alienated all my prospective neighbors. I then went through the enormous task of putting things away and tidying up while John continued his examinations and plans. He left me to the drudgery of stowing all the misplaced gear, but as he pointed out, it was better for me to learn where everything was than him. Such logic delivered John from many a tedious chore.

About a half hour later the hippie kid from the houseboat wandered down to see what was up and shook my hand enthusiastically when he found out the boat was mine. "Oh cool, you bought it man." I was impressed that he remembered our encounter.

He came aboard at my invitation. Introduced all around. Michael and John were soon jabbering together about woodwork and rigging and fuel lines and bilge pumps, etc. I continued my lowly task of cabin boy.

The hippie offered a joint and seeing how he seemed like a pretty okay guy, if somewhat spaced out, I joined them. John hadn't needed a second invitation. I don't usually do drugs with people I don't know, but I broke my rule in this

123

case. We found a six-pack of San Miguel beer in the refrigerator, cold enough. I couldn't believe the cops hadn't taken it.

That pretty much blew the better part of the day. I had left the bus at the marina the night before, so I drove John back to the police dock. He was still spending my money as we said goodbye.

Now I owned a boat and a sports car. Gee, if my income only suited my life style.

Chapter Twenty-One
Should Auld Acquaintance Be Forgot...

I packed Gunter's personal effects and called his attorney, who told me he would inform Gunter. There was no phone on the boat, but I left my home phone and the office number. Gunter left a message that he would be by Saturday afternoon around three to pick up his stuff.

I acquired the habit of showing up at the office late Friday afternoons. I could pick up my check for the previous week's work and meet up with Barbara.

The AAA gang were usually regulars on Fridays at *The Office*. Barbara, Mary, Layla, Bernice, occasionally Dixie, sometimes Darryl and the assistant (Lisa? Lilly? Something like that). Bill and Jan were pretty much regulars too, but Van, Harry and Dorothy- never.

This Friday, in a booth in back, Barbara was on my left, on the inside and Bill sat on my right. Mary, Layla and Bernice were on the opposite side. Carol the Cocksucker sat in a chair at the end of the table. (Of course, we did not call her that to her face. Just 'Carol'.)

She was a delicate blond, seemed pleasant and was pretty in an ordinary way. Not gorgeous, but not a dog. She seemed truly taken with Bill.

We talked, laughed, drank and ate for an hour or so, then Bill and Carol left. It was time for him to go see his bookie, no doubt.

Barbara got our attention. "Did any of you notice anything strange about Carol?"

I hadn't, but the women all started laughing. "What's so funny?" I asked innocently.

They laughed even harder and finally Layla sputtered, "She's a guy!"

I didn't believe it. But the women all swore they could tell. "Christ, you think Bill knows?"

That started us all laughing. "How could he not know?" I said.

Bernice said, "There's ways, honey. There's other things than pussy, you know." I blushed.

For no apparent reason, Bernice slid in next to me when Bill left. After a moment, I felt a hand come to rest midway between my knee and hip. I could feel the heat of it through my jeans. Bernice, quiet middle-aged lady. And molester of young men, apparently. Her hand was sliding up and down my leg, slowly, sort of an absent-minded caress. She was talking and listening to the others and feeling up my leg at the same time. Interesting. My mind harkened back to the little three-way kissing spree we'd shared. That was enough to get Mr. Happy perked up.

Then her hand is doing improper things to my groin.

Barbara noticed her attentions. Her hand casually slid under the table as well, and onto my left thigh. Quite high up. She looked at me, smiling and talking about something. I had lost the thread of the conversation a few minutes before and just sat there smiling and trying not to let on.

My cock was straining against the polyesther fabric of the leisure suit, which stretched quite readily. I carry to the left, by the way. When their hands met, they both started laughing, pretending it was something Layla said. But they were both exploring the bulge with their fingertips and not being at all shy about it.

I was telling the story of the stranded Lincoln when Layla suddenly interrupted. "*What* are you two *doing* down there?" she said, loudly, laughing. "You're feeling him up!"

I blushed again. Bernice and Barbara's hands froze for a second, then they started laughing and both of them squeezed it harder.

"You should feel it, Layla," Barbara said, lighting a cigarette with her other hand. "It's fucking huge and hard as a rock. Isn't it Bernie?"

Bernice smiled quietly and her eyes were soft and hot. "It's very nice. I haven't felt one like it in years."

"*Jesus!*" Mary choked on her drink. "I don't believe you guys." She shook her head, but she was laughing as well, and looked at me with an appraising stare.

"I want to feel it too," Layla announced. She was on the other side of the booth, though, and couldn't reach. Bernice was closest to the outside, and obligingly slid out.

"Go ahead, honey, cop a feel. I'm don't think Dougie will mind."

"Hey, guys, now wait a minute..." It was useless. Layla was sitting next to me in an instant and laid her hand right on my crotch. She took a second or two to examine the length and thickness and slid closer to me.

"*My God,*" she looked at Mary. "You won't believe this thing." She started giggling, then stuck her tongue in my ear and whispered, "I've got to try this out." From another table, a woman who was watching started to laugh, then nudged one of her girlfriends and started whispering.

Barbara got a serious look. "Okay, ladies, let's go somewhere."

"You want to get a hotel room?" Layla.

Mary said nothing, glanced at her watch, and then, as if satisfied that she had enough time to accomplish something, smiled. "Hotel's good."

Bernice said, "Let's go to my place."

"Have you got a big enough bed?" Barbara, ever practical.

"Oh, well, maybe not."

"Hotel it is. Let's go."

They piled out, Barbara pushing me out of the booth. We spilled out onto the sidewalk, the women taking my arms on either side. We staggered across the street and into the Palace Hotel.

Barbara, ever practical, instructed the women to wait in the lobby while she got the room. They steered me over to the gift shop and we admired the trinkets for the few minutes it took Barbara to obtain a key. Downtown hotels are used to people checking in with no luggage. We made it a short, giggly ride in the elevator.

Before I knew it we were in a double room with two queen beds. Mary was on the phone with room service ordering a bottle, Layla was already in the shower, and Barbara and Bernice were half undressed, admiring each other's bodies. They turned to me, each took a hand and they sat me on the bed. Bernice took off my shirt while Barbara attacked my pants. Bernice was running her hands through my chest hair, murmuring something about hairy men, and Barbara wasted no time pulling off my shoes, socks, pants and shorts. Then she was on her knees next to the bed and taking me into her mouth. She slowly started sucking while Bernice and I kissed and fondled.

Mary finished on the phone, ran over, flinging clothes as she came. She leaped onto the bed and started licking a nipple and caressing the part of my cock that wasn't in Barbara's mouth.

I surrendered to them. I guided whatever body parts came my way- a nipple into my mouth here, an encouraging adjustment of a leg there. When Layla came out of the bathroom she joined Barbara and the two of them worked on me. My poor cock was straining with the attention, but they knew what they were doing and kept me from getting too far along too quickly.

When room service came with the bottle and ice, Barbara greeted him at the door buck-naked, took the bottle and ice bucket, and handed him a five. When she closed the door, we all burst out laughing. "You should have seen his face," she giggled.

We sprawled on the bed, rolled around, laughed and gasped and moaned. They touched me, each other, shared sensations, bragged to each other how good they felt. They took turns trying various sensations. I lost track. They fed me and each other liquor from time to time, never too much, but enough to maintain the crazy mood. Pot magically appeared and we took turns smoking and fucking, the ladies holding the joint to my lips from time to time.

I have never done anything like it before. But sometimes magic does happen, and for that special time and place I was in love with four women and they with me. They were ecstatic with each other's eroticism, encouraged each other on and on. Even after I came we kept going and when I relaxed and quit trying to control myself or them, I came again and a third time. Each time I came they screamed with a sort of truimphant yell.

Eventually we pulled up the bed covers, snuggled together and fell asleep. Somewhere in the middle of night I woke to find Barbara and Bernice moaning and kissing each other frantically. The sight of them, their white and brown skin interlaced in the streetlight coming through the window, the shadows rippling over them, was so powerfully erotic that I was hard again instantly. I joined in and soon the five of us were slowly writhing and squirming together, Mary showing a decided interest in the women and Layla took on the role of director, encouraging each one to try each new sensation. She would interview the recipients for their reactions. It was interesting, to say the least.

We woke up around nine with major hangovers. Mary was fretting about getting home before her medical-student husband got off duty, Barbara calmly showered, applied what make up she had with her, ordered coffee and breakfast from room service and smiled. Bernice looked a little embarrassed. Layla was singing to herself, called her boyfriend and told him she partied with her girlfriends (which was mostly true).

I ferried everyone home, briefly considered working, gave up that idea and headed to the boat. My feelings about women would never be the same. I can't put what I felt into coherent thought, but I was somehow less of a man and more of a man at the same time. They revealed a Dionysian depth that I had never experienced. They shared some of their secrets with me. And left me exhausted.

I arrived at the boat at ten and ate a leisurely second breakfast. I puttered around, drinking coffee and fussing with things. Gunter hailed me from the dock at three. He let himself in with the key he still carried. I motioned him aboard; he hopped on with familiar ease. He handed me his key. "I suppose I won't be needing this." He looked rueful when he said this.

He gave me a little tour, giving me tips on how to operate the galley and various devices. We were sitting in the wheelhouse when we felt the boat bob in response to someone climbing on board.

I stood up to see who it was and faced two men, both aiming automatics with silencers. They looked very fit and their faces looked as though they brooked no nonsense. They waved me back into the wheelhouse with the pistols.

I put my hands up and backed into a seat. When Gunter saw me followed by the two gunmen he shrank back, and lifted his hands as well. He didn't look surprised, more resigned than afraid. Myself, I was terrified.

One gunman positioned himself at the door to the wheelhouse, we would have to get past him to get out. The other took a seat facing Gunter and me.

He looked over to Gunter. "You are a loose end. We are going to cut that loose end before anything more becomes unraveled." He turned to me.

"You, on the other hand, are simply a pain in the ass. Three dead comrades are what you have to answer for."

"I suppose you can't accept that they were hors' d'combat and let it go at that?" He shook his head no.

"Mossad?" I had to know.

He didn't answer. "We are going for a little sail." His partner prepared to cast off while the first guy supervised Gunter's starting the boat. We were cruising down the slough and headed for the Bay much more quickly than I would have liked. Once we entered more open water, the gunman in the wheelhouse told Gunter to head for the Golden Gate. A burial at sea seemed to be in store.

It was a nice day for a sail. Clear sky, a stiff breeze blowing in through the gap in the hills that forms the passage from the Bay into the Pacific. We motored, without sails, the boat riding up and down the choppy swells easily. The view as we passed under the Golden Gate Bridge was terrific, had I been in the mood for sightseeing. As it was, I was trying to think my way out of this mess.

Gunter manned the wheel, steering naturally and skillfully, keeping the bow aimed into the increasing swells as we came to the more open water beyond the bridge.

This part of the passage between the Bay and ocean can be quite treacherous. The shallows to either side of the deep water channel into the Bay are called the Potato Patch, and are a nasty bit of confused water, made difficult by being shallow, filled with rocks, and the unpredictable effects of tides, currents, winds and the swirling eddies created by the shore and water being funneled into the narrow gap of the Gate. The boat bobbed and weaved, but the two gunmen had their sea legs under them and rode easily. They resumed their stations, one in the seat behind Gunter at the wheel, with me a short arc of his pistol to the left. The other was outside, in the cockpit, facing the wheelhouse door. He commanded the exit from there.

I decided to speak up, not seeing how anything I said could make matters much worse. "I didn't really think you guys were this casual about killing."

"What guys are you referring to, Mr. McCool?"

"Why don't you tell me?"

"I suppose that will do no harm, under the circumstances," he shrugged in a casual way. "We had an arrangement, a deal, I suppose you would say, with Mr. Gunter's partners. Midland Surplus was supposed to obtain some radar equipment for us. The Iranians were to act as intermediaries, although they perhaps did not realize that was their role. We were to obtain the radar equipment and take it to its final destination."

"Which was not Iran, I gather, but Israel." I wanted to get to the point, frankly.

"Well, actually, that is the, I believe you say, 'fly in the ointment'?"

"Yes? How were the Israelis the 'fly in the ointment'?"

"It seems that while Mr. Gunter's partners were working with us, Mr. Gunter here was working with the Mossad. He arranged to put the equipment in question on the ship they designated, and thus put the radar devices into their hands. Is that not so, Mr. Gunter?"

Gunter looked back at the guy for a moment and said, "They were paying a substantial amount for the favor and I thought I might as well sell the same crap twice, that's right. I fucked you, fucked those two bit partners and I fucked the Iranians."

"And now, Mr. Gunter, it is your turn to get fucked," the agent said.

"And what was the intended final destination anyway, since we're all about to get fucked." I was feeling a little testy about all this double and triple crossing with me in the middle.

"Oh, the Soviet Union, of course. It was our operation to begin with. But we did not have access to the kind of hard currency that Midland demanded for selling out their own country. So we got a third party to pay for it. If the Iranians had not been so malleable, I'm sure the Iraqis or the Syrians could have been manipulated as easily."

The boat was clear of the narrow channel between the San Francisco peninsula and the Marin peninsula, the two fingers of land that are joined by the fabled Golden Gate Bridge. We were heading toward open water. She was bouncing around quite a bit more now, and Gunter swayed at the wheel to keep his balance.

A huge oil tanker was coming into the Gate and Gunter steered well to the south to avoid it. In about ten minutes it passed us and Gunter aimed the bow to meet the swell the passing ship's wake created.

I didn't know that Gunter had anything in mind, but I was trying to look for any advantage, some distraction. I stood up slowly, looking at the view. I could see the wake heading towards us, as a rolling four-foot high ridge of water. Gunter looked over at me for second, and then, when the wave was just about upon us, he spun the wheel hard to the left, putting her broadside to the wave.

It hit us at that moment and rolled the boat far onto her beam, the deck almost vertical to the water. Gunter braced himself with the wheel, but the wheelhouse gunman lost his balance and fell back. Since I was now above him, I flung myself on top of him. As I landed the gun went off with a hoarse cough. The smell of gunpowder enveloped us. I seized the wrist of his gun hand and drove it onto a brass railing with all the force I could summon. You could hear the bones crunch and the gun fell from his fingers.

But this was no untrained or unprepared civilian. He was an experienced field agent and he fought for his life. His left hand seized my throat and his knees were driving toward my belly instantly. I brought my head down into his nose, which gushed blood and he was momentarily blinded. I grabbed his hair with my right hand and fumbled at his left to get it off my windpipe, smashing his head into the deck at the same time.

He drew his knees up and was about to fling me off of him when I heard another *pop-pop* and he lay still. Gunter whirled toward the wheelhouse door anticipating the other agent outside, but there was no one there. The boat was bobbing wildly back and forth, up and down. Gunter dropped the gun and grabbed the steering wheel, which was spinning back and forth crazily. He struggled with it and managed to get the boat to respond. I dragged myself up in time to see the wild dance of white caps and hear the roar of the waves breaking on the shore. Gunter whirled the wheel to the left to bring us back toward the channel, there was one terrific crash when we hit something in the water and then we were back under control. Gunter throttled back and leaned against the wheel, breathing hard. There was no sign of the other gunman. Apparently he had been catapulted over the side into the maelstrom.

I realized my sleeve was wet and looked down to see blood soaking through my shirt from the left shoulder. I felt dizzy and sank into a chair. Gunter threw me a first aid kit and I stuffed some gauze into a neat little hole in the flesh of my upper arm. I was lucky that these guys carried small caliber guns, probably .22 or .25. The bullet entered the meat of the muscle and was lodged in there somewhere. It was starting to hurt like Hell.

As we motored back Gunter and I discussed what we should do with the corpse. Neither one of us was in favor of going to the authorities with this guy and getting into an even longer story than before. So we took the easy way out, wrapped him in a tarp and chaining one of the boat anchors to the bundle, we putted around until dark and then quietly slipped him into the water. When he slid into the blackness, Gunter said to me, "You'll have to buy another back up anchor. That was the only spare."

"A small price to pay for peace of mind," I mumbled.

131

When we got back to the slip and were tied up I did a better job, with Gunter's help, of binding up the arm.

"So you have the money the Israelis gave you stashed somewhere safe, I suppose?"

"Oh, well. My retirement is quite safe, thanks. And I have all that potential business in Central America to look forward to. I think I'll set up in Costa Rica. Lovely country. You know, they have more teachers than they have policemen there. I can work out of San Jose quite well." He took the box of personal stuff in one hand and held out his right hand to me. "Take good care of her. I'll have to order another one when I get settled. And I hope you enjoy the car, it's going to be harder to replace."

With a little wave of his hand, he hopped onto the dock and vanished into the night. Goodbye Gunter. I hope your business deals go more smoothly in the future, and if not, I hope I don't get involved in them.

It was a chore to drive the bus back to the apartment and drag myself up the stairs. When I stumbled through the door, I called for Rick upstairs and asked him to come down. "Bring your doctor stuff."

Rick clucked his tongue when he saw my arm, put me on the bed and went to work. It was not fun, having the bullet removed with only a little morphine for pain, but he did a workmanlike job of cleaning up the wound, put in a dressing to wick the bloody drainage up and out and then bound the whole thing up. By the time he was finished I was bitching and moaning. Rick was not sympathetic.

"You know," he said, sounding irritated. "There's no reason for you to be bitching. And I'm getting tired of patching you up. If you could stop being stabbed and shot for a month or two, I would really appreciate it." He pouted in the chair.

"Take some more of the cocaine and leave me alone," I ordered.

"All right, I will!" He flounced over to the freezer, took about ten grams of coke and put it in a plastic bag. Then he turned and winked at me. "At least when you get in trouble, it works out well for me." And out he went, promising, or perhaps it was a threat, to look in on me after while.

I lit a cigarette and sat in my recliner taking inventory: nine corpses, two police investigations stymied, two million dollars won and lost, one boat, one car and a new girl friend. Not bad for a few weeks work. I'm beginning to like this detective stuff.

On the weekend of October twentieth Nixon carried out the Saturday Night Massacre and Elliot Richardson gave up his job rather than bend to the President's pressure. Big deal, it's not like he was worried about getting another one, was it?

Chapter Twenty-Two
No Matter Where You Go, There You Are

It was mid-November. OPEC announced that they would stop exporting oil to the West, accusing them, especially the US, of having waged war by proxy, using the Israelis against the Arabs. I suppose, from their point of view, it looked that way. The fact that the Arabs were viewed as a bunch of fanatical, genocidal maniacs by the West didn't help.

As gasoline prices soared, those of us who depended on our cars for work were hurting. I was frequently unable to work-no gas for the bus. I served paper downtown using public transit, but that took a long time and with the San Francisco Municipal Railway, you could never quite predict whether the bus or streetcar would show up anywhere near the time needed. Muni, as it was known for short, was a corrupt and dilapidated organization, paralyzed by a management that could not care less about efficiency and a union that seemed more interested in thwarting public transportation than promoting it. A rude, uncaring, unhelpful, downright hostile attitude from the drivers and operators was the norm. There were frequent assaults on the drivers- after a month of using Muni regularly, I was ready to punch a driver or two myself.

I was sitting in Van Duzee's office one morning, reading the *Chronicle* as usual. The Microbus was parked with a full tank of gas, and was "on reserve" for any special that might come by. AAA started this "on reserve" category for our customers so they could count on a server being available, with gas, to run a special. We were paid five bucks an hour to sit around and wait. It was okay; Jan, Bill and I would sit in *The Office*, trying not to get plastered before three, and wait for a page.

I was becoming a newshound, with nothing much to do but read the paper cover to cover. A headline caught my eye, near the bottom of page thirteen: *Arabs Accuse CIA of Transferring High Tech Weapons to Israel*. Seems that the Syrians had taken fantastic tank casualties in the Yom Kippur war and were claiming that the Israelis had been secretly given a new targeting system from the US. I smiled a little.

A couple of pages later another article caught my eye, this one about a Senate subcommittee investigation into "improper technology transfers" to Israel. Seems that Jesse Helms, the idiot senator from North Carolina, had his panties in a bunch over the Arabs' claims of secret help to the Israelis. Witnesses were to be called from the various US intelligence branches about the case. I didn't imagine that

Helms would get anywhere, but he could make a couple of spooks' lives miserable in the meantime.

While I was reading I heard the front office door open and Barbara talking to a couple of deep voices. Then I heard Harry come out and talk with these guys for a minute. Then Barbara came into Van's office with her eyes wide. She came up to me and half whispered, although Van could plainly hear her anyway, "There's a couple of FBI guys here asking for you."

My heart sank for a moment. Fuckin' FBI for *me!* Then, because I couldn't think of a reason the FBI would care a fig about me, I told her: "Well, show them in, honey, show them in." I even put the paper in my lap.

Ten seconds later two mugs walked in.

I swear the Feds breed these guys on a farm somewhere in Kansas. They could have been brothers. Both slightly over six feet, maybe six two or three, but not taller than six four. Athletic, but with a little paunch from lots of deskwork. No glasses. Matching suits, ties, and shirts. They could have traded clothes. One guy even wore his hair in a flat top. Christ, I haven't seen that haircut since 1963. They looked a lot like those NASA engineers, without pocket protectors or slide rules.

I stayed seated and looked at them over the paper. For some reason just the sight of them pissed me off. I guess because I didn't like the feeling that they gave me. Like I was afraid of my own government.

"Doug McCool?" Mr. Left said.

"What do you think?" I thought I might as well start off well. I could always fold my hand if they were too tough.

They simultaneously flipped open matching badge holders with picture ID and the shield. They held them open about half as long as it would have taken to read. Agents Something and Something Else. I don't remember. It wasn't important.

"Whoa there, speedy! I didn't see your ID's. You could be junior G-men for all I could tell. Let me see those again." When threatened, always attack first.

I made a great effort of studying their badges and names, even writing them down on a scrap of paper. "Okay, now that everyone knows everyone else," I continued after about five or six minutes of document inspection. "What can I do for you guys?"

"We would like you come with us to answer some questions in an investigation we are conducting." Mr. Right.

"Oh, really, I thought you guys were here to get my advice on how to protect democracy from the Facist police state." They were getting warmer.

"It's a national security matter. We will try to take as little of your," he sneered, "*precious* time as possible."

Okay, the gauntlet!

"Sure, I'd love to go with you to the Gay Pride Parade if you want. *If* you've got a warrant or a subpoena or something."

They looked at each other with their eyes only. Then launched into tactic number two: "We can get one if you want."

"Am I under arrest now?" This is an important question to ask law enforcement types.

They both sighed. "No. We are not arresting you. We just want to ask some informal questions."

"Mother McCool did not raise any sons stupid enough to answer questions, 'informal' or not, in front of the FBI and tape recorders and deputy United States Attorneys General without a lawyer. So unless you assholes have a warrant for my arrest, I suggest you both go back to whatever hole you crawled out of and do it fast." I was quaking with fear inside, but if you play poker, you know how important playing out the bluff can be. Either that or shut the fuck up and fold your cards.

They opened their mouths, closed them again silently, spun on their collective heels and walked out. Van was staring at me as though I had turned into a pumpkin. I folded the paper and left it on Dixie's desk. After all, it was her paper. With Van still staring open mouthed, I walked through a totally silent office. The girls were all poised, fingers in the air, staring. Harry stood behind Barbara's desk, looking very grim. I sauntered out, my knees shaking. I tossed the scrap of paper into a wastebasket on the way out. Two points.

Down to *The Office* for a quick pop. I was drinking a lot lately, mostly out of boredom. At least this time I had a reason.

Two days later I was in *The Office*, as usual, sitting at the bar, idly chatting with Sharon about football. It was looking like the young Heisman trophy winner O.J. Simpson was going to break the NFL single season rushing record this year, he was on his way to over two thousand yards. Sharon thought that he was "sexy". I ventured a guess that his broken field running style may have been acquired in youth, escaping the clutches of the law, perhaps. She accused me of being a cynic. Me?

A man came in from the Market Street door, stopped for a moment while his eyes adjusted to the dim light of the bar, and casually looked about before he took a stool. Ordered an Irish coffee and chatted with Sharon about the cool weather, the gas crisis and other mundane chitchat.

Seeing my glass empty, Sharon asked. " 'Nother Doug?" I nodded.

The newcomer turned to me. "You're Doug McCool, aren't you?"

I was startled, and I suppose my face showed that. "Who wants to know?" I answered, not very friendly that day.

The stranger slid to the stool next to me as Sharon plunked a new drink down. I started to slide a five over to her, but the stranger said, "Let me get that."

"What do you think the price of a drink is going to get you?" I said challengingly. Why should this mutt buy me a drink?

"How about ten minutes of talk about Midland Surplus?" That got my attention. I motioned to a booth away from the bar, in the middle of the place, far from either door.

We took our drinks and moved. I sat, he sat. We appraised each other for a moment. The stranger was a young fellow, maybe a couple of years older than me, give or take a year or two. Gray suit, striped tie, "styled" hair, a sharp intelligent look, with grey eyes and sandy brown hair. Something about him said "prep school; Ivy League, Berkeley or Stanford Law School." He stuck out a hand and said, "Brian Haggarty, I work for the Senate Intelligence Affairs Committee."

Oh fuck. I was waiting for a nasty piece of paper to come out of his pocket but it didn't happen. He saw the look of apprehension on my face.

"Look, Mr. McCool, may I call you Doug, call me Brian, we're not going to subpoena you or anything like that. I'm just trying to get some background information."

"Uh huh, and Nixon doesn't know anything about Watergate."

"Look, I'm sorry about those two FBI goons. They were just supposed to bring you over to my office. I gather they were a little heavy handed."

"Let's just say they didn't say the magic word."

"The magic word?"

"You *know*, the *magic* word."

"And what, Mr. McCool, is the *magic* word?"

"Why *please,* of course."

Haggarty took a breath and launched into his spiel. "We ran across your name in some files that relate to a certain incident involving Midland. We have also been trying to interview some of the others involved in that case, but without much luck.

"Mr. Belli has been subpoenaed to appear before the committee, and we really don't want to subpoena you, but we can." He let the threat dangle.

"I'm just trying to get a line on what happened here in August and September. The Committee is trying to dispel the charge that we, I mean the United States, gave the Israelis a laser targeting system by clandestine means.

"The CIA denies any involvement in the matter. But certain facts don't seem to fit that position and I believe you can clear that up."

136

"Look, Mr. Haggarty, Brian, I'm a process server. I'm not an investigator, and I'm certainly not in the spy business." When in doubt, deny everything. I subscribed to San Francisco defense attorney Louis Nizer's philosophy - never plead guilty.

"Well, yes, I understand. However, that doesn't explain the fact that property awarded the Iranian government in that case wound up being transferred to you. And the fact that 'independent operatives' known to work for the CIA on occasion died in a firefight here in San Francisco that happened to occur in the area of the marina where the boat that was ultimately transferred to you was docked."

That was a new piece of information. Thanks, Brian.

"And," he was piling it on, "a concealed weapons permit was issued to you, *as a private investigator,* working for AAA Legal Process the day before that firefight.

"Jim Gunter, the former owner of your boat, and car, I might add, has left the country and is currently believed to be in Costa Rica or El Salvador. You had some association with him, we believe, and your boss, Harry Silver, has been active in organizations supporting Israel for years." He seemed to feel that if the logic of these 'guilt by association' charges wasn't that strong the weight of them would make up for it.

I took my time answering him. I lit a cigarette and took a long pull of my drink. He sipped his Irish coffee and looked at me, waiting calmly.

"Okay," I finally said, "what's the big deal? Yes, I did some work for Belli's office. Harry is my boss and if he says jump, I say how high. I served Gunter an Order to Show Cause, you know that. It was an important case with a lot of money on the line. Belli and his client were appreciative. The gunfight at the marina was a drug deal gone bad, according to the police. I don't know anything about your CIA guy. Never saw him, wasn't there, had nothing to do with me. I had already served Gunter by the time that took place." I could pile it on myself.

"Yes, that's true. The service took place on a Sunday, and on Monday afternoon you were issued the permit. Two corpses were found in the water with their inflatable boat..." he pulled a file out of his briefcase and flipped it open, "...'death was instantaneous in the first case, caused by massive trauma to the head, presumably by a large caliber bullet,' and...'death caused by exsanguination secondary to large caliber bullet wound to the left shoulder area, severing the brachial artery.' You know what weapons you had registered to you, of course." Yeah, I knew.

"The slugs could not be recovered, naturally, as they both passed completely through tissue and were lost in the water. The forensic examination concluded that they were probably fired from a, I'm quoting here, '.44 or .45 caliber weapon, probably a pistol, but rifle fire cannot be ruled out.'

137

"The committee wants to know what the fuck went on with you and Gunter, and by God, we're going to get some answers." The profanity and harsh tone were out of character; he seemed urbane and polite until now. "Now you can either give me the straight story, here, off the record, or you can appear in front of the committee, with a lawyer if you choose, and take the chance that you will be facing a contempt of Congress charge. Your choice."

His hardball shift in character concerned me. I didn't need this kind of shit. And who was going to pay for the kind of lawyer that sat next to you at Senate hearings and put his hand over the mike while whispering in your ear? Not me. I was broke. Mel? Harry?

"Look, Brian, I'm not trying to be a hard ass about this, honest. But you have to understand that I'm only a bit player here. I have people to answer to if I start blabbing to you. Those people might not want me spilling my guts to Congressional investigators. You can understand that?"

He shook his head yes, but his eyes didn't soften and I could see that I was getting no sympathy with my workingman bit.

"I'll tell you what," I offered. "Let me have a day or two to talk to my boss. Then, I'll give you a call and meet you in your office, tell you what I can and we'll go from there?"

Haggarty considered. He didn't want to let me off the hook so easily. "If I do that, you will have to give a formal statement to me. If that statement does not fully satisfy the committee, you will be called to testify. Or you can talk with me informally now."

This formal and informal crap didn't mean squat as far as I was concerned. He was holding all the cards and making all the decisions. "What you're saying here is that I spill my guts to you, and if *you* think it's what you want to hear, *you'll* keep it 'informal'. How do I know that whatever I say will be 'satisfactory'? You'll turn around and call me anyway. You're gonna have to do better than that, *Brian.*"

He thought for a moment. "Okay, go talk to your boss, if you want. I'll wait here. You've got an hour."

I decided he could sit there until Hell froze over, if Harry had a way out for me.

I jiggled impatiently as the old elevator creaked its way up to the fifth floor and then I burst through the office door. I saw that Harry and Dorothy were in their office alone and without preamble I threw the door open, walked in and took a seat, flipping the door closed behind me. It banged shut harder than I meant it to. They looked at me with mouths open and eyes squinting.

Too Many Spies Spoil the Case

"Sorry about the door." I hadn't meant to startle them. "Look, there's a guy named Haggarty down in *The Office* right now threatening to subpoena me before the Senate Intelligence Operations committee if I don't talk about the Gunter-Midlands deal."

They exchanged looks but both kept poker faces.

"And you said...?" Harry led.

"I said 'go screw yourself'. For now. But unless you're prepared to get some high powered legal gun to get me off the hook, I'll sing like Sonny and Cher."

"What exactly did he say?"

So I recapped the conversation, pointing out that Haggarty seemed extremely well informed and had files that appeared to be copies from the SFPD and God knows where else. "Look, I didn't have anything to do with the original scam. But they seem to think that you did, Harry. Some Israel support group you belong to." I paused to see if Harry reacted, but he was a stone wall. "I told them I was just an employee doing my duty to triple A and client, but nevertheless, if they think I know something, ignorance is not going to help me out. They think I know more than I do, and I don't intend to be in this pot of hot water alone."

"Now Doug, just take it easy. These things can be dealt with."

"Start dealing with it. Haggarty is waiting for me to come back. You've got," I checked my watch, "forty seven minutes."

I stood up and walked out of their office. Barbara was giving me the fish eye as I stalked past, but I ignored her. The other women glanced at me and looked at each other, but they did not want to know anything that would put them between me and the bosses.

I walked up behind Dixie and whispered in her ear, "Mom, don't you have to go to the bathroom right now?"

Dixie looked at me and winked, got up and went out. I looked at Van. "Van, I think you have to go to the bathroom too." Van's head wobbled a bit, but he stood up and walked out.

I picked up the phone and dialed Rick's place. "Heeellllooo" He answered. Thank God he was home and not screwing for a change.

"Rick, listen up. This a condition red." I waited for him to mumble that he was up to speed.

"Okay, what's up?" he said, after a beat.

"Go down to my pad. In my closet on the floor towards the back is a gym bag. Take it out of the closet. I wouldn't open it if I were you. Put the things in the freezer in the outside pocket. You know the things I mean?"

"Sure."

"Throw three changes of clothes into my duffel, it's in the closet too. Make sure you put in something warm for me to wear. Then, quick like a bunny bring it to," I paused to think for second, "the Palace Hotel. It's on Market and New Montgomery."

"Yeah, I know where the Palace is."

"Okay, they have a bar, off the Market Street entrance, it's real dark and usually empty, so meet me there. This is a crash emergency, you dig?"

"I'm steady and ready, Freddy," he answered and hung up.

I checked my watch. I had thirty minutes until Haggarty's deadline. I walked back out to the outer office. Harry and Dorothy were talking, looking serious. I opened the door without knocking.

"Change in plans, folks. If I leave now, I'll have a twenty-minute head start or more on Mister Congressional person. I'm blowing town. You don't know where. I'll call you in a few days. I might even be out of the country, for all you know." I closed the door on their surprised looks. Let them think about hanging my ass out to dry.

I took the elevator down to two, then took the stairs to the lobby. The elevator opens right across from *The Office* but the stairs let you out on the Sutter St. side. Even though the Palace was kitty corner from 450 Market, I walked around the block the long way, and down Market on the opposite side, entering with a busload of Japanese that conveniently appeared.

Chapter Twenty-Three
Two Weeks Before the Mast

I had enough time to kill two gimlets in quick succession before Rick showed up. Quick work on his part. He hopped up on a stool next to me, setting his load down gently on the floor.

"Did you look in the bag?"

"No."

"Good, then you have one less lie to tell."

"Where you goin'?"

"Not even you, pal, not even you. 'I don't know' is the easiest answer to give. No matter how long they question you, you don't know where I went. Suffice to say, away from here for a few weeks. This'll all blow over. By the way, don't leave your stash out in plain view, and don't let any suits intimidate you into letting them in the house or the apartment. Not without a warrant."

"Natch."

"Okay, just making sure you dig. They may have some very impressive badges."

"I don' care 'bout no stinkin' badges." Rick's best Mexican accent.

"Later."

I took the gear he brought and went out the back door of the Palace. My bus was parked right on the alley. I took a careful look around, but I really didn't think they'd know where I parked. I tossed the stuff in the back and took off, heading for Van Ness Avenue and the Golden Gate Bridge.

I got off the freeway in Sausalito and drove through town until I got to the area known as Gate Six. John's boatyard was just to the south. The area was dirty and disorganized, a mish mash of small industrial buildings, car repair shops, a marine supply store and sundry small businesses. There was a ramshackle collection of floating (and not floating) houseboats and strange vessels docked at Gate Six. The hippie types that lived there were known as the Red Legs. Don't know why.

I found John's boatyard at the end of the muddy drive, past a chain link fence topped with razor wire. John himself was in the cockpit of a huge motor yacht, circular saw screaming and sawdust flying. He called to me when I finally got his attention, "Be down in a minute."

He clambered down the rickety wooden ladder that was propped against the side of the boat, which sat in a cradle of timbers, each one eight inches thick. He enveloped my hand with his huge paw and ratcheted my arm up and down like a bilge pump.

"Hey, it's about time you came to my place." He waved his arms about expansively, "What to you think of my domain?"

There were boats of all types scattered about the yard, and several more tied up at the slip. They were in every condition, from some that looked either half built or half destroyed to some that were in pristine condition. There were three men attending to various tasks, a small portable building that served as the office and four or five cars scattered around as well, two or three of which might actually be running.

"Looks like business is good."

"Christ on a crutch, Doug, I can't keep up. I've got three haul-outs waiting right now, my crane needs parts and I'm waiting for a lumber delivery that was due two days ago. I've got to put a new diesel in that Grand Banks over there, and I'm pulling a Chevy V8 out of that old ski boat and putting it into that little Chris Craft runabout." He shook his head. "What brings you to my neck of the woods?"

"Can we get some coffee in your office?"

"Sure, we can get better than that."

We wound our way through the maze of marine clutter until we were seated in his office. John pulled a couple of Bud Longnecks from the refrigerator that sat outside under a tarp. We took long pulls before I spoke.

"I need to make myself disappear for a few days, maybe two weeks. I was thinking you might have an idea where I could go. I was thinking about taking the boat and putting up somewhere."

"Who's after you now?" John was used to my pulling a disappearing act now and again.

"The Congress of the United States, or at least, part of it." John's eyebrows shot up and he looked afraid.

"Jesus, what did you do now?"

"They want me to talk about things that I'd rather not talk about. In connection with the way I happened to get a hold of the *Jolly Jim*." There was apparently no limits to Gunter's ego. "Trust me, you don't want to know anymore than that."

John held up his hands, "Don't say another word. If you say I don't want to know, I don't want to know." He put on his 'hard thinking' face. There was one thing about John, his face was as readable as a large type book. He always lost money when he played poker.

"You can just anchor it over here, at the Red Legs' dock. They'll never find you. Are the cops looking for you?"

"No, just this fuckin' committee and maybe a couple of FBI."

John started laughing. "You've got the FBI looking for you now? Oh, Doug, this is best fuckup of yours yet!" He roared.

"Never mind that. Will it be cool with the Red Legs?"

"Oh sure. I've got a couple of buddies over there. We have a deal. I let them scrounge the old stuff that comes off these boats, and in return, they leave my place alone. I make sure I put some really good stuff in their pile every once in a while, so they're happy."

The Red Legs were a group of "seafaring" hippies. They had taken over a small abandoned marina and made it a floating commune. There was every sort of craft tied up there, in a maze of boards and boats that seemed to be half sinking all the time, but never completely sank. There were all kinds of vessels tied to this raft of junk, and then some that were anchored nearby. The anchor-outs kind of trailed off, scattered like little islands from the Red Legs archipelago of flotsam and jetsam.

Their reputation was that of modern day pirates, like the oyster pirates that used to haunt this area in the old days. One did not just poke around their territory without leave. Word was that many a cargo of pot was offloaded through there at night. The Red Legs discouraged idle visitors with a polite firmness. By the same token, if you were perceived as one of their naval brethren, you were welcomed into the fold.

"I can get to work on those repairs while you're here," John added, inspired. "This'll be perfect!" He was already thinking about the projects he had planned. If I let John get his paws on the *Jolly Jim* I might not see her again for six months.

"I don't want to go back to the marina in my bus. Have you got something around here that runs?"

"Oh sure. Let's see. Corvair is apart right now, I'm rebuilding the turbo. The Nash is okay. I just bought a '39 Chevy, hey I only paid three fifty for it, but I don't think you should drive it..." He inventoried cars and projects for a few minutes.

I wound up with a choice- a white '59 Nash station wagon John called the Kelvinator for obvious reasons, or his old '63 Dodge Lancer from high school. It was a Frankenstein of a car, having suffered through innumerable mechanical experiments, not all of which were humane. Currently it was sporting a new rattle-can black paint job, wide chrome rims and a 426 Hemi transplant. John had not gotten around to beefing up the front end for that load, so it sat at a rakish angle and steered like a dump truck. With the cherry bomb dual exhaust it sounded like something Mario Andretti would be driving. Perfect, a discreet ride. I just couldn't bring myself to drive the Kelvinator.

I locked my stuff in the van, took the keys to the Lancer from John and headed back to the City.

I drove slowly up to the marina parking lot, the Lancer just burbling along at idle. Once you got used to the nose-heavy handling, the car was kind of a kick to drive. It would accelerate so fast that you could disappear in a cloud of exhaust and tire smoke that was just like a James Bond trick. The brakes were totally inadequate and I had to leave plenty of room in front of me so I wouldn't rear end someone when coming to a stop. The four speed stuck up through a hole chopped in the tunnel, with a Hurst shifter and a skull knob. I felt sixteen again.

I didn't see anything suspicious when I pulled up, but as soon as I got out of the car, I saw two guys in a Ford sedan straighten up. They were sitting across the street, headed up toward Third. I gauged the distance to the locked gate. Once through there, I was home free, but it was too far. They had the doors open and were on their way. The same two FBI twins that braced me in the office.

I jumped back in the Lancer, locked the door, pulled the seat belt tight and fired it up. They were across the street and into the dirt of the parking lot when I jammed the shifter into reverse and roared past them backwards. I slid to halt, shoved the lever into first, looked to see if the street was clear, and popped the clutch.

The rear tires launched a hail of gravel and dirt behind me, I eased up on the gas until the tires gained traction, and then leaped across the street and down Fourth towards Third. Once I hit the pavement the tires threw up a cloud of smoke.

When I reached Third, I stopped to look behind me. Through the dissipating clouds of dust and smoke I saw the big Ford sweeping around the corner.

I gave them a chance to catch up and then pulled out onto Third Street. The beginnings of a plan formed in my mind. The traffic was thick in places as the afternoon commute was building up and Third is an arterial. I thought I might lose them in the traffic.

I merged with a tight knot of cars and matched my speed to theirs. The Ford pulled out about a block behind me. They started working their way through the cars, not pushing it, but steadily gaining. I made a couple of quick lane changes and was now out in front of the pack. There were knots of cars ahead of me, and light signals too, so I couldn't just floor it and take off. I would have to find some way of losing them without relying on sheer speed.

We maintained this relationship for several blocks, them hanging back a few car lengths so I couldn't turn off and lose them that way. They were waiting for a break that would let them cut me off. Once they got me stopped, all they had to do was put the subpoena under my wiper. I knew, since I have done the same thing myself countless times.

Too Many Spies Spoil the Case

I came to a stop at a light. They were four cars back. The traffic was a little thinner, the knots of cars getting broken up by the signals. There was a long open stretch ahead of me, the next signal not even visible.

When the light turned green I accelerated away smartly, trying to get them excited. They wove the Ford through the last remaining cars, worried that I was going to get away. I kept the speed down from the car's true potential and let them get closer.

Up ahead, coming the opposite way was a knot of cars. I floored the Lancer in third gear and it leaped forward like a scalded cat. I glanced in the mirror to see the Ford surging forward, but now at least three car lengths behind. The approaching traffic was half a block away.

I let the engine wind out in third until I was going at least seventy. Then I mashed the brakes as hard as I could. As soon as the rear wheels locked, I cranked the wheel to the left and the Lancer brodied around, pivoting on the front wheels. I let up on the steering wheel a little and was now facing the opposite direction, in the right lane going back downtown. I dropped the gear lever into second, floored the accelerator again, and shot passed them. They were stuck. They couldn't follow without causing a horrendous accident. They didn't want me badly enough to destroy eight or ten civilian vehicles trying to catch me. I shot down Third, thankful no cops had witnessed my driving exhibition, let up on the gas as soon as they were out of sight, and motored briskly back to the marina.

When the gate slammed behind me I took a deep breath. The Lancer squatted in the parking lot, the poor abused steed run hard and put away wet. They don't make 'em like that anymore.

Chapter Twenty-Four

Living Among the Red Legs

It was dark by the time I reached John's small dock area in Sausalito in the *Jolly Jim*. He met me there.

"I'll show you where you can anchor," he called. "You can use this dinghy to get back and forth." He putted off in the dinghy and I followed him. He circled an open area about thirty yards away from the nearest Red Leg vessel tied to their docks. He tossed me the painter and I tied him up to the *Jolly Jim*. After supervising my anchoring, he plopped himself in a seat in the salon and we opened beers. San Miguel, of course. I just love those commercials by Scott Beach.

"I talked to Bob over there," indicating the hippie hangout with a nod of his head, "and he's cool with you tying up here. You can take the dinghy over there to get to shore. Nobody will bother it, they know it's mine. You can use the Kelvinator to get around in until we have a chance to rescue the trusty Lancer." John liked to refer to his possessions as though they were living beings. Once he laid hands on something, it became imbued with whatever personality he decided. "You can't get out to the road through my place at night, the gate's locked and I don't have an extra key for you. You need anything?"

I couldn't think of anything that couldn't wait until tomorrow. I ferried John back to his place and returned to the boat. The dinghy was powered by a one cylinder Seagull outboard that sputtered and choked incessantly. I hoped it would not prove to be the same unreliable piece of crap every other British mechanical device turned out to be.

With the boat anchored bow and stern to keep from swinging in a circle I was almost as safe as though she were in a slip. I didn't sleep that well, though, as the boat was much more active tied in the open water, and every major change of movement woke me up. I even dreamed that the boat was sinking, that water was covering the floorboards, and woke up in a panic, but after checking everything and seeing it was fine, I laid back down and dozed until midmorning.

I was excited to wake up 'at sea' for the first time. It was a very gray day, the clouds forming a roof so low they obscured Tiburon, just across the bay from Gate Six. The water danced in small waves, barely showing white at their tops, a moving caldron of water at slow boil. The *Jolly Jim* jounced at her moorings, but remained secure.

After a hot shower, courtesy of the diesel generator, half a pot of coffee and some cereal I lounged outside in the cockpit, enjoying the salty breeze on my face and fine mist that blew up from the water. This was a fine morning.

By afternoon, however, it was getting downright dull. John waved from his dock in the morning, but I didn't go ashore. I knew he was busy and didn't want to interfere with him. Since I was restless, I put on a coat and took the dinghy over to the Red Legs dock, tied it off securely, and then mentally marked the path through the maze of floating riffraff that constituted the Gate Six community of free thinkers.

This "marina for hippies" just appeared, seemingly from nothing. The city fathers of Sausalito were very unhappy, but the land was actually in the county, and privately owned. The eviction process became complicated when the original owner decided that the whole situation was too much trouble, and deeded the land to the Gate Sixers. They now had a legal right to be there, and the county would have to condemn the area for a reason. Additionally, since this was Bay shoreline, the Bay Area Conservation and Development Commission was in on the act. It would take years to clear up the mess.

Of course, there were plenty of reasons to throw them out. The intense density in which this accumulation of houseboats, half-built creations of dubious inspiration and castoff derelict vessels had grown made it a fire hazard of extreme proportions. If the city and county waited long enough, the residents would probably burn the whole place down one night themselves.

Sanitary facilities were nonexistent. There were a few reeking port-a-potties in the parking area, scattered among dead and dying vehicles. It looked like a junkyard, but every once in while, one of the moribund mechanical creatures would stir itself for a trip to the outside.

As I threaded my way toward solid land and the parking lot, eyes peeked out at me from windows and portholes. It was a lot like walking through some village of natives who have never seen a white man. They seemed to be torn between curiosity and fear.

As I drew closer to the shore, the more obviously landlocked structures became. They were larger, in some cases the superstructure overhung the sides of the hull by two feet on each side. If most of these things were to be rendered independent of the others, they would capsize immediately. But being shored up by their proximity, they remained more or less upright, depending on how vigorously the owners' bilge pumps were working.

Heavy-duty extension cords ran along the surface of the dock, with branches that ran to each home. There were some lights that hung from wires strung along a row of two by four planks that gave the walkway a hesitant form of lighting at night.

The smell is best left undescribed. If you have ever been to South East Asia, say Bankok, you will know what I mean.

There was a guy hanging out on the deck of a rather nice A-frame built on an old barge. As I drew up he nodded and motioned me over.

"You must be Doug." I allowed as how I was with a nod. "I'm Bob. The Swede said you were okay." That was their term for John.

"I appreciate you letting me hang out here for a while." My dear old gray haired mother always said be polite.

"Hey man, anyone can come or go. It's the freedom of the high seas, man." He asserted this last with fervor.

"Yeah, right, cool. Well, got to run some errands." I wasn't ready for a conversation about man and freedom at this time. Maybe later.

He nodded goodbye and I continued my careful trek. I found the Kelvinator parked at the very outer layer of cars in the muddy lot. Its white paint was now gray and brown from grime. That's the trouble with white cars. It did look like a fifties refrigerator tipped on its side. The little straight six fired up immediately and I eased it into the road.

I had no phone on the boat. Ship-to-shore telephone calls were very expensive. I wouldn't have made one with the boat radio unless I was in peril. So I needed some place on shore I could establish a temporary hangout, without getting in John's way all the time.

Sausalito used to be a little Portuguese fishing village, relocated to the end of the Marin peninsula, tucked into the hills on the inside shore, close to the Gate for fishing vessels, but a lovely protected anchorage, with the hills of Marin cutting off the fierce Pacific storms that sweep in during winter.

If people had shut up about it, it would have remained a real town with real people. As is usually the case, word started getting around, next thing you know that spoiler of all good places, Herb Caen, is shooting his mouth off, and the area gets "trendy". Restaurant prices quadruple, traffic quintuples, tourists come, bringing with them shops that cater to the kind of dreck tourists are forever hauling back to Wichita or Sioux Falls, the original local businesses can't afford the higher rents and move out, the businesses that depended on those businesses fold- next thing you know, the goddam area is one big stinking Disneyland version of what used to be a real town. They did it to Fisherman's Wharf, and they were doing it to Sausalito.

Too Many Spies Spoil the Case

I came back after this depressing tour of what had been my favorite place to get paella and bouillabaisse and found Zack's by the Bay waiting for me with open arms. Zack's was obviously a little too 'maritime' in its decoration to be authentic, but they featured a big bar and good food and best of all, phone booths were you could go inside, sit down and close the door. As soon as I saw these I knew I was home.

I ordered a gin and tonic from the barman and went into the booth to call Harry. Harry had talked to Mel, Mel was talking to people who were talking to people and I was counseled to be patient. Harry was kind enough to indicate that he would pay me for my time while thus remaining indisposed, although at my ten dollar an hour rate, times six hours a day, Harry figuring that was a reasonable average. I couldn't argue with sixty bucks a day. Since I wasn't racking up gas and wear on my car, it was pretty much what I netted when working.

Thus effectively put on paid vacation, I turned my mind towards keeping myself amused while staying out of sight.

Unfortunately for us, Barbara didn't drive. Taking the bus to Sausalito was possible, but not until the weekend. I would not be foolish enough to go into the City and start hanging around places I usually go, including her place. We made a date for Saturday but that left me with idle time on my hands. I say this just to explain how I wound up getting briefly sidetracked.

Chapter Twenty-Five

When In Rome...

Having acquitted myself of any further work-related activity I went about making myself comfortable in Zack's. The barman, Dave, was a likable sort, rather like Bill, friendly, talkative, but not very deep. Just the way I expect a bartender to be.

Dave told me where I could find a quiet bookstore and a decent coffee shop that served a good breakfast without gouging. I ate lunch at the bar, an entirely passable hamburger and then went and stocked up on reading material. I figured I was in for a long spell of hermiting. I took my time at the bookstore and scored the seven volume *History of Western Civilization*, by Will and Ariel Durant. I figured that would keep me busy for a while.

About five thirty or so the bar business began to pick up tempo. The room filled with a young crowd of junior executive types, both sexes wearing their solid color suits, the men with their ties loosened. They jabbered loudly about their lives of work, tennis, golf, shopping and parties. The men worked very hard at chatting up the women and the women worked very hard at making the men jump through hoops.

I was certainly not dressed in a suit. In fact, I suppose I looked a little salty, with my jeans and running shoes, waterproof coat thrown over my barstool. John had insisted I take a old Greek fisherman's cap he had laying around. It fit me and I couldn't get out of it. He was thrilled and declared I looked a proper old salt already. I wasn't much of a hat guy, but I did like the rakish way the cap sat on my head.

When the crush of yuppies became too thick at the bar I fled to a table in a corner overlooking the water. There I could read, drink and smoke in peace. I could even see the *Jolly Jim* from where I sat, through a forest of masts, bobbing at anchor. It was reassuring to keep an eye on her. I had turned on the anchor lights the night before and hadn't bothered to turn them off. The generator would charge the battery whenever I needed.

At six a waitress came on duty, relieving me of the need to even stir myself for a drink. She was a lovely girl, wearing a 'pirate' outfit that left little to the imagination except whether she was a natural blonde or not. We struck up a conversation afterwhile, I tipped her extravagantly and by dinnertime, we were friends. Her name was Michelle.

I learned her history in snatches of conversation as she attended to my wants or she came into the area for the other patrons. When the exuberant pairing in the bar quieted down, she took her break talking to me.

Turned out she was a Red Leg girl, although the management didn't necessarily know that. She told me when I pointed out the boat to her.

"Oh cool, that's a beautiful teak lady! Can I see her sometime?"

"Anytime you like." I was not picky about company as attractive and friendly as she. We ended up agreeing to meet after she got off work, midnight.

As we walked through the junkyard parking lot and onto the boardwalk of the marina, Michelle stopped me. "Hey, there's a party at this place tonight. Why don't you come and meet some people?"

I was lonely and bored and the idea of a party with these free spirits sounded like fun. We wended through the maze until we came upon the A-frame where Bob spoke to me earlier. "This is the Pirate King's place," she said, seriously.

"Oh come on, the Pirate King?"

"No, really. Every year, one of the men is voted Pirate King for the year. Sometimes he gets voted for more than one year. Bobby's been King for three years already."

We entered a pleasant house, built on an old barge. This was one of the original houseboats, before the more motley types moved in. It was a two story A-frame, shingled on the outside, wood paneling inside. Large windows looked out over the kingdom of Gate Six.

There were people everywhere, standing, sitting on pillows, dancing on the outside deck. The air was thick with smoke- tobacco, incense and the ever-present marijuana. Music blasted so loud the wooden structure vibrated to the bass beat. Michelle introduced me to a lot of people, most of whose names I never heard in the din, but there were smiles and handshakes all around. Someone handed me a roach holder with a smoldering joint and soon Michelle and I were laughing and talking with a group of people I didn't know. Word got around that there was coke in one of the upstairs rooms and Michelle led me there by the sleeve. When we got to the room there were dozens of people crowded around a table in the middle of which sat a sizable bowl of cocaine. People were helping themselves, laying out line after line, snorting them up, and then others taking their place.

Turns out that Bobby was Robert P., lead singer for a hot rock group. If I tell you his last name, he'll sue the shit out of me. He sat at the head of the table, a benign smile on his face, watching dozens of freeloaders sucking up his expensive cocaine.

In the Bay Area, circa 1973, cocaine was everywhere. Young, and not so young, executives snorted. Musicians and artists snorted. It was the drug of choice among the huge gay population, especially for its reputed aphrodisiac powers, and it was said that any man could get laid in the City just by going into a singles bar and letting it be known that he possessed a gram or two to share with the right woman. Or women. There was something about having sex while on coke that many women were crazy about. It was supposed to give men incredible stamina. I thought that it did have a delaying effect on my orgasm, and of course, it gave you unreasonable energy. My theory on drugs is that the better it makes you feel, the worse it is for you. Cocaine made me feel so good, I knew it was bad. But, like the song says, 'they say it'll kill you, but they don't say when". I could take it or leave it myself, but there were a lot of people who couldn't.

Anyway, before I knew it, Michelle laid out lines and handed me the rolled up dollar bill. Those stories about using a rolled up hundred are pure exaggeration. Cocaine is God's way of telling you you make too much money, but if Bobby wanted to buy his friends, who was I to say no?

Naturally the evening became a blur. I remember meeting a lot of laughing people, making a lot of jokes that seemed to go over well, dancing with Michelle, and then a whole succession of women, who seemed to wear less and less as the night wore on.

At some point we wandered into another room where in short order it became clear to me there was an orgy going on. It was lit only with a black light and a couple of lava lamps, so the skin tones took on a *camera oscura* quality that made the whole thing surreal. I felt disembodied, like I was observing myself, an effect of too much cocaine and pot, not to mention brandy. Michelle pulled me onto a huge beanbag chair, next to another couple that were already entwined. After that it just dissolves into a writhing mass of bodies turning about. I'm sorry, but that's all I really remember of it. I assume I enjoyed myself.

I seemed to have eventually gotten back to the *Jolly Jim* in reasonable good order, but I had no problem keeping a low profile for thirty-six hours. I slept and read quietly. The world on shore was sometimes too strange for me to comprehend. On board the boat I was free from entanglements and relationships. If I could have thought of a way to make a living, I would never go further onto shore than a dock.

Days passed this way: I read a great many books, most of them about sailing and adventure. I longed for strange tropical ports with exotic people. What I got was cold, wet days. I refused to call Harry more often than every three days. Thus

I placed three calls in nine days. In the last call I'm afraid my temper may have been a little short.

I roamed Sausalito restlessly, exploring the town's limited resources. I found that once you left the main tourist area it was a vaguely Mediterranean town of homes all staring longingly at the view, built clinging to the rocky hillside. One could only hope that when the Big One came, all this would not be simply wiped from the face of the slope in a great smear of rock and earth, like a dissatisfied artist with a rag of turpentine. The native dweller of the land of earthquakes must learn fatalism or denial. We should pray to the gods San Andreas, Hayward and the other great faults, perhaps sacrificing a virgin once a year. Maybe the suicides off the Golden Gate Bridge fulfilled some purpose after all. Perhaps their spirits kept the great earth more or less still for almost seventy years.

I came back to Gate Six late one night. I had dared to drive into San Francisco with John to bring back the Lancer. John was proud when I told him the starring role it played in evading the FBI. He even patted the hood affectionately. He had a strange relationship with objects, I tell you.

I had forgotten my flashlight in the dinghy and thus was making my way slowly in the dark, still not completely familiar with the maze. I hesitated at several turnings, not wanting to stumble around the rather treacherous paths more than necessary.

As I stood in the dark for a moment getting my bearings, I heard noise from a houseboat nearby. I recognized Michelle's geodesic dome roofing over an old landing craft hull. It was certainly the sound of a man and woman arguing, and there was something in the note of her voice that caught my ear. I moved a little closer and focused my attention on the muted voices.

I know the sound of that distinctly male harangue: it has a certain pitch and cadence that tells me instantly that some fellow has taken complete leave of his senses. I guess it comes from having heard it so many times myself.

Michelle's voice was not distinctly audible, but the tone of her words were unmistakable. She was pleading with him to calm down.

The first blow left me undecided. Should I stay out, mind my own business? But the second blow took the wind out of her with a groan. My body made a decision before my mind.

I mounted the steps up to her door, yanked it open, removing the flimsy thing from the hinges. It hung in my hand. I threw it down on the dock and sprang inside.

The electric lights were on and the tableau was stark. Michelle was sprawled across a coffee table, littered with bottles and the remains of their coke. I remembered that she told me she had an 'old man' who came and went at will.

The man that stood over her was tall and long limbed. His tank top revealed a whipcord musculature. His rage was clearly visible in his glaring eyes and foam-flecked lips. He swung his gaze at me as I stood at the doorway, taking the scene in one glance. "Get the fuck out of here!" he roared.

I wished for one of my pistols, but I was not carrying. And I really didn't want to kill him. But I was not going to walk on by while he beat his woman senseless or worse.

I knew it would be useless to try reason. But I tried anyway. "It's time for you to go. You're all coked up and you need to chill for while. You don't want to do something you'll be sorry for later."

He literally growled at me. I've seen guys out of their mind on drugs and testosterone before. There is no more dangerous combination. He charged at once.

Fighting hand to hand looks cool in the movies. That's because they choreograph every move. They do all kinds of cool flips and stuff breaks. This fight was not being directed and was messy. I sidestepped his charge, but took a right to the side of my head that bounced it off a post. I pushed him away and he stumbled and fell. We wrestled and grunted together like a couple of bull deer. He had me in both size and strength. A couple of times I thought I was going to lose.

He was doing a pretty good job of throttling me when Michelle walked up behind him and smacked him over the head with a small wooden folding chair, which disintegrated on impact. He fell like a rag doll.

I took Michelle back to the *Jolly Jim* for the night. The next morning we returned to her place to find a small crowd gathered around. They parted as Michelle walked up to her door. Bobby, the Pirate King, was there, along with a couple of other men and two women. The boyfriend lay where we had left him. *Livor mortis* had turned his face and chest an ugly color. He was quite dead.

We were herded into the King's main room on his houseboat. They then held a strangely distorted version of the trial process.

One of the women sat holding my hand as I testified. I was allowed to speak my piece then questioned by one of the Pirate King's outliers. Michelle and the rest were examined in the same way.

Everyone was removed and the group closed themselves in deliberation. I was uncomfortable with the lack of formality, but had been ignored when I suggested we just call the police.

"We handle our own problems," was all they said.

They did not apparently seem to need a lot of time. There were sounds of chanting and music. I have no idea by what means they arrived at their decision.

They called us in early that afternoon and Bobby, rock star and Pirate King, pronounced us innocent of fault. Michelle's old man, it was concluded, had killed himself by generating so much negative karma. I never found out what they did with his body.

I got the feeling that I would quickly outstay my welcome if I didn't move on. I felt cheated. I had done what I thought was right. Everyone, it was more or less agreed, thought that I'd done nothing wrong. Michelle told me she thought most people didn't blame her for striking what turned out to be the fatal blow. Nevertheless, a few days later, Michelle's boat was boarded up and there was no sign of her. I didn't even feel good about asking anyone where she'd gone. They stared at me with a carefully neutral expression, and I thought I heard people whisper after I passed.

I called Harry for the fourth time in a fortnight. I felt I needed to bring a little more pressure to bear. I came to the decision that the weakest link in the chain was Belli. He would be the most interested in my silence, but I was leery about trying any pressure with such an experienced and subtle tactician. So I decided to try to get to Belli through Harry.

"It's time to shit or get off the pot, Harry."

"What's on your mind, Doug?"

"The Intelligence committee is on my mind, Harry. It's only a matter of time before they serve me with a subpoena and then I'll have no choice. If I don't talk to them fully and completely they'll have my tit in the wringer."

It was silent on the other end for a moment. "I realize that, Doug. But what can I do for you? I don't..."

"You can call your pal Mel Belli for starters and tell him to get the subpoena quashed. Or else you can tell him to fill me in on the whole picture, so that I can figure out what I can say and what I shouldn't. Because if I go in there like the half dumb little lamb I'm looking like right now, they'll roast me."

Harry was quiet so long I had to ask him if he was still on the line.

"Okay, Doug. I'm here. Why don't you let me do that? I'll try to talk to him today and see what we can do for you." Like they're doing me a big favor. "Why don't you check back with me around three and I'll let you know." I couldn't tell if he was giving me another stall or not. But I was thinking that I would just call Hagarty in the morning and go on in and tell everything I knew or guessed. I couldn't continue to live on the fringes.

At three I was told to come into the office after five thirty for a meeting. I agreed and hung up. After I walked out of the cafe I realized that it seemed pretty odd that Belli would meet there, instead of his fancy digs. Mel Belli in that seedy little office? I wasn't going to call back just to ask Harry about that, though.

Chapter Twenty-Six

...and Never Brought to Mind

I drove the Microbus downtown and parked, then napped in the back the rest of the afternoon, and about five fifteen started to walk to the office. I was feeling paranoid and wore the PPK in the ankle holster.

The office was silent when I got there. It seemed like I had been away a year and everything had changed. Of course, the only thing that had changed was me.

He waved me into his office and to a chair. I took the one in the left hand corner, furthest from the door so as not to impede our guest when he entered the cramped space. I crossed my legs, conveniently bringing the Walther at my ankle a little closer to Papa.

Harry looked tense and unhappy and wasn't trying to hide it. He even told me to go ahead and smoke, and shoved an ashtray that he exhumed from under a pile of papers to me. I told him I'd wait until Belli got there and he just nodded.

We sat there looking at each other for a couple of minutes, chatting a little about the energy crisis and Harry brought up Werner Erhard and did I think there was anything to this EST thing. I told him I thought Erhard was the greatest con man of modern times and he looked a little disappointed, like I'd told him the Easter Bunny wasn't real.

The outer door opened and a figure walked in. It was not Mel Belli. It was Farrar. My mouth hung open for second, I'm sure.

Farrar walked into the office with a familiar ease, shook hands with Harry warmly and then with me, smiling. He took the chair by the door.

"Okay," I looked from one to the other. "I'm ready for a really great story." The two of them looked at each other for a moment, Harry tipped his chair back as though settling in to listen as well, and Farrar focused his weird hazel eyes on me.

"I am glad to see you are well, Doug. This has been a bloody damned affair and I would have regretted your getting injured," pause, "or killed."

"Getting injured or killed would have hurt my feelings awfully," I lipped back.

Farrar ignored my withering sarcasm. "I'm going to tell you some information that not very many people know. Or know only pieces of. But we don't want you to go before the committee unprepared. And we really don't want to kill you ourselves." That last comment got my attention.

"Now that I imagine I have your complete attention, I'm going to lay out the story. Bear with me, and save your observations and conclusions for the end, as I believe your boss has told you to do before." I understood that he and Harry were in regular communication.

He handed me a plastic identity card. I suppose I could have gotten a really good printer to make something like it, but it was a pretty official-looking card, with a watermark and a band that ran through it that made forgery difficult. The card identified a Major David ben Solomon, Israeli Intelligence Service. Mossad. He was talking while I examined this revelation.

"About five or six years ago it began to be plain to us that the tide in Washington D.C. was slowly turning against us."

Farrar, or rather, ben Solomon smiled. "Ironic that I'm only a captain in the SAVAK. I guess I don't work hard enough to get another promotion."

I digested this while he went on with his narration. "The Republican Party has never been as helpful to us as the Democrats. Too much anti-Semitism there. And with Nixon, well, we found we were having a very difficult time obtaining the kind of advanced tactical weaponry that previously allowed us such a decisive edge over our many enemies.

"Especially in air power. The ability to blunt any massive tank attack with air-to-ground strikes is crucial to our defensive strategy. But we were unable to obtain *Kali*. We tried to bring political pressure to bear, but could not get the Administration to relent. We were aware of what it could do for us. We had other supporters who informed us of its existence and capabilities."

"Agents in the US." I interrupted.

"Well, of course, just as there are CIA agents in Israel. The Johnson administration knew we had nuclear capability through their own agents. We were not unhappy to allow Washington to eventually release that information, just so our neighbors understood that we intend to be the last man standing.

"So, it became clear to our intelligence leaders that the only way to obtain the system was to steal it. This we were able to do thanks to my position in SAVAK.

"In case you are wondering, I am Iranian. And a Jew. Although of course, no one in SAVAK knows that. It would mean torture and death if that was discovered."

He tossed off the idea of torture and death as though they were everyday risks of the commute to work.

"The rest you know, more or less. The Russian approach was a stroke of brilliance on the part of one of our planners. By muddying the waters sufficiently, we hoped to create enough confusion that no one would ever know for sure who had gotten what, if any of this were to come out.

"And of course, the best part was that we did not have to raid our tottering treasury for three hundred and fifty million dollars. The oil rich Iranians paid the

157

bill for us. We did have to pay off Gunter, but that was not anywhere near the first amount." Solomon laughed quietly. It was pretty clever. Sounds like something I would have done.

"We did not anticipate the degree of rage on the part of the Iranians. You are probably not aware of the large anti-American sentiment growing in Iran. And toward the Shah as well. Fundamentalist Islamic priests are preaching against the Shah, his attempts to modernize Iran and blaming the changes on the US."

"It seems that no one loves us anymore," I said. I was getting tired of hearing about how my country was reviled by every poor piss-pot peasant in every God forsaken corner of the planet. I guess that's one reason why the American public likes Israel. At least they stick by us. Fat lot of good they were as an ally; like the British, they were only good for moral support. But I liked them better than the fucking French.

"So that more or less brings us up to the present. You now understand why certain relationships and names should be kept silent. We are doing our best at the diplomatic and Congressional level to keep Senator Helms big mouth shut, but he seems to determined to get to the bottom, irrespective of the risk to the relationships involved. Should the rest of the Middle East find out for a fact that we obtained *Kali*, there would be some who would accuse the US of having given us the system, and claiming it was stolen to protect the US diplomatic position.

"A great many people's careers are on the line, in several capitals, and given the current situation at home, any instability could be fatal. We only just survived this last attack. I can tell you that the decision to use nuclear weapons was twenty-four hours away. The alert had been issued and the weapons were ready for launch.

"What a nuclear attack would do to the oil situation is not clear, but major oil fields are certainly targets. We intend to die on our feet, not our knees. Never again!"

I could not but agree with the last idea. I would have felt the same myself even without being half Jewish. But the idea that the Middle East would be involved in a nuclear war, with Israel starting it was unimaginably frightening. It didn't take much vision to see the Russians sticking their nose into that mess, and if the Russians went in support of the Arabs, would the US just sit by and let the Russians move in troops and weapons? Not hardly. That black shit was what made the industrial world turn and without it we would be out of the ballgame.

"This is all well and good. I agree and I understand. But how is this going to get the committee off my back?" After all, I still have my problems.

"We are working on that. We're quite sure that in another week or so we will be able to convince staff members that if they pursue this any further, the risk will be greater than the reward. We're hoping that Senator Helm's attention span is short enough to become distracted by something else. President Nixon's Watergate problems can only get worse. If we can just buy some time, say until after the New Year."

I turned to Harry. "Where do you fit into this whole mess?"

"David contacted me here while he was attending school, sent here by the SAVAK. His mission for the Mossad was to recruit helpers in the United States and he became aware of me through my activity in pro-Israel organizations. It was David that contacted Mel Belli and secured him to represent the Iranians, not knowing whether he would be successful for them or not, but knowing that Mr. Belli's discretion was absolute. Mel is man of many layers, not all of them readily apparent."

David focused his intense eyes on me. "We always have contingency plans. This is just the most, ah, discrete plan. There has been too much wet work already." I recognized that term.

"Oh yeah, speaking of 'wet work'. I didn't mention it to anyone, but Gunter and I were jumped by a pair of guys who said they were KGB. They tried to take us out, but they got wet themselves."

Harry and David looked startled. "You'd better fill us in on that," David said. He pinned me in my chair with his eyes. So I ran over the escapade quickly.

David sighed at the conclusion of my narrative. "That is our fault, for trying to be too clever. I would guess that someone in the KGB was in trouble when this plan backfired, and perhaps in order to save a career these men were sent. By the way, Gunter's two partners were killed in an auto accident in Switzerland four months ago. I think we can chalk that up to the Russians as well. They are notorious for resorting to violence quickly." That much I knew to be true. I remembered a news account about a Russian intelligence man who had been kidnapped in Beruit by the Palestinians. The next day, two Palestinian officials were taken, and later found dumped on the road, dead, their genitalia stuffed in their mouths. The Russian was released that afternoon.

"Oh great! So that means that it was the Russians that were trying to whack Gunter that night. And they may not take a hint when this last team doesn't return."

David and Harry looked at each other for a long minute. Harry spoke: "It means that we all need to be cautious. Mel and I have taken what precautions we can, and David's cover is as strong as ever. You need to disappear again."

I rolled my eyes. The idea of another boring exile was not appealing, and I had worn out my welcome at Gate Six.

Farrar, or rather, ben Solomon, stood up. "Doug, you can figure out what you're going to do and then do it. I don't really want to know where you are. Just do me one favor..."

"What's that?"

"Try not to be taken prisoner. It would be better to be dead than have any parties get a hold of you for questioning."

"Does that include the Mossad?"

"It might." He nodded to the two of us and walked out.

Harry tore a check out of the business checkbook and handed it over. Four thousand dollars. "Take this and go back on vacation. I don't want to know where you are. Check in with me regularly. I'll keep you posted. In an emergency, I'll page you."

I tucked the check into my pocket and left, no happier than when I entered. In fact, a lot less happy.

Chapter Twenty-Seven
A Friend In Need Is a Friend Indeed

I drove back to John's boatyard, thinking mightily along the way, but not accomplishing much creativity. I figured that I needed to get completely away from the Bay Area, and leave behind everything and everyone that connected me to me.

That meant I needed to trade the Microbus for another set of wheels and abandon staying on the boat. While the boat was hard to trace, it wasn't impossible. And the car had been seen by too many people, too many times. While it was only the dumbest luck that would have them spot me in it, I harbored no intention of trusting my dumb luck. Luck is like a rich aunt, just when you need her most, she isn't around to bail you out.

I negotiated with John for repairs to the *Jolly Jim*. "What about the name?" he asked. "While we've got her out and are painting, now's the time to change it."

"I haven't thought of an inspiration yet. Maybe it should stay the *Jolly Jim* for now. It's a fitting tribute to her former owner. Look at all the happiness he's brought into the world."

"He did?" What John knew of Jim Gunter was not such that he thought of him as the bringer of glad tidings.

"'Every cloud has a silver lining', me dear old gray haired mother used to say." John argued. "I met your mother. She's a redhead."

"But is it hers or is it Clairol? Only her hairdresser and my Dad know for sure."

I brought the boat to John's dock so he could hoist her out with the giant sling and crane the next day.

I packed my clothes, guns, drugs and other such necessities of life. I had to come up with a different car. The Cobra was out of the question. Might as well hang a sign on my back, "I'm too dumb to live, please shoot me now."

I couldn't take one of John's for an indefinite period, his wife needed the Kelvinator, the Lancer was not the kind of car you took on long trips to who knows where. Rick needed his car to get to work.

It was either rent one or scrounge one. Renting costs money. Between my Irish genes and my Jewish genes, scrounging was a shoe-in. Only people who have been really poor appreciate the value of money.

I called Jerry at Bugworld, only slightly desperate.

"Jer! It's Doug. Hey, how's my standing with you these days?"

"Hi Doug. You're a good customer. What do you need?"

"I need to borrow a car for a few days. I need something super reliable and preferably fairly fast and good handling. I'm having a little trouble these days, and I don't know what to expect."

Jerry knew that from time to time I was in mild trouble of one kind or another. The last time was an angry husband, but that blew over without serious incident.

"Well, Doug, I can't have you going out and destroying one of my cars."

"I'm not planning on destroying it, but I wouldn't want to kid you, it might get used hard. If you don't have something like that, no sweat."

I could hear Jerry struggling with his conscience. "Okay. You can take my car. I've had for a while and it's stone solid. You'll be happy." He hesitated. "I really don't want this car screwed up though."

"I promise to avoid that at almost any cost. If I trash it, I'll pay to get it fixed. What is it?"

"You can have the Porche."

A '59 Speedster. Oh goody. I struggled to keep the greedy thrill in my head from coming into my voice. "Jerry, I will love you forever."

"That's what my last wife said. Two years later, she took half of everything I owned."

"Oh, sorry." I guess that's why he'd been living above the shop for the last six months.

We arranged for him to meet me at the marina parking lot. I wanted to leave the bus there, where it could be easily spotted. With the boat out of the slip, and the bus parked there anyone watching might think that I was returning some time soon and camp on the area. That would tie up a team in useless waiting. I asked Michael the hippie to move it every once in a while. He didn't ask why, took the fifty I gave him eagerly and promised he wouldn't forget to move it from time to time. "Try to do it at night, so nobody sees who it is. And if you want to take it for drive sometime, that's fine. It's insured." I would love it if he took it out for the day without being seen clearly. He and I were similar in general appearance. Next to each other we were very different, but at night you would only see our silhouettes. The long hair and casual dress would be enough to fool someone who didn't know us well.

After I dropped Jerry back at the shop, my gear stowed in the boot of the little inverted bowl of a car, I went out to eat and decide where to go.

I didn't want to leave California. I didn't think it was necessary to go that far. With the Speedster at my disposal I figured I might as well have fun and go north along the coast on Highway One, then cut inland to Eureka and come back down through the redwoods. I could stop in Garberville and visit my buddy Steve the hippie for few days.

Too Many Spies Spoil the Case

It would be shame to make such a nice trip alone, I thought. Barbara would be needed at the office; she never took off more than a day or two. She couldn't just suddenly take an extended vacation. So I tried to think of anyone I knew who might be available for a little impromptu tour of Northern California and liked a little romping at night.

I called Jeanie. It was her husband that had been at the root of a recent problem, the one that Jerry helped me with before, but I thought he was now in Alaska, working on the pipeline. Don was a skinny little wannabe biker with a heroin monkey on his back. Not first class husband material. But Jeanie was not quite ready to make the break. As long as Don was out of sight, he was out of mind, in her thinking, so why bother with a divorce?

As for Don, well, every welder I have ever known, and for some reason I have known a few, every welder I meet is either a druggie or an alcoholic. I'm not saying there aren't perfectly sober and hard working welders. I just haven't met one yet.

Jeanie was ready, as usual. She didn't mind our on-again off-again arrangement. Our relationship was pretty much confined to calling each other up to see if the other one wanted a fuck that night. I don't know, maybe worse arrangements could be made. We liked each other okay, but as Jeanie once said, "What's love got to do with it?"

She needed an hour to pack and dump her kid with the grandmother. I'm afraid that motherhood was kind of an on-again off-again thing for Jeanie, too. I'd met the little girl once or twice and she seemed none the worse for wear, but then, everybody's childhood is fucked up one way or another.

I picked her up at nine. I squeezed her duffel in the boot. Jeanie was a freckled, Irish lass. I think she was twenty eight or nine, nice figure, long straight auburn blond hair and green eyes. She was quiet, undemanding, pretty much a laid back, take-it-or-leave-it kind of person. She fucked with a grim determination, but I had no complaints in that department. She liked her men hard and strong, her nails drawing patterns in the skin on my back.

So for the next three days we pretty much set up a rhythm of driving, taking in spectacular views, dining in restaurants that averaged a solid 'excellent', staying in small motels, fucking. Once, at a motel with a hot tub nestled in the woods Jeanie and I frolicked naked with two or three other couples. It was kind of fun to be naked with perfect strangers. Once we were alone in the tub, Jeanie gave me an urgent blowjob that left both of us gasping. Part of the thrill was the chance of being caught, of course.

163

In the early morning chill we would roar up to the next stop. I would take the curving roads at speed, keeping well within the limits of the Speedster. I had no desire to mimic James Dean. And anyway, he'd been driving a 550, not a Speedster, as legend claimed.

Every morning I would pull in somewhere and call Harry. It was one of these casual two-minute calls that turned out to my last conversation with him.

We stopped in the area around Garberville, where Steve lived. This is in the heart of redwood country, a hilly, dry terrain good only for limited cattle and sheep grazing, an ever-dwindling supply of lumber, and fishing along the coast. But in the past few years, another cash crop had been discovered.

When the Haight died, officially in '68 and for real by '71 at the latest, many of the first hippies headed for 'the land'. This concept of 'the land', spoken with reverent tones, was a complete covalent bond with hippie philosophy: you could be independent, 'natural', organically garden and get in touch with Nature, with a capital N.

The fact that none of these people had any experience with agriculture, that the area they picked was overpriced land worthless for almost anything except the above mentioned industries, that they had no money and no credit, none of this dissuaded the Love Generation. What could not be done would be done. Vision would replace practicality, hope would substitute for reason, faith was more than adequate against rational analysis.

Desperate for cash and wanting to make up for the interrupted supplies of imported grass, they began to grow their own. At first, just small gardens for personal consumption and maybe some informal barter with others. It did not take long for these capitalists in tie dye to see a good thing when they stumbled into it. Easy to grow, worth a thousand dollars a pound, in high demand. And the cops didn't have much of a clue. The few busts were more accidents than investigation. Soon there were whole fields of the stuff, waving in the summer heat, being harvested with great celebration in the fall. Think of it as when the people in Kansas figured out how to grow corn. Eureka! Indeed.

So we arrived in Steve's area at a time of great joy. Harvest festival, literally. Everyone who had successfully brought in a large crop was relieved and flush with money. Steve and Cindy, his lady of the moment (a long moment, about six months), guided us from party to celebration to dance to community banquets. I was a good guest, making free with a goodly amount of my heisted cocaine. I was even able to trade some of it for a replenished stash of pot and Steve sold some for me, for which he received a commission, paid in kind, not cash. I was trying to figure out what exactly I was going to do with the stuff. I didn't want to be a cocaine dealer in the slightest, but I didn't think I was going to flush it down the toilet, either.

After settling down with drinks and joints during a break in the social whirl of Southern Humboldt, I brought Steve up to speed. This entailed a long, necessarily confusing repetition of events leading up to my impromptu visit. When I opened my gym bag with its guns and drugs, Steve whistled softly and held the cocaine bag in his hand speculatively.

"How much is there?" He asked me.

"I don't know. I'm guessing around a half a kilo. I've given quite bit away."

Steve immediately pulled out a gram scale. After weighing and calculating he came up with a number: "You've got twenty six point four ounces here. That's seven hundred and thirty nine point two grams. At one hundred dollars per gram, that's," the calculator spit out a number. Steve looked up at me with a huge smile. "Seventy three thousand, nine hundred and twenty dollars." He rested from his labors.

I was shocked. I hadn't bothered to really figure it out, but I had known it was a goodly amount. What was a burned-out coke freak in the Western Addition doing with one hundred thousand dollars worth of cocaine? And would there not be people who would like to know where it was? I found myself hoping my trail was adequately covered from that little escapade. A hundred grand was enough to get one killed in a very unpleasant fashion should the original owner show up.

We chewed over the story of how the unfortunate Mr. Jackson and his platform shoes had resulted in my being blessed (or burdened) with the drugs and cash. Steve went over my story step-by-step and allowed as how he could see no failure on my part, either morally or in covering my role in the affair.

"Look, you didn't intend to kill him, did you?" He answered his own question before I did. "No, he pulled the knife on you. How's your butt, by the way?"

I showed him the vestigal scar, to his satisfaction.

"So this guy just had an accident. He was bound to have gotten killed eventually. Now, as to why he was holding this much blow, well, that's odd. My guess is he ripped someone else off, and was dealing it out quickly to get rid of it. When you showed up he was so coked up he couldn't think straight.

"You probably shouldn't have taken it. Well, shit, I would have too, so don't get me wrong." He laughed. One thief to another. "But you know," he became serious, "this process serving gig is generating a lot of bad karma for you. You should really get into some other line of work."

I knew better than to get into a debate about the relative karmic penalties of process serving versus felony cultivation or other assorted charges I knew Steve to be guilty of. Steve could always justify his actions with logic so convoluted that to follow it was to get lost in a maze from which there was no retreat. I know, I've tried before.

Jeanie was in hog heaven. After the second night at Steve's she discovered much to her pleasure that Cindy was not the jealous type, and that she and Steve were not averse to a trade now and again. Jeanie seemed bent on making up for a long drought in the sex department. Frankly, I was grateful for Steve taking up the slack. A man can only do so much. Cindy provided me with a welcome break. Her demands weren't quite so urgent. And frequent.

On the fifth day of this distinctly, and uniquely California tour I made my usual check-in call to the office.

Chapter Twenty-Eight

Send Lawyers, Guns, and Money—The Shit Has Hit the Fan

When I called in, I got Van instead of Harry. "Doug, where are you? Harry and Dorothy aren't here and things have gone to Hell in a handbasket."
"Uh, Van, I'm not sure I want to go into that on this phone. Where's Harry?"
"I don't know. Look, the police were here looking for you."
"What for?"
"Something about your van. Your car...well they said there was an explosion. Doug, someone was killed."
Oh God. Michael.
"Who, Van, who got killed?"
"I don't know. They just said some fellow started it and it blew up. The police really want to talk to you and they were pretty unhappy when they couldn't find you. Where are you?"
"Where the Hell is Harry? Does he know about this yet?"
"I haven't heard from Harry or Dorothy. Things are a little crazy here." I could imagine.
"I'll call you back." I hung up in a daze. Oh shit! Where the fuck was Harry in all this mess?

I decided I would try to get a hold of Harry at home but there was no answer. After another hour I tried the office again.
Barbara's voice was breaking when she answered. She just said, "Talk to Van," and transferred me over.
Van was stuttering he was so anxious. "Doug, oh Christ, Doug. Harry's dead."
I was so surprised I dropped the phone. I fumbled it back next to my ear. "When, how?" I couldn't decide what I wanted to know first.
"Dorothy called from the hospital. I guess he went out to pull the car out of the garage and when she came down to the driveway, he was slumped behind the wheel. She called an ambulance and I guess they think he had a heart attack. Geez, Doug, you need to get back here. "
" I'll be there as soon as I can."
"Yeah."

I hung up. I started to walk away from the phone, but then turned back. It took me several minutes to get Mel Belli's number and then place the call. Then wade through the receptionist to get to his secretary.

"I need to talk to Mr. Belli right away. This is Doug McCool."

"He's in conference, may I give him a message?" Meridithe said, her voice that aggravatingly patient tone that personal secretaries have perfected over the years.

"Go in there and tell him that Harry Silver's dead, my car's been blown up and he's going to be dead too if he doesn't get on this phone." She went and delivered the message. In a minute, Belli's familiar rumble came on the line.

"Doug, you mean to tell me Harry's dead? How?"

"I don't know. Look I'm a long ways away at the moment, but if they came after me and they got Harry, you're next. You've got to call the police and get them working on this thing with all the details. Christ, Mel, people are dropping like flies! Some poor kid that never hurt anybody is dead because he started my car."

"I will get right on this. Are you returning to the City?"

"Today. You're going to have to get bodyguards and a top security man to go over your cars, your house. Don't drive and don't go home!"

"I will get a hotel room in the name of someone else. Don't worry. I know how to take care of myself. You be careful, Doug."

We were back in San Francisco by the that afternoon. I dropped off a disappointed Jeanie and went straight to the office. While things seemed strained, the state of crisis had abated. Dorothy was not there. Barbara kept things organized. I went into Harry's office and closed the door. I reached Belli's office, but he was not there and the self-important Meridithe wouldn't tell me where he was. That was at least some minimal security. I left a message for him to call me but the number I used was for the bar downstairs. I told Barbara where I'd be and went to wait until I heard from the lawyer.

Three gin and tonics later Sharon handed me the phone. "Mel?"

"Hello Doug. This is not the office phone."

"The office phone is probably not safe, Mel, I'm calling from a bar. And yours are certainly not clear either. We need to get together."

"Come to the Hyatt Regency. An assistant will meet you in the lobby, by the fountain and escort you."

"I'll see you in half an hour."

I walked down Market to the hotel and stood around the lobby. A black fellow cat-pawed his way across the lobby, looking from side to side. He was as wide as a door and looked like he could stop a bullet with his teeth. When he saw me he altered course and walked up. We exchanged greetings.

He: "McCool?"
Me: "Yeah."
He: "Follow me."

Mel was set up nicely, of course, with a secretary in an adjoining room, two bodyguards and three phones. One phone was to his ear. He motioned me to a chair and waved at a tray of sandwiches. I took one to soak up the gin.

Mel put his hand over the receiver. "A bomb was found on my car, and a sweep of the office revealed several listening devices. The FBI denies having obtained warrants or placing them. We are assuming intelligence agencies. The police are currently staking out my house and office."

"Doug, I'm sorry about Harry. I don't think anyone of us realized how desperate someone is to put this affair into the dustbin of history."

He motioned to one of the bodyguards, who opened the door to the other room and in walked a man who looked like a cop. He acknowledged me with a nod and sat with us.

Mel introduced him. "Inspector Ron Thompson, this is Doug McCool." We shook hands.

Thompson was the head of the SFPD Intelligence Division. Naturally, this was not a unit focused on international operations, but they served a similar function for local issues. They kept track of gang activities, foreign criminals and domestic radical political groups. I was leery of him, as I didn't necessarily approve of all of his unit's activities.

Belli sensed my reluctance. "Ron is a personal friend of mine, Doug, and in this situation, his interest is in bringing this series of murders to a rapid end. I have received his assurance that he is not interested in, what's the phrase, 'jamming you up'."

Thompson spoke up. "Mr. McCool, Mel has given me the background on this case. I realize that you have done nothing that wouldn't be considered self-defense. I'm not happy that we have been left out of the loop for so long, but that's neither here nor there now. I want to lure these guys out and nab them. Once we have suspects in custody we can sort out who's done what to whom. I assure you that we will not be looking to prosecute you. Mr. Belli would be your counsel in any event, and I wouldn't want to go up against him in court with this case anyway."

"As long as we agree that you aren't investigating me, I'm prepared to cooperate with you guys in any way." Sometimes you just have to have trust. I certainly couldn't face this alone.

We spent the rest of the afternoon and far into the evening talking, even making charts on large sheets of blank newsprint. Finally, we came to a halt. We had chewed over the whole thing so many times we were beginning to hate each other. We took a break to eat.

"The answer is to suck them in and take them out. Whoever they are." I was for trying to get some other agency involved, but we eliminated all of them since we didn't know who we could trust. Belli had persuaded the staffers on the Intelligence committee to withdraw the subpoenas temporarily. But there was someone who was determined to bury this whole story. Literally.

Thompson thought that the way to get the killers out into the open was to give them an opportunity to strike that was so appealing they would be unable to pass it by. This involved putting Mel and I into a situation together where they could try to take us both out at once. Thompson figured that this was the best way to go.

I was leery of this idea. "If they succeed, they'll get two birds with one stone. I don't want to insult you Inspector, but you're asking us to trust you and your team."

Thompson agreed that it was a great risk, but the opportunity to draw them out in a predictable location was attractive.

"Don't you think that will make them suspicious?" I thought that we were making it a little obvious, myself.

"There are a lot of reasons for you and Mel to decide to hang out together. Safety in numbers. Avoiding phone taps. We left the listening devices undisturbed." Thompson countered. "There's no point in trying to read their minds. Either they go for it or they don't. They have to realize that you guys aren't dumb. You know you're the next targets. So they will expect you to take some precautions. We will try to funnel their attack to an opening that we create and control."

"You two will hang out at Mel's place tonight. We will have a team of SWAT officers in the parking lot across the street. We'll have cars on the east and west ends of the block. I expect them to try for you when you enter or exit, but they might try to get you inside the building.

"I'll put two men inside with you guys. If the shit hits the fan, all you have to do is dive for the floor."

It sounded optimistic but I couldn't think of another idea that was better. We wrangled over my being armed, but in the end Thompson agreed that I could carry. "You have the permit, so I will allow it. But if you fuck up and shoot one of my men, I promise you we'll have your ass." Cops didn't like armed civilians involved in their set ups and I couldn't blame them, but Thompson was satisfied with my experience. "You took care of those two guys at the marina pretty good."

"Did you ever find out who they were?"

"Yeah, we eventually found them through fingerprints and service records. They were both ex-Marines. No arrests but their passport records showed they did a lot of traveling in Europe and the mid-East. We don't know who they might have been working for."

Thompson might not have, but I was beginning to smell the fragrance of CIA.

Chapter Twenty-Nine

Into the Valley of Death Rode the Six Hundred

We broke up around nine and Mel and I headed for his place by taxi. The taxi was being driven by a SWAT guy in plain clothes. His nine-millimeter was lying next to him on the seat. I thought, in passing, this would be a good way for cabbies to get much bigger tips.

Mel's place was on Marina Boulevard, right across from the St. Francis Yacht Club and the Marina Green where Carol Doda, the famous dancer, first displayed the topless bathing suit nine years earlier. Her twin peaks put North Beach and the Condor Club on the world map.

The townhouse was two stories, with huge windows in the front that gave the lawyer a fabulous view of the Marina and the Bay. Of course it was dark now, and neither one of us had any intention of admiring the view in front of large windows. The back of the townhouse opened onto a small garden, with another townhouse backing onto this. There was no rear entrance into the garden; the only way to get to the rear was through the front. Nevertheless, there were two SWAT guys camped out in the back yard. Another team was stationed in the marina parking lot, not directly across the street, but the only place a van could be parked without attracting undo attention. There were units on the side streets on either side as well. Thompson himself was in the townhouse with us, along with another SWAT guy. We were as secure as we could be, but I was worried that the killers would make the cops and not try anything.

Belli was between wives, at the moment, and he sent his current companion away for the duration. His place was nice, of course. You entered a small courtyard through fancy black wrought iron gates with gold trim. The entrance on the ground floor led to a huge living area with fireplace, a dining room off that with a table that could seat at least twenty without crowding. The kitchen completed that side of the house. On the opposite side of the hall was a large library/office, a bath and a family room with the TV and comfortable chairs. This opened onto a brick patio and the Japanese style landscape in back.

The upstairs contained three bedrooms, the master with its own bath, and two guest rooms that shared a large bath of their own. There was a narrow staircase that led to the roof, with a deck and spa. You could sit up there and enjoy a warm night when the fog didn't freeze you to death.

The four of us hustled through the gate and into the townhouse. Belli led us to the kitchen where he proceeded to fix us all a late night feast. Belli's refrigerator was stocked like a restaurant. Soon we were stuffing our faces on reheated *dim sum*, spring rolls, *char sui bao* and other Chinatown goodies. Belli washed his down with beer, the rest of us settled for coffee.

Barry, the SWAT man, set up in the office room that was just off the entry hall. Thompson chose the TV room in the back. That covered the ground floor front and back inside. Thompson decided that the roof entry would be the most attractive. The team in the backyard was assigned to cover the roof. If the attackers took that bait and came over the roof, bam, they would have them surrounded.

Belli went to bed after showing me the guest rooms. I chose one, and took off my coat and shoes with relief. I had the gym bag with me carrying the Ruger and my service Colt. I decided to keep my pants and shirt on, with the Browning and the Walther in their respective places. I didn't want to hang the Ruger around me, it was heavy and uncomfortable, so I just put it on the nightstand. I laid the .45 next to me on the bed.

It was nearly midnight and I was tired. I propped a chair against the door to the bedroom, but I would have to move heavy furniture to block the door to the shared bath. I fixed myself up in bed with pillows and the latest James Bond book. Chewing gum for the mind.

Despite coffee and tension I fell asleep. I don't know exactly when, but it was inevitable. I was too comfortable in the big bed, surrounded by cops inside and out.

Something woke me up. I glanced at the bedside clock- three forty five. I reached up and turned off the reading lamp and listened for a repetition of whatever the sound was that disturbed me. Nothing, silence.

I slipped off the side of the bed away from the doors. The door to the bathroom was across from the foot of the bed; the door to the hallway was to the right. I took the extra pillows and made a pillow man under the blankets, then knelt on the floor between the wall and the bed, letting my pupils adjust to the dark. It might be an old gag, but what the Hell. I held the Ruger in my right hand and the Colt .45 in my left. I could have killed a charging rhino.

Then I heard the faint sound of someone turning the knob to the hallway door. There was a creak as they gently put their weight against the door, but the chair prevented them from opening it. There was only one try and the sounds stopped.

I turned my head toward the bathroom door. I brought the guns up to bear on the middle of the door, cocked both hammers and waited.

There were no other sounds or movements to give me warning. I saw the door move, a shadow moving in the dark. The guns in my hands went off and I fell backwards, ears ringing, eyes blinded by the flash. Gun smoke floated in the air.

I could see clearly after a second. The door to the bathroom had two chunks blown out of the middle.

I heard three quick shots and shouts down the hall a moment later. I pulled myself back up to my knees, the pistols wavering in front of me. I could only hear muted sounds, but there were no other shots.

I heard Thompson call from the other room to someone else, "This room's clear. One suspect down." Then to me. "Doug, it's Thompson. It's okay, come on out. It's clear."

The door to the bathroom was half opened but I could see nothing. I got to my feet slowly, ears still ringing and opened what remained of the door.

Thompson was standing in the doorway to the second guest room, his service pistol casually pointed at me. We faced each other for a second and then lowered our weapons. He shrugged, "I had to make sure it was you. You okay?"

I pointed to my ears. "Can't hear very well."

Between us on the floor was the body of the assassin. Both slugs had hit him, blowing a couple of really impressive holes. The bathroom walls were dripping gore. I made a face.

I backed out of the bathroom and moved the chair to the door so I could meet Thompson in the hall. He pointed to Belli's room. "The other one's in there. I've got him cuffed." He pulled a radio from his suit pocket and called his other units telling them he was clear. We went into the bedroom where his prisoner lay on the floor, bleeding from a wound to the right thigh, cuffed and on his belly. He was all in black with a ski mask discarded on the floor alongside an Uzi with a long silencer. The wall and bed were torn up with many bullet holes and the air was thick with smoke. Thompson ignored him to check on Belli.

The door to the master bath opened and Belli peered out. He looked rumpled, his long white hair every which way, paisley robe and pajamas covering his bulk. He looked at the dead man and then to Thompson and then to me. He then stepped over the body and placed himself in a chintz upholstered wing back chair.

Before he could speak there was the sound of many footsteps on the stairs and Thompson turned to the doorway. He directed an ambulance crew to the prisoner. Teams of cops were soon busy cataloging the scene, taping rooms off and taking pictures.

Belli and I left them to do their work and went down to the kitchen. Belli started up a huge coffee urn, which was soon burping and gurgling. He sat across from me at the kitchen table.

"I guess I have to thank an aging prostate for saving my life," he chuckled. He was remarkably calm for a man who had narrowly escaped death.

"How's that?"

"When you reach my age, young man, you find your rest interrupted by one or two nightly trips to the toilet. I was relieving myself when our intruder attacked. I suppose he didn't stop to see if I was in the bedroom or not."

Saved by your bladder. Well, why not?

"They must have obtained a plan to the house. I wonder how they knew we were in those rooms. They seemed to have found us easily."

Thompson and a couple of other inspectors joined us and Belli served coffee all around. "Let's go in my study across the hall, where we can all be accommodated comfortably."

Once we were all arranged, Thompson gave us his take on the action.

"As you may have guessed, these two evaded the trap. They came across the neighboring roofs. But they surprised and killed the team in the backyard. Once inside they checked the bedrooms, assuming, I suppose, that's where they would find you two. Barry and I heard nothing downstairs until Doug's shots. I suppose they intended to kill you two and retreat undetected. You can see the silencers."

"Your man couldn't get in through the door you'd blocked, Doug, and so came through the bathroom door. My God, what did you shoot him with? It sounded like cannon fire. Barry and I came flying up the steps. Barry took this guy in the leg. He's on his way to San Francisco General now. We'll catch up to him there and see what we can get out of him and ID the dead one."

Belli and I had no questions for him. Thompson and his men left. One SWAT officer stayed behind just as a precaution. By now it was nearly six, so we gave up any attempt at rest, showered and dressed. Belli took his car to his office and thoughtfully dropped me at 450 Market on the way.

Chapter Thirty

Through a Glass, Darkly

On December 23rd the Shah of Iran announced that OPEC would double the price of oil. Merry Christmas. What a pal.

The police were through with me. They got nothing out of the prisoner from Belli's townhouse except an identification from the Pentagon records that showed him to be a former Navy SEAL, three years post discharge. The armed service background of these guys seemed to point to CIA involvement, but nobody was talking.

I retrieved the *Jolly Jim* from John, three thousand dollars poorer than before, but with a beautiful refit. I felt truly at home with the lovely motorsailer now. John pestered me to think of a new name. Inspiration eluded me, so I told him to be patient. "Buddha will provide," I assured him. He just looked at me as though I had lost what little mind I had left. For now, the ketch would remain the *Jolly Jim*.

It was a tough winter. Gas was nonexistent and waiting in lines frayed motorists nerves to the breaking point. My bus was totaled, of course, and I was looking for a replacement. Until I got one, I couldn't work, so the matter was pressing. I was living off my ill-gotten gains.

I returned the Speedster to Jerry unmolested, much to his relief. I told him I needed a replacement for the bus. He assured me he would let me know when he found a suitable candidate.

Over the course of the next three weeks I was able to sell about thirty thousand dollars worth of the cocaine. Steve put together a 'consortium' that took some, and Rick sold some to his endless supply of friends.

I bundled the loot up and strolled down the dock to Michael's former houseboat. His girl was there, still not quite understanding or believing that he was gone for good. I felt terrible.

We talked the afternoon away and she made chamomile and valerian tea. "It's supposed to calm you," she informed me. I didn't feel much of anything, but I drank more anyway, hoping that it helped her more than it was doing for me.

I handed her the bundle. "Michael's insurance money."

She looked confused. "Michael had insurance?"

"I guess he didn't want to talk about it. Anyway, take it, it's for you." I trusted to her confusion to keep her from questioning the story too closely.

"Oh wow, this is a ton of money!" she exclaimed on opening the package. "God, I didn't think Michael was the life insurance type." Me neither, go figure.

Too Many Spies Spoil the Case

I gently suggested that she might want to consider moving up to Humboldt. She needed to live there, among her own kind, so to speak. She took Steve's number from me.

"Yeah, I can't stay here. This is just too heavy a downer for me, you know." I told her that she could certainly find some healing up there. She was cute enough to inspire any number of like-minded men to volunteer their comfort.

Jerry finally called me. "Hey Doug, you still looking for another bus?"

"Yeah. Haven't found one I like yet. Got a lead for me?"

"I've got a lien on this one in my shop. The owner ordered all this work done and now he can't pay."

"How much you got into it?"

Jerry hemmed and hawed for minute or two. He started to tell me about all the work he'd done. "Look, this thing is really nice. I put a Corvair motor in it, beefed up the transmission, replaced the shocks with Bilsteins..." I interrupted his recital.

"Bottom line, Jerry?"

"I'm into it for $3,500 parts and labor. Can you gimme three grand?"

"I'll come by and take it for a drive."

I took the Muni across town to get there and was damn sick of public transportation. When I got to Jerry's he took me around back. I saw a nice green and blue '71 Microbus sitting in the back. It looked odd, sitting lower than the normal height, with the fat Corvair exhaust sticking out the back. Jerry fired it up and showed me how clean the conversion had been performed.

I took it for a spin and by the time I went around the block I knew I'd found a new car. It was incredibly fast with the big Chevy flat six and Jerry's suspension work improved the handling to that of a normal car. It didn't have the camper interior and I thought I would miss my little stove and refrigerator, but Jerry assured me he could rig up another one for a reasonable price. I loved the snazzy two-tone paint and we exchanged cash for title on the spot. I was back in business. Of course, I wouldn't get as good a mileage as with the regular engine, but the thought of being able to travel fast overcame my sense of practicality.

I hung around the office helping Dorothy out and was getting paid for that. She took a couple of weeks off after Harry's death, but she couldn't stand sitting around the house. Work was as good a therapy as she could find. I helped Van manage the servers until I got my wheels, then went back into serving fast and furious.

The Intelligence Committee hearings faded away when the Watergate hearings got going in full swing. It was beginning to look like the White House was rotten

177

with crooks and plotters from top to bottom. I wondered how long Nixon could hold out, since his impeachment looked like a forgone conclusion to me.

One day I realized I'd forgotten about Jerome. I felt badly about him. So I went back to Gunter's former building and the new doorman gave me the name of the property management firm. I stopped by there and convinced the owner that I was not nefarious in any way and secured Jerome's emergency contact name and number: a Carol Burgoyne, on Broderick.
   That night I had a pow wow with Rick.
"I want to off the rest of that coke."
Rick's eyebrows went up a notch. "Giving up a bad habit?"
"Not necessarily. I just need to convert it into something more socially acceptable."
   So Rick agreed to arrange to sell it. It took him a week, but with all his merry friends it wasn't difficult. I kept a couple ounces in the freezer for the future. One night Rick brought me down a shoebox filled with hundreds. When we got finished counting there was about forty thousand dollars. I put twenty in a plastic bag and added it to my frozen stash.
   I set out in my new bus for Jerome's next of kin's. I found the address and a pleasant middle-aged lady greeted me at the door, looking curious as why this longhaired white boy might be standing on her porch.
"Hello. You don't know me, but I knew Jerome."
Her eyes reflected surprise that I would know a relative of hers. "How did you know my uncle?"
"I had some business with him. I'm very sorry to know he's dead."
Her eyes teared up for moment. "Can I do something for you?"
"Would you mind if I came in for a moment?"
"Oh, of course, excuse me." She opened the door for me and stepped into the hallway. I followed her into a cramped livingroom where she sat on the couch. I took a seat in a chair across from her that had been repaired with duct tape.
"He was my Mama's sisters' husband. I lived with him and my aunt for while in Mississippi when I was a child. He was a sweet man, Jesus knows."
"Yes, he was a nice fellow. Did he have children?"
"They had three, but they all dead now."
"Oh." What can you say?
"My sons were fond of him as well. They were broken hearted when I told them about..." she swallowed, "...about what happened." She looked at me closely. "Can you tell me why those men shot him like that?"

"No, ma'am. I'm afraid I can't. Where are his nephews now?"

"They're at college, God bless 'em. They're going to City College now and then they're gonna transfer to San Francisco State."

I pulled a fat envelope out of my jacket pocket and put it on the coffee table that lay between us and stood up. "This is some money I owed him, so by rights it's yours, as far as I'm concerned."

I turned around and walked out before she could open it. There ought to have been enough in there to cover two years at SF State for two boys, if they were careful.

I was lounging around on the *Jolly Jim* one Saturday afternoon when a familiar figure came bobbing along the dock. Farrar, or ben Solomon, whichever, waved to me and I waved him aboard.

"Nice boat," he looked around.

"Have a seat here in the sun. Beer?"

"Thanks." He took the cold bottle. "San Miguel. I love this beer. Too bad it is so hard to get. I miss drinking beer. I'm getting tired of being a Moslem. I can only drink when I'm in Israel or abroad." He took a long swallow of beer to prove his point.

"So to what do I owe this visit? You didn't come all the way from Tehran to drink beer with me."

He shook his head. "No, although this makes the trip worthwhile," he tipped the bottle back and drained it. I fetched him another. I could sympathize with being barred from drinking.

"I thought you might like an epilogue to last fall's events."

"I'd like to know why eleven, no thirteen, people died over that whole mess, yeah."

"Okay. Here's the deal. I got my hands on a classified report from the committee. Don't ask..." he cautioned. I shook my head.

"You know William Colby took over as director in September of '73? No, well, he did. And it seems that he started poking around in the various operations that were ongoing or just concluded when this lawsuit attracted his attention. So when he finds out what happened, the shit was going to hit the fan, as you Americans so picturesquely put it.

"I will not tell you how exactly this came about, but let's just say that we originally had help from inside the Company. However, when it appeared that this was going to be revealed because of the Iranian suit and the subsequent judgment,

179

let's say that our helper went off the deep end. He was desperate to cover any trail that led back to him or even gave a hint as to who and what was involved.

Ben Solomon sighed. "I'm afraid that this is not some game, Doug. You know that these things are played for keeps, you were in intelligence work yourself."

"Yeah, maybe so, but not running around shooting civilians in major US cities. That's a bit much."

"Well, things got out of control. The men who did the killing were contract people, ex-military who were basically mercenaries, but generally working for the Company. They were the kind that took their instructions and did as they were told. They got paid to do that kind of thing."

"All I can say is that you were very lucky not to have been killed yourself." He paused. "Well, luck does have something to do with it, but you were pretty smart."

"I was just stumbling around in the dark. It's a miracle I didn't get killed. So you're telling me a rogue CIA guy was responsible for Harry, the receptionist, Sammy, Peter, Jerome, Michael and those two cops at Belli's?"

"The men who did those things were acting under contract."

"And who might this person be?"

"That is something that you can never know. Take my word for it, we will have nothing more to do with him. He has proven to be too unstable to trust. If he becomes a danger to our security, we will deal with him ourselves. For the time being, he has been reassigned to Research. We don't believe that Colby's investigation has revealed him, yet."

David stood up, draining the second beer as he did so. "Look, thanks for the beer. I thought you would like to know that it wasn't us." He looked into my eyes with those pale irises of his. "I'm sorry as Hell about Harry. He was a good friend. Someday, I will even the score, but for now, it is better to bury the dead and go on. It is up to us, the living, to do what we can to preserve what we believe in. I know what I believe in. I wonder, Doug, if you know in what you believe."

I wondered about that myself sometimes.

About the Author

Miles Archer

Miles Archer is the pen name of a Pacific Northwest writer who cut his mystery teeth on the classics in the genre, ie. Christie, Gardner, Chandler, Hammett, Stout, et al. Like many authors, Archer has had a checkered career: reporter, sales clerk, process server, free lance undercover operative, sales executive and registered nurse. More than enough careers for three lifetimes. He lives on five acres in the woods and loves the rain.

More Clocktower Books you'll enjoy

You can find more exciting Clocktower Books at clocktowerbooks.com. Most of these titles can also be ordered at Barnes & Noble (barnesandnoble.com) and Amazon (amazon.com), as well as your local bookstore. If you are a fan of Science Fiction, Fantasy, and Horror, check out our free Web-only magazine *Deep Outside SFFH* at outside.clocktowerbooks.com.

Murder Online by Beth Anderson. A widowed mother in downstate Illinois teams up with Chicago police to solve the strangulation/rape murder of her daughter, True, shortly after True moved to Chicago to begin her first job. The only clue is a chat room. Her mother goes into the chat rooms using her dead daughter's identity to try and track down the killer. When she finds him, she has no idea who he is or where he is. But he knows exactly how to find her. ISBN: 0-7433-0068-8.

Devil is in the Details, The by Ariana Overton. Holidays are supposed to be a special time of year, but the holidays in this town are turning into nightmares. What is even worse is the killer is leaving no evidence behind or clues that may help the authorities catch this person. The Devil is in the Details takes you into the mind, and activities, of a serial killer with a different twist. ISBN: 0-7433-0087-4.

Night Sounds by Beth Anderson. A world-class recording contract and a beautiful, hot woman - both on the same night. What more could a young jazz pianist want? Joe Barbarello stumbles into a nightmare of murder, sexual obsession, and international crime involving seven inhabitants of Chicago's Gold Coast, all of whom could have committed the murder. ISBN: 0-7433-0097-1.

Soul of the Vampire by Minda Samiels. A reluctant vampire tries to redeem himself while a forensic pathologist works with police to uncover the vigilante who might believe he's a vampire. ISBN: 0-7433-0095-5.

Doubletake by Sutton Miller. The quiet community of Twin Lakes, Texas is rocked when Susan Delgrave, wife of the high school English teacher, is brutally murdered. What sort of evil crawled into their town when they weren't looking? Homicide detective Barbara Hobkins, is thrust headlong into the investigation.

A product of the 'new direction' in law enforcement, her strength comes from a degree is psychology and a natural instinct for solving crimes. Neither attribute is looked upon highly by her boss or the political powers that pull his strings. Convinced the real killer is also responsible for a series of murders in Dallas, Hobkins tracks him to his seedy hidey-hole. There, her investigtion turns into a chilling race for her life, and she almost becomes a victim of DOUBLETAKE. ISBN: 0-7433-0058-0.

Tapestry by Ariana Overton. Everyone at one time or another wishes they could go back in time and change their life. The problem is, when it actually happens, the results can be surprising, dangerous, and life altering in ways we could never imagine. ISBN: 0-7433-0079-3.

9 780743 301121